SURVIVING THE REVOLUTION

T.L. ALLEN

Contents

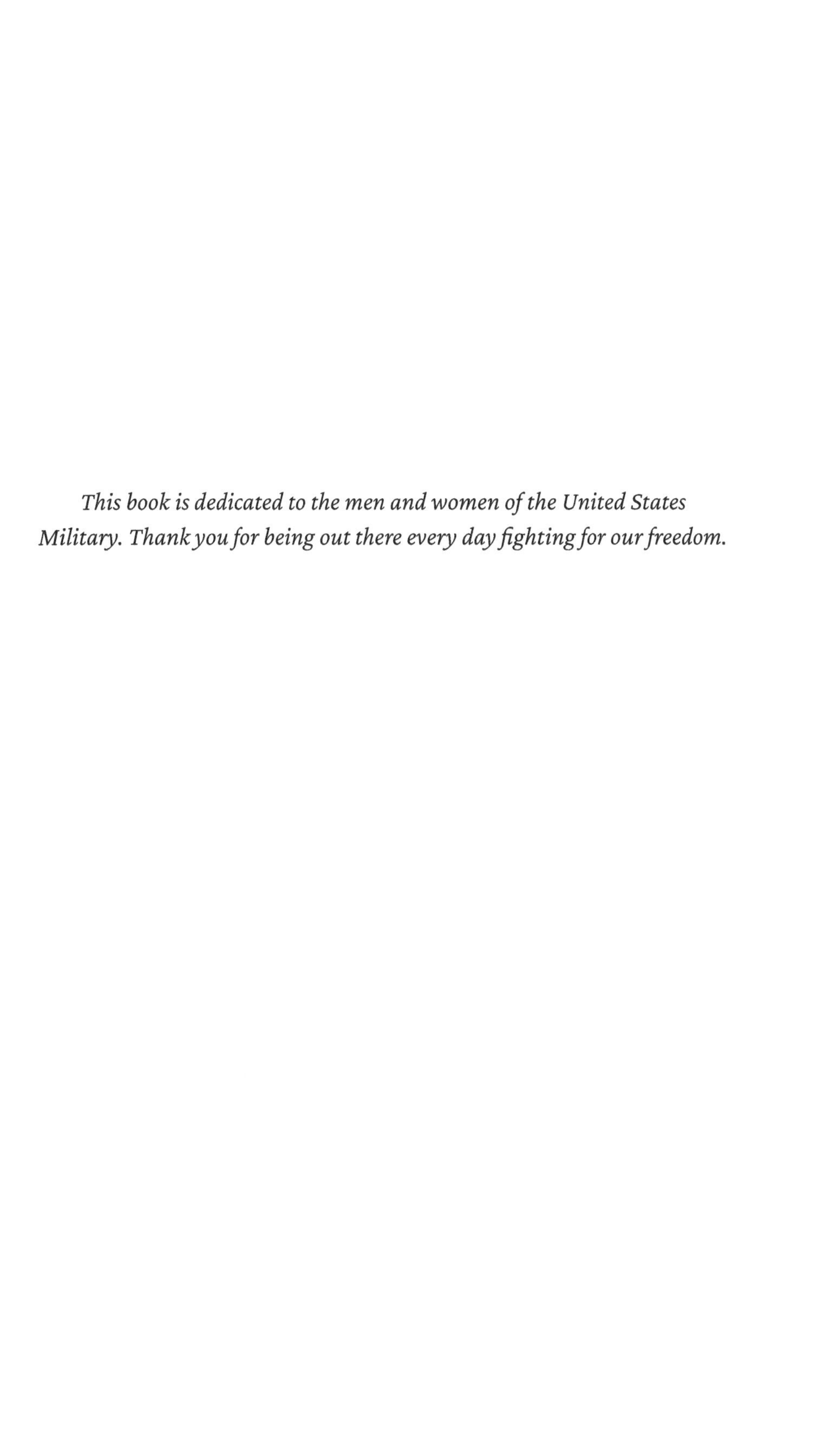

This book is dedicated to the men and women of the United States Military. Thank you for being out there every day fighting for our freedom.

SURVIVING THE REVOLUTION

Copyright © 2024 by T.A. Allen

First Edition

The opinions and or/views which are expressed in this work are solely those of the author and do not necessarily reflect the views or opinions of the publisher. Their appearance in this publication does not constitute an endorsement by Tactical 16 Publishing, its affiliates, or its employees. The contents and information conveyed herein is based upon information that the author considers reliable, but neither its completeness or accuracy are warrantied by the publisher, and it should not be relied upon as such. Tactical 16 Publishing hereby disclaims any responsibility or liability to any party for the contents of this publication.

This is a work of fiction. Names, characters, places, and events are either the product of the author's imagination or are used fictitiously. Any resemblance to actual persons (living or dead), events, or locations is entirely coincidental. No references made are intended to represent (and neither should they be inferred to represent) reality.

Published by Tactical 16 Publishing

Colorado Springs, Colorado

www.Tactical16.com

ISBN: 978-1-943226-96-2 (hard cover)

978-1-943226-97-7 (paperback)

978-1-7367651-1-1 (ebook)

CHAPTER 1

THE BEGINNING OF THE END

"Hey, Sergeant Walker, why are we going to this crappy little village again?" Asks Specialist James Jacobs, JJ for short.

Tim Walker glares at the blistering sun through his scratched up sunglasses and wipes a bead of sweat from his cheek. "To find this Imam named Mohamed bin Khalifa. Our informant said that he knows the location of some Al Qaeda assholes hiding in the area."

JJ snickers and grins at the other soldiers. "There's only one person named Khalifa that *I* want to see right now, and she's definitely not here."

Smiles from the others mean they knew exactly who JJ was talking about.

"Focus JJ. You can get back to your girlfriend Mia, as soon as we get back to camp."

"Roger that!" JJ replies with a little jump in his step.

The sandy road leading to the village was dead quiet this

morning. As they walk along, the only noise emanates from their combat boots hitting the dirt and the light jingle of their gear. The village was about two and a half miles from their combat outpost, so the they decided to take a walk today. As the squad hikes over the final hill, a small Iraqi village appears in the distance. Buildings made of cheap bricks surround a singular spire erected next to the village mosque. It might have been the heat of the sun or the mirage playing tricks on the ground, but something seemed out of place. The typically busy marketplace was devoid of its usual shoppers walking around.

Tim looks around cautiously and motions for his five-man team to proceed. "The place seems quiet today. Keep your eyes open for anything suspicious."

As the squad reaches the edge of the village, the stench of burning plastic and rotting flesh fills the air. To the left is a butcher shop with a big piece of meat hanging on a hook in the window, and baskets of fruits and vegetables sitting on the ground. To Tim's surprise, the vendor wasn't standing at the window to greet them. To the right is a linen shop lined with colorful scarves and dresses swaying in the calm breeze. Again, without anyone begging them to buy their goods.

JJ leans in close to one of the shop's dusty windows and laughs. "Oh look, a Folex. I wonder how much they want for that knockoff?"

The main street was about fifty yards long, with two-story buildings along either side. Each building has a store or restaurant on the lower floor and a small balcony extending from the upper residence. On a usual Wednesday afternoon, there would be children running back and forth in the street as vendors tried to pull you into their shops to buy their cheap stuff. The Imam they were looking for was in a mosque at the center of the village.

"I don't like this," nervously comments Private Chadwick from the back of the formation.

Tim pulls the butt of his rifle tight against his shoulder and looks around cautiously. "Me neither. Spread out and stay alert."

All of a sudden, a single shot rings out from somewhere close by. Instinctively, the team spreads out, taking cover alongside the buildings with their rifles aimed in every direction. The echo from the buildings makes it sound like the shot came from all different directions around them.

"Where did that come from?" Tim yells out.

"Don't know. Somewhere to the front, I think," replies JJ from the other side of the street.

Tim points over at Chadwick and motions to his radio. "Get on the radio and call back to command. We need QRF to come out and help us clear this place."

Just as Chad reaches for his radio and starts to make his call, Tim spots something moving out of the corner of his eye. He looks up to see an object tumbling end over end from the rooftop. A short piece of pipe spins slowly through the air as it falls toward the ground. He looks on in horror as it drops in slow motion, hitting the dirt street right in the middle of his men.

"GRENADE!" Tim yells as he sits up in bed. Breathing heavily, he frantically looks around the dark room as a bead of sweat drips from his forehead.

His wife Mary, who was sleeping next to him, wakes up and grabs his arm. Tim jumps as he looks at her and realizes that he's back in his bedroom, and dreaming of this never-ending scenario again. The room slowly comes into focus as tiny beams of light shine through the window from the streetlamp outside.

Mary rubs his arm and speaks softly. "Was it the market again?"

She had been here many times before when Tim's flashbacks woke him up in the middle of the night. She reaches for the nightstand and hands him a glass of water.

As his heartbeat begins to slow, Tim takes a sip and hands the glass back to her. "Yeah, I hate that place."

He slowly spins and puts his feet on the cold hardwood floor. The little green light from the baby monitor on his nightstand blinks, so he leans in close to hear if Victoria was still sleeping. The only sound he can hear is some heavy breathing, followed by a little fart.

Tim smiles and thinks to himself, "Yup, still out. For a two-year-old, she could sleep through a hurricane."

He slowly stands up and walks to the bathroom to clean the sweat from his face. The joints in his knees and ankles creak and pop from years of abuse. He turns on a small night light in the bathroom and splashes some cold water on his face.

Leaning in close to see his bloodshot eyes and two days of stubble on his face, he points at himself in the mirror. "Chill out, you psychopath."

This dream often haunts him in the middle of the night, but there was nothing he could do about his PTSD. Every time Mary forced him to see someone about it, the doctor would throw another bottle of pills at him and send him on his way. After serving in the Army for twenty-two years, he needed to retire and calm his nerves. They were now living in the suburbs of Dallas, in the great state of Texas. Mary was working as an English teacher at a local high school, and Tim was a stay-at-home dad battling the little monster of a toddler for a living. Not much "calming down" was being done, but it was better than fighting insurgents in Iraq. He didn't have to clean up after the Al Qaeda as much as he did with this little Tasmanian Devil, though. All in all, it was a good life.

As he dries the water from his face, something catches his eye outside the window. It looked like someone was shooting off fireworks in the city. He pulls the blinds away and sees large balls of light, but not in the sky where fireworks should explode. It's coming from the ground, silhouetting the buildings. He rubs the sleep from his eyes and takes a closer look. Following one of the explosions, what looks like stream of tracer rounds from a machine gun fly through the air.

"That can't be good," he thinks to himself.

He quickly leaves the bedroom and goes to the living room to turn on the TV. It's rare to see something truthful on the news recently. Ever since the new president took over, things had been a mess.

He hits the power button, and the room lights up with the bright red glow from a banner scrolling across the screen reading, "BREAKING NEWS!!"

A reporter stands in the street in oversized tactical gear. Just as he tries to speak, he flinches and ducks down as another exposition erupts from behind him. "Downtown Dallas has turned into an all-out war zone as an armed group of men is attempting to take control of City Hall. All across the city, police are battling hundreds of people as they pour into the streets. We're receiving multiple reports of rioting and looting of stores following the recent events at the Capital. The National Guard has been called to the scene to attempt to halt the violence."

Another loud explosion goes off that shakes the plates in the cupboards, followed by Mary's footsteps running down the hall.

She comes out into the living room and stops in front of the TV. "What was that!?"

Tim leads her over to the front window and pulls the curtain aside. "All hell is breaking loose downtown. Some kind of militia group is attacking City Hall. We need to leave the city now. We can go to my parents' farm up north. It's far enough away from the city that we'll be safe until things calm down."

Mary stares out the window with a look of shock on her face as another ball of light erupts from downtown. "Ok, I'll get the baby," she says, quickly leaving to get Victoria from her crib.

Tim turns and heads for the kitchen. Any prior serviceman is a prepper at heart, so he goes right for the go bag under the sink. It was already full of enough dried food and water for a day's drive, and a first aid kit just in case. He knows that supplies are essential, but the most important thing for this journey was waiting back in the bedroom. He sets the go bag on the bed and kneels down, pulling a black lockbox out from under the bed. He punches the code into the keypad, and it pops open, revealing his custom Colt 1911 pistol.

It sparkles in the light with its polished stainless steel barrel and dark oak grip. Engraved in the wood is Tim's old unit insignia with expert detail. Deeply etched is a black octagon with gold outlining. Over the center is a gold ink quill surrounded by four gold lightning bolts. On the bottom is a gold ribbon with black letters spelling out words in Latin. *TRIUMPHUS PERSUASIONIS* (Triumph of Persuasion.) It was a retirement gift from his good friend and commanding officer.

He carefully plucks it from its fitted case and pulls the slide back just enough to see the live round resting in the chamber. With half a smile, he releases the slide and inserts it into his holster then stuffs it into his bag, followed by two loaded magazines and an extra box of rounds.

Tim quickly zips up the bag and throws on some clothes. Within a matter of minutes, Mary is waiting next to the front door, holding the baby. They take one last look around and lock eyes in the doorway. Without saying a word, they leave the house and lock the door behind them.

Being a military family for so long, they had learned that things are just things. They learned not to get attached to anything because the military will have you move so often that it was common to lose many possessions and friends along the way. They leave the house without hesitating to think about the seventy-inch plasma TV on the wall or the box of jewelry left behind in the bedroom. They had what was important to them in their hands and were ready to do what was needed to keep their family safe.

Tim loads the bag into the back seat of his truck as Mary straps in the baby. After a quick check around the truck, Tim jumps in and starts it up. The fuel gauge shows less than a quarter tank, which was not enough to get to his family's farm.

"We'll need to stop somewhere and get gas once we get through the city. I hope we can make it that far."

As they back out of the driveway, he notices that his neighbors had the same idea. This only meant one thing. Traffic jams through the city. Improvise, adapt, and overcome is something they teach you in the Army. From this moment forward, he knows that his military training will be the key to surviving this. He takes one last look at the house and speeds off down the road.

Heading out of the suburbs is an expected mess. People are stacking suitcases on top of their cars and filling them up with all sorts of useless crap. One man was even trying to stack his dining room furniture in the back of his truck.

Mary points out the window and shakes her head. "Really? Do you really need that chair, dumbass?"

Finally, they make it out of the suburbs and onto the highway leading North toward Oklahoma. After driving for fifteen minutes, the traffic on the highway comes to a dead stop. Cars are lined up as far as they can see. Tim rolls down his window and crawls out, standing up on the seat to get a better look. Off in the distance, he can make out an overturned semi-trailer blocking the entire road, with cars backed up for miles in both directions. He sits back down and looks nervously at the fuel gauge. This is the deciding moment that would make or break the entire journey. Wait here and run out of gas, or take their chances going through the downtown area.

He looks over at Mary sitting next to him, and sees the fear on her face as she stares back. "You trust me, right?"

She looks back at the baby sleeping in her car seat, then turns to him, nodding her head.

Tim turns the wheel sharply to the right and hits the gas. "Here we go. Hold on."

The truck slides off the main road and onto the grass embankment, heading for the off-ramp. Mary holds tightly onto the roll-over bar with one hand and the baby's car seat with the other as Victoria peacefully sleeps in her seat. This was just another innocent car ride for her. They make it to the off-ramp and follow it down to the inner-city streets.

The streets are quiet and look normal for a few blocks. Things soon begin to evolve from typical inner-city slums to post-apocalyptic chaos as they pass shops with smashed-in windows. Trash cans and cars are spewing flames ten feet high. When he thinks they're past the worst of it, they turn a corner and find themselves face to face with a mob of rioters. Colorful ones, holding skateboards and metal pipes. Some have bright red and blue hair, trying to look tough with gasmasks and helmets on.

"Bunch of hippies," he says, watching them marching around like entitled children. He turns to Mary and points at the bag in the back seat. "Reach back and grab the pistol out of my bag. I might need it to scare some of these crazies out of the way."

She hands him the pistol, and he lays it on his lap as they slowly make their way around the crowd of yelling rioters. They seem preoccupied with breaking windows to steal TVs, until one rioter stops and looks up at them. He had just finished smashing in a glass door with a metal pipe and is now staring at them, breathing heavily. He points his pipe at the truck and jogs into the street. Before Tim has time to react, the rioter jumps out, waving his pipe above his head and yelling something incomprehensible.

He looks like he was enjoying the chaos as he flaunts a rainbow-colored t-shirt under a black tactical vest with BLM in white letters across the front. Tim is forced to stop the truck, and they stare at each other through the windshield for a second. The little punk doesn't look any older than sixteen as he stares blankly through his gas mask with a cracked lens.

Tim honks the horn and waves for the punk to get out of the way, but the kid raises his pipe and brings it down on top of the truck's hood, leaving a sizable dent. As the kid rears back to swing again, Tim cuts the wheel hard and hits the gas. The front bumper grazes the kids hip, sending him falling backward into a pile of trash. Before he has a chance to get back up, they speed down the road away from the crowd. Tim looks back through the rearview mirror to see the kid jump to his feet and run toward them, but gives up after a few steps.

Tim reaches over and grabs Mary's hand. "What is wrong with these people?"

"I don't know," she replies with fear in her voice.

They make it about a block past the angry horde, but are halted by a line of police officers heading toward the rioters. They're all geared up for a fight with riot shields and batons at the ready. Behind the officers is a massive truck with a high-pressure water cannon on top.

Tim looks over at Mary with an evil smile on his face and points. "I've seen one of those in action before. They can spray you right off your feet if you're not ready for it."

"Good. Those crazy people need to cool off." She replies.

An officer notices their truck trying to pass, so he walks up to Mary's window.

He motions for her to roll it down and lifts his face shield. "What are you doing inside the city? You need to go east of here to avoid any more dangerous areas. Follow this road and don't stop for anyone except police personnel."

Mary nods her head and waves back. "Thank you, officer."

He waves them past and slams his face shield back down in anticipation of the mob they were heading into. The officer's information must have been wrong because two blocks away, they come face to face with something even more terrifying than rioters.

Up ahead stands a wall of fifty men dressed in all-black tactical gear, surrounded by trucks and motorcycles. There's no other way to go except through them. If they turned and started to run, the men might fire at the truck.

Tim grips his pistol tightly and looks at Mary. "This must be the militia that the news was talking about. Keep calm and let me do the talking."

From this angle, they definitely look like a formidable fighting force. Machine guns are mounted on the back of pickups, and everyone has an assault rifle in their hands. Tim knows that this could go very badly if he doesn't play it right. Lucky for him, he had a couple Special Operations stickers on his truck's windows and his old maroon beret sitting on the dashboard.

As he attempts to slide past their line, one of the men approaches his window and motions for him to roll it down. Tim slowly rolls down his window as the man walks closer and waves. He has on a dirty black collared shirt with the sleeves rolled up, revealing tattoos covering his arms. His black tactical vest is full of pouches, but instead of extra magazines, he has a few beers stored in the front. His face is tanned with a long black beard. As he chews on a wooden toothpick, Tim can see dark holes where teeth were missing in his smile. On his head sits a brown, ragged, and faded cowboy hat with an American flag sewn on the front.

"We don't want any trouble," Tim says, pointing forward. "We just need to get through."

"What's your name and rank, soldier?" He grumbles with a deep, raspy voice. He sounds like he smokes five packs of cigarettes a day, but smells like it's closer to ten.

"My rank's retired. We're just passing through."

He reaches up and strokes his long, tangled beard. "Looks like you still have some fight in ya. You sure you don't wanna piece of this? It's about to start getting good. We got those lazy bureaucrats on the run."

Tim can't help but smile at the man. "No thanks, maybe another time. I just want to get my family out of the city and to a safer place."

"Suit yourself. Go through to the right and out the rear. The streets should be clear from here on." He reaches up and grabs the tip of his hat, tilting it while looking at Mary, then turns away.

As they pass, the man slaps the back of the truck like an old western lawman would have slapped the back of your horse to get it moving faster. Passing the line of militiamen, most of them look the same as the first guy. They look like they just came from a ZZ Top concert at a biker bar. The rest of the way out of the city is surprisingly clear. The police must have evacuated this area before the major fighting started.

Finally out of the city, it's time for them to find a place to rest and get some gas for the rest of the journey north. On the side of the road, sits a gas station with a Krispy Kreme doughnut shop attached. Tim had always been a sucker for doughnuts, so this was *obviously* the best option.

As they drive closer, Mary rolls her eyes and says, "*Okay*," before Tim even has a chance to ask.

"Winning!" He says proudly as they pull into the gas station.

While filling up the truck, Tim hears a familiar sound coming from the highway. The all-familiar roar of diesel engines over-revving, banging metal chains, and squeaky brakes slowly approaches. Sure enough, when he turns around, a convoy of tan and green National Guard trucks cruise by heading for the city. Most active military had some type of disdain towards National Guard soldiers, but they don't really know why. It's disappointing to see someone who wants to be a professional soldier, but still wants to flip burgers at McDonald's for a living. Now, looking at these "Part-timers" mobilizing with live ammo was kind of scary.

Tim watches as the sloppy convoy slowly passes. "Good luck, boys. You're gonna need it."

After filling up the tank and letting Victoria walk around a little after her glorious night's sleep, they get back in the truck and wait for Mary to return from the doughnut shop. Soon after, she comes out of the shop carrying a big box of doughnuts and a couple of coffees. She almost drops it all when she looks up and sees Tim through the window licking his lips and rubbing his hands together. She jumps into the truck with a smile, and Tim immediately digs into the doughnuts and continues their journey north.

Not even five miles down the road, a National Guard Humvee sits on the embankment, looking like a wheel had fallen off while driving.

Tim waves at the poor soldiers as they drive past. "Smile and wave, boys. Smile and wave."

Tim's parents' farm is usually a three-hour drive from Dallas, but today there was a lot more traffic than on a typical Wednesday morning leaving the city, for obvious reasons. All sorts of people were trying to get away from the madness. As the sun rises, the landscape turns from urban city to country grass fields, which was a reassuring feeling. No one's going to be rioting out here. There was nothing to loot, and if they tried, they would quickly get shot and sent back home to the city. Carrying a handgun at all times in this part of Texas is standard practice. Mainly to protect yourself from snakes, coyotes, and the occasional wild boar, which are exceptionally ferocious.

Soon, the pavement turns to gravel, then to dirt, which means the farm wasn't much farther. They pull into the driveway, and Tim instantly feels safer being at the house he grew up in. Mary called ahead to let them know they were coming, so Tim's parents were waiting on the front porch as they pull in.

As they park, Tim's mom, Nancy, comes walking toward the truck with her arms open. "Thank God y'all got out of the city safely."

Followed closely by Tim's dad, Marco, "Dallas is getting worse by the minute. The National Guard is making a real mess of things down there."

"Yeah, we saw a bunch of them attempting to make their way into the city," Tim says, looking at him with a smile.

"Come here, my little bug," Nancy says as she takes Victoria from the back seat. She's still half asleep with powdered sugar all over her face.

"Good to see ya, Son. Come inside and get comfortable. You might be here for a while."

Tim grabs the bag from the back seat and follows them to the house. "Good to see you too, Dad."

CHAPTER 2

HOMESTEAD

"Hey Tim, what's this game called again?" Asks Tim's younger cousin Jason as he walks across the backyard with his hands full. "I don't know if we should be playing with these."

Tim looks around the back yard and waves to Jason as he hunches down behind the garage, trying to be sneaky. "Jason, come here." He whispers. "Don't let my mom see you. Did you get all of them?"

"Y-yes, here," Jason whimpers, and hands the strange metal things to Tim.

"Ah, Jason, you're my favorite little cousin. You're nine years old now. Are you ready to become a man?"

"S-sure, but I'm nine and a half."

"Have you ever seen these before?"

"N-no. What are they?"

Tim grabs one of the tiny metal rods with three yellow fins. "These are called lawn darts. My dad bought them last week."

Jason looks at the lawn darts, knowing already that he's not going to enjoy this game. "H-how do you play?"

"Well, we're not going to play the way our parents do. The kids at school taught me a better way to play." Tim says, looking into his cousin's scared eyes with an evil smile. "I promise I won't hurt you. It'll be fun. You can trust me."

Jason would never trust his cousin when his family came to visit the farm. He was always getting him into some kind of trouble. That's what older cousins are for.

"Ok, Jason. Come here and stand inside this circle. Take those two lawn darts. I'll take these two. When I say now... You're paying attention, right?"

Jason stares at the shiny metal darts in his hands as his upper lip begins to quiver. "Y-yes."

"Ok, when I say now, we'll throw the lawn darts in the air as hard as we can. Make sure to throw them straight up. Then we'll run as fast as we can out of the circle. You don't want to get hit in the head with one when they come back down."

"WHAT?" Jason shrieks with wide eyes.

"Never mind that last part. Are you ready? Three... Two... One... NOW!"

———

Beams of bright yellow sunlight peek through the window curtains of the old house. Tim opens his eyes slowly to a strangely familiar room. He recognizes the ceiling of his old bedroom, which was now his parents' spare bedroom. Everything about the room felt weird, from the musty smell, to the ancient mattress they were sleeping on. Every movement felt like both of them would be tossed onto the hardwood floor.

He sits up slowly and looks around. It had been a while since he had stayed at the farm, because they lived close enough to drive home after they were done visiting. Mary was still fast asleep on her side of the bed, while Victoria rested inside of her lovely little castle they had made out of a couple of couches pinned together with a cargo strap. The sweet smell of maple-cured bacon lingered in the air, calling him to the kitchen. He slowly pulls on his clothes and makes his way to the kitchen to see what his mom was cooking up.

The old floorboards creak with every step on the way down the hall. As he rounds the corner, the sounds and smells of a glorious Southern breakfast bring back memories. On the counter is his mom's favorite old stainless steel coffee pot. It was probably thirty years old, but it worked better than any fancy new cappuccino machine. Thick strips of beautiful bacon crackle loudly in a huge cast-iron skillet sitting on the stove. Next to it, a big pot of sausage gravy bubbles, and in the oven, a fresh batch of buttermilk biscuits are turning a beautiful shade of golden brown.

His mom's kitchen was full of all sorts of cool, old stuff she had collected over the years. There's a spice rack from the Dark Ages that Tim shipped to her from Eastern Europe. On the shelf above the oven are white and blue porcelain bowls that he shipped to her from Holland when he was stationed in Germany.

The old farmhouse was the same house his mom's grandmother lived in when she was a child. His parents spent a lot of time fixing it up and modernizing it - well, at least to a 1990s modern style. The living room still had the old cast-iron wood-burning stove in the corner. It didn't work, of course, but it was still neat to see. One excellent addition was the old western-style bar placed in the hallway. On top are all of the shot glasses that Tim collected during his adventures around the world. There were probably fifty different ones with country names and patterns on them, all lined up for display.

In case you ever forgot that you were in Texas, there were about twenty different antique rifles and shotguns lining the walls around the house. Standing tall in the hallway is a beautiful wooden gun case with a big glass door displaying all of the newer guns. In the living room, his dad's armchair has Tim's old Army unit blanket draped over the back. His mom's armchair sits next to it, with a pile of books and her eyeglasses on the little side table.

Prowling the living room is a little furry creature named Missy. This cat is the sweetest and cutest little thing for her mom, but everyone else in the house is her sworn enemy. This little trickster will act like she loves everything in the world, and walk right up to you in the nicest way. Then, out of nowhere, she attacks you like you were the devil.

In the south, it's okay to wear your shoes in the house without causing any offense. In this house, if you wanted your toes to survive the day, you'd better wear them at all times. Nancy would usually lock the little terrorist in her bedroom when the family was visiting, but it looks like Missy managed to escape this morning.

Tim looks at the mischievous little furball, then down at his bare toes on the floor. With her eyes on the prize, Missy jumps from the couch and casually strolls toward the kitchen. Luckily for Tim, his mom comes through the back door just as Missy starts her attack run. Nancy smiles while wearing a bright yellow flowered blouse and blue jeans, holding a wicker basket full of colorful eggs.

She pushes the malicious cat away with her foot and sets the basket on the counter. "Good morning, Dear. Did you sleep well?"

Tim stretches his back awkwardly with his hands in the air. "Not too bad, I guess. How old is that mattress?"

Nancy looks at him with that motherly look, meaning he shouldn't complain. "I don't know. It was here when we moved in."

"Ha, lies. Where's Dad?"

"He went out to feed the horses. I have some fresh eggs for breakfast. I just pulled them from the chicken coop."

"You're going to kill me with all of this food, Mom. You know that, right?"

She tosses another piece of bacon in the pan. "You're looking a little scrawny anyway. Go tell your dad that breakfast is almost done."

Tim slips on his boots and steps out onto the back porch. As he leaves the house, he pauses for a moment and closes his eyes. The smell of horses, chickens, and murky pond water brings back memories of his childhood. He takes a deep breath and can feel the big city smog leaving his lungs as he exhales.

Behind the house is a wide-open yard filled with green grass and a massive oak tree right in the center. The towering tree acts as an umbrella, casting its shadow over some metal lawn furniture at its base. The horse barn is about fifty yards to the left of the backyard. It's a two-story barn with big double doors on either side, painted red with white trim.

He walks across the grass toward the barn and looks inside the open double doors. The upstairs loft is full of hay, and the horse stalls in the back have a couple of curious heads poking out. One is a beautiful dark red color, and the other is tall with white and black spots. He spots Marco walking through the rear doors carrying a bale of hay. He's already sweating through his white T-shirt, under an old pair of dirt-stained denim overalls. Marco spent his younger years in the Navy and learned a lot about survival and living off the land from his father. He's obviously still in good shape for his age, by the way he throws the heavy bale of hay around like it's nothing.

Tim walks through the barn, patting one of the horses on the head. "Mornin'."

"Mornin', Son. How'd ya sleep?"

"Good, I guess." The horse lets out a pleasant neigh and nods its head. "The barn looks like it's still in good shape."

"Oh, don't let the new coat of paint fool you. This place is seventy years old and needs to be rebuilt. Most of the things around here need some TLC. Good thing you showed up with some time on your hands." He lets out a satisfied laugh. "It's time for you to get to work, Boy."

"Breakfast first, then we can talk about chores. It's been a while since I had a good Southern breakfast, and I'm looking forward to it."

Tim helps his dad close up the barn, and they walk back to the house. His stomach growls as they reach the back door. After everyone wakes up and fills themselves with a superb breakfast, they decide to go outside and get some fresh air. The farm hadn't changed much since Tim was a kid. In front of the barn is a large garden filled with all sorts of colorful vegetables growing. Victoria points out some ripe, red tomatoes and orange peppers hanging from their vines. They stroll over behind the barn to the fenced-in field where the horses can run freely. Out in the middle of the field is a large bale of hay for the horses to eat.

About fifty yards directly behind the house is a small lake, with a little boathouse on the shore. A long dock made of moldy planks stretches out over the water. At the end of the dock sits an old, torn-up armchair so Marco can fish comfortably. There weren't many fish in the small lake, but he enjoyed throwing out a line and having a cold beer anyway. The lake was mainly used for pumping water to the garden and for watering the horses. Along the right side of the lake is the huge, old oak tree that Tim used to climb as a kid. It still has an old tire swing attached to a branch just over the edge of the water. He looks up and smiles, recalling the fond memories of almost dying in that old tree.

They complete the circle as they walk past the chicken coop and the old wooden tool shed to the yard's right side. The tool shed has a new metal garage covering attached to the side to park the truck under if they were expecting hail.

Marco waves to Tim excitedly and points to something on the ground. "Come here, Son. I want to show you something. We added something new to the farm recently. Seeing all of the craziness going on in the country these days, we decided to install a little underground shelter."

Hidden discreetly on the backside of the tool shed is a concrete pad with a set of metal doors attached to it. Marco reaches for his keys and opens the lock. He motions for Tim to help with opening the metal doors, and they pull them to the side and watch as they fall out of the way. Under the rusty flat doors is a newer-looking round hatch with a wheel, like you would find on a ship. Marco spins the wheel, releasing the locks, and swings the hatch open.

Tim stands there in amazement, looking into the dark hole with a metal ladder leading down. "This is so cool, Dad. I heard about shelters like this, but I never had the chance to go inside one."

Marco looks up and smiles. "Well, get in the hole, Boy."

Mary grabs Victoria's hand tightly and pulls her closer. "We'll go play in the yard. You boys have fun in your creepy, dark hole."

Tim, who was already waist-deep, looks up with excitement. "Oh, I will. Bye."

Tim reaches the bottom of the ladder in the dark, as Marco climbs down after him. The air smells stale and musty, like it hasn't been opened in a while. Marco steps down from the ladder and reaches for a small power box on the wall with a red handle. He pushes the handle up, and the fluorescent lights start to pop and flicker.

Tim looks on in amazement as the lights illuminate the room, which was much bigger than he had imagined. The ceiling is low, and the walls are painted gray. From the ladder base, he can see straight through into one big living room with a small kitchen to the left side. The kitchen is fully stocked with a fridge and a dish washer tucked into the corner. Along the wall, white painted cabinets hang over a full-sized sink.

In the middle of the room sits a couch and two armchairs resembling the ones in the main house, with a small wooden coffee table in between them. On the wall to the right side sits an old woden stand with a flat-screen TV sitting on top, and a DVD player next to it. The stand has a wide selection of DVDs and books stacked up on the shelves. Enough to entertain anyone for a couple of months.

Tim walks through, nodding approvingly and looking around.

Straight back is a doorway leading to the main bedroom. Inside, a large bed and a wooden dresser sit to the back. To the side is a standing wardrobe with a few pairs of clothes for both of his parents inside. Another door to the left goes through to a full bathroom with a shower.

On the left wall of the living room is a metal door leading to a large storeroom. Inside are four rows of tall metal shelves filled with canned food, boxes of snacks, and other things. The bottom of each shelf is packed with jugs of clean water and a few car batteries. There's even a tiny washing machine tucked away in the far corner. When Tim turns around to leave, he sees the most crucial part of any shelter. A gun rack with about ten different rifles and shotguns attached to the wall, and a pile of green ammo boxes stacked up on the floor below it.

Tim walks back into the living room where Marco stands, looking proud with his hands on his hips.

Marco points to the wall. "One more thing over here, Son." He opens a small closet on the wall next to the TV stand. "Here's the ventilation system. It's a basic low voltage system that pulls air from a pipe leading to the surface to supply fresh air while we're in here. If the power goes out, I can hook up a car battery and get it running again. There's also a small electric water pump for pulling water from the lake."

"This place is amazing, Dad," Tim replies, rather pleased that they can have something like this hidden on an old farm.

"Thanks. Like I've always said, it's better to have it and not need it, than to need it and not have it."

They climb back up the ladder and return to the house to find the girls sitting in the living room. Nancy brought out her reserve stash of kids' toys and poured them onto the living room floor for Victoria to play with, and she was in heaven. Tim smiles as the toddler plays innocently on the floor, but his smile quickly fades as he looks up at the TV with big red letters scrolling across the screen.

"BREAKING NEWS! Clashes between a violent militia group and

the National Guard have escalated in multiple cities around Texas, while rioting and looting have destroyed many inner-city areas. The governor of Texas has declared martial law and advises everyone still in the cities to stay inside their homes and lock their doors. Anyone caught contributing to the violence will be arrested. The Governor also advises that families outside of major cities stay clear until everything is under control.

In national news, the newly appointed president will be issuing a statement to all US citizens later regarding his new gun ownership policies. Sources say that he will be signing executive orders limiting the maximum number of firearms any one person can own, and permanently banning certain types of firearms from being owned or sold inside the United States. Despite receiving strong backlash from senators and the House of Representatives, the President still plans on moving forward with his new executive orders. More on the story as it happens."

Mary looks back at Tim with a scared look on her face. "Well, what does that mean?"

Tim and Marco look at each other, knowing exactly what this will lead to. They reply at the same time, "Civil war."

Tim's family farm was located in a remote area near the northern border with Oklahoma. The nearest town was a little place called Chesterfield, about thirty minutes' drive to the west. An hour in the other direction was the Stockton landfill. This was where all sorts of trash and scrap from the bigger cities in Northern Texas got dumped and recycled. If his parents wanted to visit somewhere more civilized, they would drive north to Oklahoma City. Dallas was a little closer, but it's so big that it wasn't worth the trip.

Marco turns off the TV and throws the remote onto the couch. "Looks like we're going to need some supplies and something to cook on the grill tonight. Want to head into town with me and get some stuff, Son?"

Tim stands still, staring in the general direction of the TV, lost in his thoughts. He blinks and replies, "Sure, let's go."

As Tim and Marco are walking out the door, Mary yells at them. "Don't forget to get a bunch of diapers!"

The men jump into Marco's old Ford pickup truck, because he refuses to ride in anything else. The old truck was the color of faded piss-yellow, with rust over every wheel. Minor dents pockmark the body from front to rear, and the tailgate was barely holding on by a thread. As they leave the house, they hit a big pothole, and everything inside the truck shakes like an earthquake. Tim looks over at his dad with a nervous grin, as Marco smiles back.

He reaches out and pats the dashboard. "Don't you say anything bad about old Bessie. This truck has worked harder and longer than any other truck I've owned. It'll outlive me someday."

"I'm not saying anything about this old rust bucket," Tim replies, with both feet firmly planted on the floor and each hand holding the door and armrest tightly.

Tim reaches out to turn on the radio, half-expecting the knob to fall off as he turns it. The only tiny speaker in the dashboard crackles to life with some old country music as they continue toward town.

Chesterfield was always a quiet little town. It's where Tim went to school and where he would hang out with his friends when he was young. Not much had changed in the thirty years since he left. The first thing they see pulling in is the tall metal water tower at the edge of town. It looks like it used to be white, but is now more rust-colored, with the town name painted in blue across the top. Most of the roads are still made of bricks, and the road signs have the same bullet holes. A few of the holes were from Tim and his friends.

There's one long main road running through the center of town, surrounded by scattered houses and a trailer park on the far side. Main Street is where all the action is, because all of the shops and businesses are clustered together on either side. All the buildings have the same old-style look, with rock walls and brown shingled roofs.

As any typical small town in the South, the first building on the street is Randy's Bar on the left. It's a small place, but it gets the job done. A couple of locals are sitting and watching out the window while drinking their beers. Different stores sit side by side along the main drag. A small thrift store full of old stuff, a hardware store, and a bank with only one teller. About midway down on the left is an old church painted white, with a bright gold cross on top of its steeple. Across the street from the church is the local elementary schoolhouse. Grades one through eight went here, and the high schoolers went to a newer building on the outside of town.

After the church, on the left is Bert's Grocery Store. It's a relatively new building with large glass windows, plastered with signs boasting the sale of the day. Just outside the door sits a little red rocket for the younger kids to ride by putting in a quarter. Next to the grocery store is the only good place in town to get a bite to eat, called Rose's Diner. It looks like an old fifties diner with blue neon lights lining the roof and a big red *"DINER"* neon sign in the middle. The owners went out of their way to restore the place to look authentic. The majority of the older folks in town will come here for three meals a day. This was also one of the most popular night time hangout spots when Tim was younger. He would come to hang out in the glow of the neon lights at the outside tables.

At the end of Main Street, to the left is Molly's Liquor Store, and right across the street is the Sheriff's station. There were a couple of occasions when Tim had to be picked up from the station by his dad as a kid, mostly for little stuff. The station is two stories tall, with red brick walls and metal bars over the windows.

They pull into Bert's Grocery and park the truck. After he turns off the key, it sputters a few times before finally coming to a rest. Tim steps out onto the quiet street and looks around. The street is empty except for an elderly couple walking hand in hand toward Rose's Diner for lunch.

They walk inside the grocery store, and right away, Tim recognizes the cashier from when he was younger. He could never forget her long, curly blonde hair and those bright blue eyes. She used to hang out with the rich kids whose parents could afford to buy them new sports cars. They would drive up and down Main Street, squealing their tires and laughing at the others hanging out in front of Rose's.

Tim walks up with a smile on his face as he makes eye contact. "Kari Miller?"

Kari turns and almost drops the jar of pickles she was scanning for a customer. "Tim Walker? Well, look at you. It's been a while since I've seen you around here. What brings you to town?"

"With all of this mess happening in the city, I figured this would be the safest place to lay low until everything calms down."

Kari hands a receipt to the customer and turns back to Tim with a smile. "I agree with you there. This place hasn't seen more than a bar fight in the last twenty years."

"Who's running the town nowadays?"

"Garrett O'Connell has been the sheriff for about three years now. He's pretty much running things since the old sheriff died."

"O'Connell? That lazy bastard, how'd he become the sheriff? He was always the first to throw rocks at the cop cars back in the day."

Kari leans in close over the counter, looking at Tim with a serious face. "His family owns the biggest farm in the county, and they're buying up all sorts of places around town. I think they're looking to take over this little town for themselves."

Tim leans back with a smile and laughs. "Not my circus, not my monkeys. I'll be leaving as soon as all of this riot crap is finished in the city. Good to see you again, Kari."

"Good to see you too, Tim."

Marco was just about done shopping by the time he was done talking to Kari at the register. Tim goes and grabs some diapers, and Kari rings everything up with a smile. Marco suggests grabbing some alcohol at Molly's before they leave town, and Tim couldn't agree more. They grab some whiskey and beer, then set off back toward the farm.

Back inside Bert's grocery store, Kari is sweeping the floor in front of the soda machines as Sheriff O'Connell comes through the doors. He looks around and awkwardly waves at Kari as he approaches the coffee machine. Garrett always had a thing for Kari, but never dared to do anything about it.

He smiles at her and carelessly pushes his silver thermos under the coffee machine. Hot coffee spurts out before he notices that the lid was still closed. Coffee runs down the side of the thermos and burns his fingers.

He quickly pulls his hands back, and the thermos drops to the floor with a bang, then rolls toward Kari's feet. "Ah, damn it."

Kari picks up the spinning thermos and leans her broom against the counter. "Rough day, Sheriff? Let me get that for you."

As Kari fills the thermos with coffee, Garrett leans against the counter and crosses his arms. "Thanks, Kari. I am having a rough day. Got a call from the county sheriff's office this morning, saying they're going to send some kind of task force here later this week. They didn't say what for, only that I need to give them my full cooperation and stay out of their way."

Kari rubs her chin and looks out the window. "That's weird. What would a small town like this need a task force for? Maybe they want to make sure we're safe. I heard from an old friend that the riots in Dallas are getting out of hand."

"Who did you talk to from the city?"

"Oh, Tim Walker was in here just a few minutes ago with his dad. He's staying at his parents' farm until the rioting stops."

"Walker? Didn't he go off and join the Army or something?"

"I think so. He looked like he was still in pretty good shape," Kari replies, staring off into space and raising her eyebrows. "I always did like a man in uniform."

Garrett looks down at his tan sheriff's uniform and straightens his tie. "You do?"

Kari blinks awkwardly, focusing on Garrett, as coffee starts to overflow from the thermos. "Ah, shit that's hot."

As Garrett grabs the thermos, his finger grazes Kari's hand.

As their eyes meet, Kari's face turns red and she turns away and walks quickly to the register, where she rings up the coffee.

Feeling ashamed, Garrett looks sadly at his overflowing coffee and quietly scolds himself, "Stupid idiot." He slowly walks to the register and drops a five-dollar bill on the counter. "Bye, Kari. Talk to you later."

Kari waves without saying a word and looks back at her register, feeling embarrassed.

As Garrett leaves the store, he takes a sip of his coffee and looks around at the quiet main street. "What do I need a task force for?"

The ride back to the farm is just as bumpy as the ride out. Tim holds tightly onto the whiskey bottle in his lap so it doesn't bounce off and break.

Every bone in his body rattles as his dad's truck rolls down the dirt road, and he thinks to himself, "This old pickup needs to die."

As they listen to some good old country music on the radio and watch the cornfields pass, the radio starts bellowing out the emergency alert tone. They both instinctively look out the windows at the sky, because the warning on the radio usually meant a tornado or hail was coming. The sky was bright and blue, so they look back at each other, confused.

"This is the Emergency Broadcast System. Please stand by for an important message."

"What's going on?" Marco asks, sounding confused, as the radio plays the tone again.

"This is the Emergency Broadcast System. Please stand by for an important message: The United States is under attack. The United States is under attack. The President of the United States has been assassinated. At two PM Eastern Standard Time, Washington D.C. was hit by a coordinated attack by an unknown force. Additional attacks have been reported in multiple southern states. Parts of New Mexico, Texas, Oklahoma, Arkansas, and Louisiana are no longer under the control of the U.S. government. If you are inside these areas, proceed directly to your homes, secure your doors, and wait for further instructions. This message will repeat every hour."

Tim points through the windshield and yells, "We need to get home now. Punch it, Dad!"

Marco pushes every bit of horsepower out of the old clunker he can while flying down the dirt road. When they pull into the driveway, Nancy is waiting for them at the back door. They rush inside to see the news on the TV.

"BREAKING NEWS! The President of the United States has been assassinated. Coordinated attacks against state capitals in the South have caused a complete collapse of government control. The organization taking credit for the attacks has not yet come forward. The Vice President is alive and has been moved to a secure location. She has declared martial law for the following states: New Mexico, Oklahoma, Texas, Arkansas, and Louisiana. More information will follow as the situation continues."

"Oh my God, what's happening?" Nancy cries, staring at the TV.

Tim looks over at Marco to see the look of fear on his face as he stands with his arms wrapped around Nancy.

Marco stares back and asks, "It's happening. Isn't it?"

Tim glares back at the TV and puts his arms around Mary. "I'm afraid it is." He says nervously, then takes a deep breath. "Okay, we need to prepare for the worst. Dad, get the shelter ready for us to move in at a moment's notice. Mary, stay by Victoria and keep her things ready to move. This is going to get worse before it gets better."

Chapter 3

THE REPUBLICAN REVOLUTION

Tim watches helplessly as the Russian-made grenade hits the street in the middle of his team. A bright flash of light, followed by a powerful blast, sends sand and gravel flying in all directions. He comes to, lying on the ground next to one of the buildings. All he can hear is a loud ringing, followed by the muffled thump of gunfire. As his sunglasses were knocked from his face, he squints as he looks up to see the blurred image of a soldier running toward him.

JJ reaches out a hand and yells, "Are you okay? Get up! We need to move now!"

Tim's vision and hearing start to come back as he pushes himself to his feet. He pulls his M4 rifle to his shoulder and looks around.

One of his team members yells from the other side of the street. "Contact front! Contact front!"

Tim instinctively takes a knee and aims his rifle to the front.

"Muscle Memory" is what it's called when you meticulously train to fight and learn to respond in a specific way, so you can react without having to think about it. You just do it. Tim finds his target, aligns his sights, and fires without hesitation.

"Chad's hit in the leg and bleeding badly," JJ yells, and points to Private Marshal. "Get a tourniquet on that now."

As the dust clears, Tim rubs his eyes and looks at what was left of his team. "JJ report!"

"Rhodes is KIA. Chad's injured but still breathing. Marshal's okay, just a little shaken up. You good? Are you hit anywhere?"

Tim sweeps his hands around his legs and looks himself over quickly. "Yeah, I'm good to go. Got my bell rung is all. Call it in and get reinforcements out here ASAP. More could be coming."

JJ reaches for his radio and looks up at the other side of village as a large dust cloud raises from behind the mosque. Before they have time to regroup, three trucks come screaming through the other side of the village and slide to a stop right in front of the disabled team. A massive cloud of dust engulfs the street as men dressed in rags and scarfs jump from the back of the trucks. Like ghosts emerging from a fog, the men appear with their rifles aimed at the team.

Tim, JJ, and Marshal open fire blindly into the thick cloud with everything they have. Two men fall to the ground as the others return fire. Marshal screams out from the other side of the street as he's hit and falls hard to the ground. Tim looks over to see how badly he was hit, but the dust was too thick. Before he has time to react, the men are on top of him and JJ, with their rifles pointed in their faces. The soldiers raise their hands in defeat, because there are too many men to try to fight, especially with one member of their team dead and two injured.

The insurgents have tattered, loose clothing with large pieces of cloth wrapped around their heads, covering their faces. The only thing visible are their bloodshot eyes, staring back with such hate and anger. They grab Tim and JJ's rifles and throw them into the dirt. As the dust clears, Tim looks over at Marshal, Rhodes, and Chad lying on the ground on the other side of the street. They weren't moving, and he fears the worst. One of the men pulls the rag from his face revealing a short black beard covering scared and pitted cheeks. He scowls and looks over at the three soldiers lying on the ground. He walks over and kicks Chad in the leg, but he doesn't move.

The man looks back at the remaining two soldiers on their knees and speaks with a deep gravelly voice. "Khalas."

He points to them and yells a couple more words as the others grab Tim and JJ by their arms. They bind their hands behind their backs with zip ties and drag them to one of the trucks. One man lowers the tailgate and tosses JJ inside. Tim struggles to break free but is overpowered and tossed into the back of the truck beside his friend. The two soldiers lay facing each other, and Tim can see the fear on JJ's face as they begin to drive away.

Tim looks his frightened friend in the eyes, trying to calm him as best he can. "Take it easy, JJ. I'll find a way out of this."

Tim opens his eyes to see Mary staring back at him from across the bed.

She looks at him with a smile. "Good morning. You should really stop calling me JJ."

"Maybe you should just change your name, and this wouldn't be a problem," he replies mockingly.

She stares back at him with her best stink eye. "Yeah, and maybe I can also grow a dick, and we can be best buds."

"Deal!" Tim replies excitedly, offering her a high five.

She laughs and slaps his hand back, followed by a swift wrestling attack, sending them both rolling off of the bed and hitting the floor with a loud thud. They lay there for a second, breathing heavily like a pair of easily exhausted elderly people.

Their attention is turned to the door as Nancy knocks. "You kids okay? You better not be up to any funny business. Your great-grandma Betty died in there, and I'm sure her ghost wouldn't approve of that in her bed."

Mary stares down at Tim with a haunting look on her face. "When are we going home?"

"First chance we get. I promise."

They slowly push themselves to their feet and get dressed while nervously checking around the room for ghosts. Mary grabs Victoria out of her little fortress, and they head to the kitchen to see what Nancy was cooking for breakfast.

Marco was already sitting in the living room, staring at the TV as they enter.

"Any updates?" Tim asks, looking up at the TV.

"The news is saying someone is finally taking responsibility for the attacks." Marco replies.

Just then, BREAKING NEWS scrolls across the TV screen. "An organization has taken responsibility for the horrific attacks across the country. They're calling themselves the Republican Revolution. Earlier today, they released a video online stating their intentions. Here's what they have to say."

A window pops up on the screen with a man wearing all black, and a mask covering his face. He stares at the camera with determination in his eyes, and speaks with strong sense of confidence. "America, you have a disease. There is a sickness that has infected every level of your government for far too long. The radical left has started to twist this once-great country into a downward spiral from which there is no return. We are here to right this atrocity. We are the Republican Revolution. We are not terrorists. We are not here to scare or intimidate you. We are here to clean the swamp that has been trying to swallow this great country. As our great former president once said, "The Republican train is coming!" Our brothers and sisters in the south are laying down the railroad tracks as we speak. We have already removed the head of the snake. Now, the R.R. will sweep across this country in overwhelming numbers to eradicate the radical left agenda and bring peace and freedom back to our once great land. We will not tire, we will not falter, and we will not fail."

Nancy stares at the TV with disgust. "What is this world coming to?"

Tim stands with his arms crossed staring at the TV. "Well, one semi-positive thing we can take from this is that this Republican Revolution doesn't seem to be aimed at hurting large numbers of people. They may look like a terrorist organization, but it doesn't seem like they want an all-out war. They're just trying to get rid of specific people who don't agree with their way of life. In this case, it's the entire Democratic Party. Now, what this means for the rest of the country, I don't know yet. If they're successful, it will mean a complete change in how we live in America. If they fail, it could very well turn into an all-out civil war. Only time will tell."

Back in Chesterfield, Sheriff O'Connell sits in his office filing paperwork as a group of men wearing all black walk through the station's front door. The clerk behind the reception desk attempts to stop them, but they walk straight through without saying a word.

One of the men walks into the Sheriff's office and stands in front of his desk, looking down at him confidently. "Sheriff O'Connell? I'm a representative of the newly appointed Governor of Texas," he says officially, placing a piece of paper on Garrett's desk with an official stamp in the corner.

The stamp doesn't look like the official seal of the governor. It has a large red R.R. imprinted in the center.

Garrett picks up the paper and reads it over. "Are you the task force that the county office is sending over? I wasn't expecting you for another few days. Who is this coming from? I can't accept this without the Governor's signature on it."

The man leans on the desk with both hands and stares at Garrett. "The Republican Revolution is now in charge and orders you to hand over your town, or you will answer directly to the new governor, General Grant. You will then most likely be executed for treason."

Garrett stares back with wide eyes at the man as he leans on his desk. As they lock eyes, the man slowly straightens up and places a hand on the pistol attached to his hip. The men outside the office follow suit and assume a defensive posture, waiting for commands.

Garrett looks through the door at the scared look on his clerk's face and slowly stands up from his chair.

Without making any sudden movements, he reaches for his chest and removes his badge, placing it carefully on his desk. "I don't know what you're trying to do here, but please don't hurt anyone. We'll cooperate with you the best we can."

The man releases his pistol and relaxes. "Outstanding Sheriff. Now, have your men evacuate the town immediately. Except for the bar. I could use a drink."

Two months pass on the farm, and nothing significant changes except that all cell phone, internet, and satellite networks stopped working. What was left of the US Government was attempting to disrupt all communication between the states occupied by the R.R. The local radio stations were still working, so what little news they got came from that. The Walkers were hoping for the best, but expecting the worst.

The underground shelter was fully stocked and armed, and the garden was in full bloom with fresh crops. They even built a still for making some moonshine. Tim insisted on building it. He would sneak across the road and steal a few baskets of corn from the neighboring farm to make the mash. He put the still in the old boathouse so he could pump water from the lake to cool it.

Marco had an idea to build a disguise for the top of the shelter so no one would find it if they had to hide. He created a false hay bale to place over the top of the doors, and it looked pretty convincing. Tim had a plan to convert the old windmill into a wind-powered generator, but he needed some new parts first. Fortunately for them, the power grid was still working.

The dirt road leading to the farm was pretty far out of the way, so they didn't get too many cars passing by. It was easy for them to spot a couple of trucks coming down the dusty road from far off this evening. As they got closer, Tim could see that one of the trucks was from the Sheriff's department in Chesterfield, with lights on top and a big gold star on the side.

Tim grabs his pistol, slides it into his hip holster, and walks toward the door. "What's this all about?"

Marco moves the blinds to the side and looks out the window. "No idea. Better let me come with you."

"No, stay here and be quiet. Be ready to run for the bunker if anything happens."

Tim opens the front door and steps out onto the porch just as the two trucks turn into the driveway. They come to a stop in front of the house, and the door to the sheriff's truck opens. Tim immediately recognizes Garrett O'Connell as he steps out of his truck wearing his big, white cowboy hat and tan sheriff's uniform. As Garrett walks toward the house, three men get out of the other truck and wait. They weren't wearing the standard sheriff's uniforms, though. They were wearing all black collared shirts with black tactical vests, blue jeans, and tan combat boots.

Garrett slowly walks over to the front of the porch and stops a couple of yards back. "Evening, Tim."

"O'Connell," he replies, sounding annoyed.

"A friend of mine told me you were in the area. How's the family doing?"

"We're surviving. Is there something I can do for you, Sheriff?"

We're just wondering how you're holding up way out here. We're checking in on a few different farms in the area."

"You need a team of mercenaries to check on peaceful farmers all the way out here?"

The group of men in the back shift their positions and turn towards the house.

"Not really. These men are here because there's someone in town who wants to speak with you. He believes your previous skill set could be useful to him."

"Who are these people?" Tim asks, already knowing what they

were. "These guys look like the kind of people this Republican Revolution would be hiring."

Garrett looks at the men, then turns back to Tim. "Why don't you come to town with us so I can introduce you? He'll explain everything. I would advise you to get along with these guys. They don't like to take no for an answer."

The men in black start moving slowly from the trucks and line up in front of the house. Just then, Marco comes out of the front door with a shotgun in one hand and tosses Tim a loaded AR-15 with the other.

"GUN!" Yells one of the men, and they all draw their pistols and aim them at the house.

Before anyone can shoot, Garrett walks out in between everyone with his hands in the air. "Calm down now, put the guns down. Let's not get ahead of ourselves here. They only want to talk to you, Tim. We'll bring you right back after. I swear."

Marco whispers in Tim's ear from behind. "I don't trust these guys."

"I don't either," Tim whispers back, then looks back at Garrett. "I'll come with you on one condition. I'm driving my own truck."

"I'm coming with you," Marco says quickly.

Tim hands the rifle to his dad and takes his keys. "No, I need you here to keep the girls safe. These guys are just fancy-dressed hillbillies. I can handle them."

"Be easy with the old girl," Marco says hesitantly.

Tim leans in close and whispers. "If I'm not back in a couple of hours, get in the bunker and stay there."

"Will do. Stay safe, Son. Love you."

Tim turns back to the sheriff. "Love you too, Dad. Now go back inside and wait for me."

Tim walks off the porch, jumps into his dad's old pickup, starts it up, and drives down the driveway. Garrett pulls his truck out in front of him, as the others follow closely behind. On the way to town, Tim listens to the news on the radio.

"This is WKGN Radio with the latest news in Northern Texas. The R.R. presence has been increasing over the last month. There have been many reports of checkpoints and roadblocks being set up throughout the Dallas-Fort Worth area. Many farms have reported that the R.R. has been commandeering their crops and livestock to feed their forces. Authorities are advising everyone to avoid confrontation or resisting the R.R. in any way. They assure us that the U.S. government is formulating a means of peaceful negotiations with the R.R. to end the violence and return the southern states to order. Tune in for more news at eleven."

As they get closer to town, things look much different than Tim's last visit. A large barricade was constructed at the entrance to Main Street, with guard towers and spotlights. Silhouettes of men with rifles walk back and forth on top of the rusty water tower. The doors and windows of all the stores are boarded up. All except for Randy's Bar, of course. What's a revolution without alcohol?

The schoolhouse looks like it was converted into a barracks for all of the militiamen. The street outside the barracks is being used as a staging area, with piles of supplies, boxes of ammo, and weapons. Trucks used as tactical vehicles are lined up on one side of the street in front of the old church, facing the main entrance. At least fifty men stand around, talking, drinking beer, and messing with their guns.

Further down the street, Burt's Grocery Store is a disaster. All of the glass windows are broken, and the door is kicked in. Inside, the shelves are empty and falling over, looking like a pack of wild animals tore through them. Rose's Diner looks like it was turned into the officers' lounge. Inside are a few grey-haired old-timers wearing their black outfits, leaning over tables, and drinking coffee. Tim almost doesn't recognize this part of town because all of the neon lights outside of Rose's are turned off. Molly's Liquor has the front door half hanging off the hinges, and the lights are flickering. The shelves and refrigerators are completely raided of all alcohol. The priorities of this militia are becoming pretty clear now.

The back end of Main Street was completely blocked off with all of the town's school buses, acting like a gigantic wall sealing off the exit. Guard towers were built up on either side, with big spotlights mounted on them. The small town was converted into a well-fortified installation.

Garrett leads Tim all the way to the sheriff's station and parks his truck. Tim parks his dad's truck with the tailgate towards the building in case he needs to make a quick escape. He jumps out and looks around, taking in what the militia had done with the place. The sheriff's station was set up as the headquarters building. A large military-style antenna was mounted on the roof, and sandbags line the windows to the front. Tim walks toward the front door, where Garrett is waiting for him.

He points down to Tim's pistol. "I'll need to take your gun before you can go inside."

Tim stares at him in the eyes for a second, then slowly pulls the pistol from its holster, handing it to him. "I better get that back."

"Don't worry. You will," he replies as he holds up the shiny pistol, looking it over before stuffing it into his belt.

Tim follows the sheriff into the back of the station where his desk should have been, but instead, a tall, grizzly-looking man is looking down at a big map of Northern Texas on the table. He's easily six foot four with black hair and dark skin. A short black beard on his face hides a scar just below his lower lip. A long black trench coat hangs over a black button-up shirt and blue jeans. On his head rests a tattered black baseball cap with what looks like a railroad sign, but it's in red instead of yellow.

"Sir, this is the man I was talking about earlier," Garrett says as the man looks up at Tim and nods. "Tim, this is Colonel Jack Wallace of the R.R."

"At ease, soldier. Welcome to Forward Operating Base Chesterfield. I've heard a lot of good things about you. Your friend here speaks very highly of you. I understand you served in the military for some time?"

"I did my time." Tim replies, as he crosses his arms.

Wallace pulls a piece of paper out from under the map and holds it up to the light. "I had our people look up your service record. You did quite well in your time in the Army. It says here you served twenty-two years in the Special Operations. Seven deployments to Afghanistan, Iraq, Syria, and Pakistan, earning two Purple Hearts and a Bronze Star for valor. Very impressive, I must say. I'm in great need of highly skilled leaders in my ranks. I'm sure you had a good look at what I'm working with on your way in. How would you feel about joining our cause and being given the rank of Captain? You'll have an entire company of men under your command."

"Thanks for the offer, but I'm retired. Plus, I really don't want to get wrapped up in whatever it is you're doing here."

Wallace slams his fists down on the desk. "What we're doing here is taking back our *freedom!* This twisted democratic government is stealing our country away. Our very way of life is being compromised, and we're no longer able to keep our families safe. We *must* take it back by force."

"I've seen my fair share of war against *actual* enemies of the U.S. I won't fight my own people."

"I see. Fair enough. What if I could offer you the rank of Major, and you would serve alongside me in commanding this revolution?"

Garrett raises his hand and clears his throat. "But sir, you said before that I was going to get that position."

Wallace points his hand at Garrett. "Quiet soldier! Can't you see the officers are having a conversation here?" He barks, then turns back to Tim offering his hand with a sinister smile. "So, what do you say, Major Walker?"

Tim looks at Wallace and can tell that he's desperate for someone with half a brain to join this ragtag revolution.

He leans closer and speaks confidently enough to make Wallace think he's considering joining. "So, what if I *do* join your revolution? What then? What's your endgame here? Do you seriously plan on having us march through to Canada, taking out any Democrats we find along the way? That seems kind of pointless to me. There needs to be a bigger goal here."

Wallace's eyebrows raise and he points his finger at Tim. "Now, this is a smart man. This is the kind of mind we need in a command position," he leans forward with both hands on his desk. "We're not stopping at the Canadian border. Once we take D.C. and align the rest of the states, we'll be taking Canada by storm. Those moose-fuckers won't know what hit them. Then we'll focus our efforts on South America. With our great General Mathias T. Grant behind the wheel, we won't stop until the entire Western Hemisphere is under the control of the Revolution. We've been preparing for this for years," Wallace reaches his hand out toward Tim again. "So, what do you say?"

Tim steps back and shakes his head. "I'll never join your revolution. I will not betray my country by fighting in this civil war, and helping you with this grand scheme for world domination."

Wallace lowers his head and looks down at his map. Without looking up, he barks orders at Garrett. "O'Connell, take this man and lock him in the holding cells."

"Wait. What? You said that you would let him go if he didn't want to join us. You said that anyone has the right to come and go as they wish."

You'll keep your mouth *shut* if you know what's good for you. Unless you want to end up in that cell with him. He knows too much and is far too dangerous to be roaming around outside unaccounted for. Lock him up. That's an order!"

Garrett takes Tim by the arm, walks him to the back of the station, and pushes him into one of the holding cells. He looks through the bars with disappointed eyes as he locks the door and says nothing. Tim turns around and sits down on the tattered bed in the back.

He looks around the cell and says to himself, "Well, what are you going to do now, dumbass?"

Looking around the cell, he doesn't see much to work with. The bed was hanging from the wall by chains. There was a small window, but it's full of iron bars. Outside the cell, he can see down the hallway to a guard's desk. There's another cell next to his, but it looks empty except for a large lump under a blanket on the bed. Tim looks closer through the bars and sees a pair of boots poking out from under the blanket. It looks like someone was sleeping in the other bed.

Tim slides closer to the bars and whispers. "Hey, hey, pssst. Buddy, are you awake?"

He's probably one of the militia idiots who got too drunk and had to be detained. Unless he was like Tim and declined the offer to join, in which case he could help him escape. Tim finds a pebble on the floor and tosses it at the breathing lump of cloth.

The blanket jumps, and a head pops out. "Eh, what? What time is it?"

"Pssst, hey buddy. Over here."

The man slowly sits up with a dumbfounded, half-drunk expression on his face. He stretches his arms up while wearing a dirty brown t-shirt and torn jeans. He slowly scrapes the long, greasy, brown hair from his face and looks over at Tim.

"Who the hell'r you? Why'r you in my trailer?" He slurs.

Tim shakes his head and thinks to himself. "Oh great, this guy's hammered. He's not going to be any help, but I don't have any other options."

The man looks around the cell, confused. "Wa, where am I?

"Dude, you're in the sheriff's station jail. Wake up, will you? I need some help getting out of here. Are you part of this militia?"

"What? No, I own the bar down the street," he answers, starting to come out of his drunken stupor.

"You're Randy?"

"Yup, Randy Morgan at your service. We had a little bender last night, or was it this morning? I don't remember. It's the end of the world!! Hahaha!"

"Shhhh, you idiot. Help me get out of here."

"But why do you want to get out? These beds are *so* nice." Randy says as he starts to lie back down.

Thinking quickly, Tim remembers the one thing that would always motivate a dunk person, more booze. "Hey, I can make it up to you. I have some moonshine back on my farm. I just made a fresh batch last week. I'll give you a gallon if you help me get out of this cell."

Randy abruptly sits up straight. "Moonshine? I like moonshine. Where's your farm?" He asks, sounding a little more motivated.

"It's about thirty minutes from here. I have a truck out front. You just have to help me get out of this cell and out of town without being seen."

Randy looks over at Tim with a half-straight face and a raised eyebrow. "Oooh, that's all. You know where we are, right?"

"Yes, I know where we are. Can you help me?" Tim asks again, feeling like this is going nowhere.

He has his doubts about this guy, but he's out of options. Randy takes a deep breath and attempts to stand up from the bed and nearly falls flat on his face. He tries again, grabbing at the bars in front of him, but his hand goes straight through, causing him to lose balance and smash his face into the bars with a loud bang. Tim looks down at the floor and shakes his head, feeling that all hope was lost. When he looks back up, Randy is standing outside the cell, staring back at him through the bars with a crooked smile.

Tim jumps up and whispers to him. "How the hell did you get out?"

Randy looks back then points to himself. "Who, me? Oh, I was just taking a power nap. These beds are really comfortable. Let me go get the keys. I'll be right back."

Randy stumbles down the hallway toward the guard and falls forward, slapping both hands down hard on the desk. "Hey Richie! What's up?"

"Wow, that was a quick nap, Randy. You feeling alright?"

"Yeah, I'm good. Hey, I'm about to open the bar. We're having a strip beer pong tournament tonight. You want to be first up against the twins?"

"Oh, hell yeah. They're so hot. But I've got this guy locked up in the back, and the Colonel said to watch him."

"Don't worry about that guy. He's not going anywhere. Tell you what, I'll stay here and give the keys to the next guard I see, and tell him you had to go take a shit. Then I'll meet you at the bar later. The first round's on me."

"Hey, thanks a million, Randy. I owe you one."

The guard places the keys on the table and takes off out of the door. Randy lazily leans back, looking down the hallway at Tim, and winks. Tim shakes his head and laughs to himself as Randy snatches the keys off the desk and wobbles back down the hallway toward the cell.

Tim looks at him with a smile. "You're a crazy man. You know that, right?"

"Yeah, whatever. You better be good for that shine, bro."

"I am. Now open this thing, and let's get the hell out of here."

Randy fumbles with the keys for a second and finally finds the right one to unlock the cell. Once Tim is free, he starts looking around for a way out of the building without being seen.

"Psssttt, follow me," Randy spits, as he whispers.

Tim follows him down the hall and around behind the guard's desk.

"The bars on the window are loose. This is how I sneak a bottle to Richie when he is on duty."

Tim slides the window open and reaches for the bars. Sure enough, the bars are hinged and swing outward. He ducks under the bars and quietly slides out the window, crouching next to the building checking left and right as Randy attempts his exit.

Tim looks up at the fumbling drunk and cringes. "Oh Lord, this is gonna be bad."

First, Randy tries to get one leg through, then tries the other. After giving up on the legs, he decides to go headfirst. He starts a smooth yet limp noodle glide under the bars until his arm slips through and gets caught at his elbow. He proceeds to bend in half sideways and turn backwards so that when his ass hits the ground, his hands and feet are straight up, caught in the bars.

He leans his head back and looks at Tim with the biggest smile. "Nailed it!"

Tim helps him get the rest of his limbs through the window and onto his feet. "You good?"

"Good to go, Captain." Randy replies, giving a sloppy salute with his left hand.

"Wait a second. Couldn't you have just walked out the front door? I mean, you're not under arrest or anything."

"Yeah. I guess so." He replies, looking confused. "But what's the fun in that?"

They make their way to the front of the building and hide behind the bushes next to the street. Tim can see his dad's truck parked just to the right. The keys are still inside, so he knows he can get it moving quickly. The only tricky part was getting past all of the soldiers scattered around the town without being seen. He's not going to let this drunken idiot drive out. They would never make it.

Just then, he hears someone arguing toward the main entrance of the building.

"This is bullshit. I was supposed to be second-in-charge. How could he treat me like that? Doesn't he know who I am?"

Tim looks over and sees Sheriff O'Connell apparently arguing with himself about the conversation they had with the Colonel earlier. He stomps his way down the front of the building towards the guys hiding in the bushes. As Garrett comes to the edge of the wall, Tim reaches out from the bush and grabs him in a chokehold, covering his mouth. He pulls him back through the bushes and pushes his back against the wall. Randy then proceeds to slap Garrett's face wildly for no reason.

"Hey, stop, stop! What are you doing?" Tim says, glaring at Randy.

"Helping," he replies.

Garrett raises his hands in defense and whimpers. "What's going on? Please don't kill me!"

Tim lowers the Sheriff down the wall to the grass and kneels down in front of him, still holding his forearm against his throat. "It's me, don't scream. I'll let you go if you promise to keep quiet."

Garrett nods, and Tim releases his grip. "How did you get out?"

Randy looks at him with a crooked smile. "I helped!"

Tim stands up and steps back looking around, then back to Garrett. "Look, this Wallace guy, shit, this whole militia thing is a big joke. These idiots are going to get everyone killed."

"I know," Garrett says reluctantly looking down at his boots and kicking at the air. "I was stupid to think he was going to let me in on anything. He was just using me to get control of the town."

"Listen, help me get out of here, and I'll do what I can to get control of the town back for you."

"Did you really do all of those things he was talking about? The Army stuff and all?"

"Yes, but if we don't get out of this town, I can't be any help to anyone."

"And *I* don't get ma moonshine," slurs Randy.

Garrett stands up and stares awkwardly at Randy, then back at Tim, extending his hand for a handshake. "Alright, I'll help. What do you need me to do?"

Tim shakes his hand and dusts off some of the leaves that were still on his uniform. Randy reaches in and helps with the dusting, but Garrett slaps frantically at his hands and points at him angrily.

Garrett then reaches into his belt, pulls out Tim's pistol, and hands it to him. "Here, you might need this."

"Thank you," Tim says, taking the pistol and placing it back into his hip holster. "Ok, you see my truck right over there?"

Garrett looks at Tim awkwardly. "Yeah, is that yours? I was wondering about that. You couldn't afford anything new, seeing as you're some big war hero?"

Tim gives Garrett a quick, mean stare. "Focus. The keys are in the ignition. All you need to do is get in, start it up, and I'll jump in the back as you pull off."

Randy looks over excitedly. "What do you want me to do?"

"Just get in the passenger seat and ride along. Don't do anything out of the ordinary. We don't want to draw any attention to ourselves as we leave town. If they ask what you're doing, just say you're taking this old truck to the dump. Got it?"

"Got it," replies Garrett.

"Randy?"

He gives Tim another sloppy salute. "Got it, Boss. Nothing out of the ordinary."

Garrett slowly slides past the bushes and walks toward the truck. He goes to open the door, but as he slowly pulls, the old, crappy door lets out a loud creaking sound that echoes off the buildings across the street. He cringes his face and continues to slowly pull the door until it's finally open. He looks around to see if anyone heard him, then jumps into the driver's seat, closing the door behind him. Garrett finds the keys in the ignition and turns the old, tired engine over. It growls to life, sending a large puff of black smoke out of the tailpipe into the night air.

Randy looks over at Tim and laughs. "Epic."

Then he steps out and makes his jagged line toward the truck's passenger side, opening the door smoothly on the first try.

With his hands on his hips, Randy growls at Garrett through the open door. "Let me see your license and registration."

Garrett reaches through the cab and grabs Randy by the shirt, pulling him into the truck face-first onto the seat. Randy huffs as he sits up, and closes the door. Then turns to Garrett and punches him in the shoulder.

From his bushy hiding spot, Tim waits until the flash of the reverse lights signal that the truck is shifting into drive. He makes a run for the truck bed, smoothly sliding over the tailgate and lies down flat inside the bed. He grabs an old tarp from inside and stretches it over himself so it doesn't look like a body underneath.

Garrett continues driving down Main Street toward the staging area. Through the holes in the tarp, Tim can see the streetlights slowly passing above. As they approach some men standing around, one of them waves to Randy.

"Hey Randy, last night was the best night of my life! I'm still drunk."

Randy sticks his head out the window and waves. "Me too!"

The guy hands Randy a beer as they pass, and he proceeds to chug the beer and throws the empty bottle at another group of men standing near their trucks. The bottle smashes on the ground at their feet, and they all cheer.

"This guy is a lunatic." Tim grumbles to himself as he lies still in the truck bed.

He watches through the holes at the fading lights as the truck passes the final barrier, leaving town.

A few moments later, Randy pounds on the side of the truck with his hand. "All clear, Captain."

Tim slides out from under the tarp, looking around to make sure it was actually all clear, and peeks up through the back window. "Hey, stop here really quick. I'll drive." As the screechy brakes bring the truck to a stop, he jumps out of the bed and into the driver's seat, pushing Garrett into the center. "What was that back there, Randy?"

Randy turns to other two with an innocent look on his face. "You said nothing out of the ordinary, right? That's my norm, bro."

"I'm sure it is," Tim replies mockingly. "Let's get back to my farm and regroup."

As the guys drive down the driveway, Marco and Mary are waiting on the porch for Tim to return.

"Mary meets him with a hug. "I thought you were dead. What took you so long?"

"I got locked up for a little while, but I had some help getting out."

"What's *he* doing back here?" Marco says, looking over at Garrett with a sneer on his face.

"Don't worry, Dad. He's on our side now. And this is Randy. He owns the bar in town."

"Smells like he brought the bar with him," Mary comments, covering her nose.

"Nice to meet you too." Randy replies, wincing at her, then looks at Tim. "Now, where's my moonshine?"

"Moonshine?" Marco asks, looking at Tim oddly.

"Long story. Dad, can you grab a jug out of the shed for me? Fellas, let's go inside. We have some things to discuss."

The guys follow Tim inside the house, and they sit at the dining room table. Moments later, Marco returns with a jug of shine and places it on the kitchen counter. Tim looks over at Randy, who was eyeballing the jug and licking his lips.

He points at him to calm down. "Easy, Randy. You have to wait until later to drink that. We have some important things to discuss first."

Mary brings Randy a big cup of coffee and sets it on the table.

"Now guys," Tim says, taking a breath, "I want to thank you both for helping me out back there, but I see now we have a bigger problem to deal with. Once those guys find out I'm gone, they're gonna come looking for me. There's no way we can outgun these guys, but I'm pretty sure we can outsmart them. We might need some more people and supplies, though. I can't have my dad and the girls out there risking their lives. No offense, Randy, but I don't trust you with a gun."

"None taken," Randy replies, taking a big drink of his coffee with his middle finger extended.

"I might be able to help with that." Garrett says. "My dad has about fifty hired hands on his farm. You know, tending to horses and working the fields and whatnot."

"What's your dad's opinion of this militia? I saw how quickly you were to join their cause. Can we trust him to help us and not turn us in?"

"I think so. It's been a while since I talked to him. Wallace has been taking a lot of this year's crops from his farm. Come to think of it, those guys did shoot up a bunch of his cattle the other day. Yeah, I think he'll be willing to help."

"Good. Now, Randy. You have the most important job of all."

Randy sets his mug down and looks up with an excited grin.

"You need to drive back to town and continue doing what you normally do at the bar."

"What?! I was hoping for something more explosive. Something that requires karate chops and stuff," he replies while chopping at the air.

Tim stands up and grabs a couple of radios off the shelf. "I need a man on the inside. Take this radio. Your call sign will be... Whiskey Tango Foxtrot. Mine's Toolman. Turn this on every day at two PM and wait for me to call you. It's imperative that you never mention any specific locations or names while talking on the open radio. You never know who's listening, so only use code words.

Here's the plan. I'm sure you hear all sorts of stuff from those guys while they're drunk in your bar. That's the best way to hear their latest plans. Keep them drinking and keep them talking. Also, a hungover soldier is easier to trick. When I have a new plan, I'll let you know. Got it?"

Randy takes the radio and the truck keys off the table, then looks at Tim. "Got it, Captain."

"Like hell, he's taking my truck!" Marco says, standing up and grabbing for his keys.

"Don't worry, Dad. You'll get your truck back in one piece. *Won't he Randy?*"

"Of course, like new." Randy says, smiling at Marco. "Well, like it is. Still in one piece... of crap."

"Now, for the rest of you, we can expect them to be here first thing in the morning once they notice I'm missing. Dad, is the shelter ready?"

Marco, who is still staring angrily at Randy, turns to Tim. "Yes, it is."

"Ok, I need you guys to make this place look like we packed up and left town in a hurry, then get inside the shelter and put the disguise over the entrance. Be ready to stay there for a couple of days. I'm confident they're not smart enough to find the entrance. I'm going with Garrett to his dad's farm. I'll keep my radio on me at all times. Let me know when it's all clear."

Tim gives Randy a to-go cup of coffee and sends him on his way back to town. Marco and the girls gather what they need for a couple of days in the shelter and hunker down inside. Once they make sure the bunker is properly hidden and secured from the outside, Tim and Garrett jump into Tim's truck and leave for the O'Connell's' farm. Tomorrow will be a long day, and they have a lot to do if they're going to survive this.

Chapter 4

THE O'CONNELL'S

The heat from the Iraqi sun blasts down upon Tim and JJ for what seems like hours as they unwillingly bounce around in the back of the pickup.

JJ looks at Tim and whispers, "How are we going to get out of this?"

"I don't know," Tim replies, looking around the dirty truck bed. "Just hang in there for now. We'll find a way."

Suddenly, everything goes dark as the truck drives into what looks like a tunnel, but it turns out to be a cave of some sort. The truck comes to a quick stop, and they hear men coming around the side.

"Yalla, Yalla!" Yells one of the captors, as another grabs Tim by the ankles and pulls him out of the truck.

He slams onto the dirt and watches as JJ comes crashing down next to him. Without remorse, they pull the soldiers to their feet and strip all of their tactical gear off. Another man pats them down, takes both of their pocket knives, and shoves the soldiers deeper into the cave. As Tim's eyes slowly adjust to the darkness, he notices dim yellow lights hanging from wooden poles against the walls. The thick smell of salt and clay fills the air as they stomp through muddy puddles.

Once he realizes what they were being dragged down into, he thinks to himself, "This is an old mine."

They reach what looks like a big metal cage in a large cut-out room at the end of the mineshaft. Lying in a puddle of water on the floor of the cage are three other men. They're soldiers from the looks of their tattered uniforms and combat boots. One of the captors unlocks the cage door and tosses Tim and JJ onto the muddy floor. He slams the rusty door shut and locks it with a big cast-iron key. Their captors stand at the door, looking through the bars for a few seconds, nodding to each other. Then they walk back up the tunnel and out of sight.

The light is too low to make out the other soldiers' name tapes, but it's obvious that they were Army by the camouflage pattern on their uniforms.

Tim sits up in the mud and whispers to the men. "You guys alright? How long have you been in here?"

The soldier sitting closest slowly turns his head and looks at Tim, with dried blood covering half of his face. "We've been here for days, a week maybe. It's hard to tell without sunlight."

Tim motions to the other two soldiers. "Are those two alright?"

"Yeah, we're alive," one of the other men says, sloshing the muddy water around as he sits up.

"What do these guys want?" Tim asks, trying to stay calm.

"Don't know exactly. There's one guy who speaks English, as far as I can tell. He takes us up to another area one by one and asks us about where our unit is located and how many men we have."

Tim looks the exhausted soldiers over, and speaks calmly. "What unit are you guys from?"

"We're from the First of the Five-O-Fifth, out of Fort Bragg. Our patrol was ambushed, and they brought us here," he replies with a crackle in his voice. "I'm Maxwell, and that's Sharp and Jenkins."

"We're from Ninth Group, also from Bragg. Don't worry, guys. We'll find a way out of this. I'm Tim, and this is JJ. Will you guys be able to fight when I need you to?"

Jenkins sits up straight with his hands tied behind his back. "Group guys! Thank God. Yes, we can still fight. Please get us out of this shithole."

"We contacted our unit just before they took us. They should be able to track us down quickly. We're so deep in this mine, though. We'll need to get out of this cage and protect ourselves once our rescue gets here. Have you seen a way out of this yet?"

Sharp slams his back against the metal bars. "No, it's solid steel, and they always keep it locked."

Tim looks around at the end of the tunnel as his night vision starts to come back. An old, busted mine car, half-buried in the mud, sits to the left of the cage next to the wall. Stacked up on the other side of the room are three large green wooden crates.

Tim motions with his eyes toward the crates. "Have you seen them take any weapons out of those boxes?"

Maxwell looks up at Tim. "I don't think so. They brought those down here yesterday. They've been moving a lot of boxes in and out lately. We think this is some kind of supply depot for them."

"How often do they come back here and check on us?" JJ asks, peeking through the bars at the tunnel entrance.

"I think every couple of hours. I can't tell," replies Maxwell, sounding super exhausted.

Tim shuffles around in the mud to look at the three soldiers. "Ok, I have a plan, but I'll need everyone to work together. Do you guys have a knife on you?"

"No, they took all of our things when we got here."

Tim slides his hands under his butt and behind his knees. He reaches into the side of his boot and pulls out a small knife. "Then your leadership has failed you. Always keep a knife hidden on you somewhere." Tim looks over at JJ as he pulls a knife out of a hidden slot in the back of his belt. "Now, pay attention. The key is to loosen the zip tie just enough so you can get your hands out when you need them. If they come and take one of us, you don't want them to find all the ties cut off completely. They'll search us again, and then we'll really be fucked."

Tim inserts the end of the knife under the teeth of the zip tie and slowly releases it. "A little trick I picked up in survival school."

By the time he was done explaining the procedure to the others, JJ is already free and looking around. He was much more limber than Tim. Once both of them were free, Tim turns to JJ, and they tap their knives together as if they were toasting a drink.

"Ok, come here, Maxwell. Once you're free, help your buddies, then stay here and wait for my orders."

Tim hands the soldier his knife, and as he turns around, JJ is already reaching through the bars to pick the lock. Thirty seconds later, the lock clicks open and Tim slowly pushes the gate open, whispering to JJ.

"What took you so long?"

"I was taking your mom out for a drink," JJ quickly whispers back.

Tim opens the rusty door just enough to slip past and moves low and slow toward the green crates, keeping an eye on the tunnel out of the room. JJ follows him out the door but stops just outside the cage and takes a knee. When Tim reaches the crates, he looks them up and down for any type of booby trap, then lifts the lid of the top box. As he sees what was waiting inside, his eyes open wide.

It was a crate of brand-new AK-47s. He pulls one from the rack and releases the magazine to see that it's fully loaded. A slight tingle manifests in the front of his pants as he rocks the magazine back into place and turns around. When JJ sees what Tim was holding, he throws his hands in the air like he just scored a touchdown. Tim tosses one rifle to him, and JJ hands it through the door to the other guys. He passes three more rifles to JJ and closes the box slowly.

Just as Tim reaches the cage, he hears footsteps echoing down the tunnel, signaling that someone was coming. JJ quickly closes the gate, and they shove their rifles under the mud and sit on them. Everyone slides their zip ties back on and go limp like they were toys from Toy Story, and a kid was coming. The captor walks up to the cage and stops, looking at the soldiers closely through the bars. He turns to the room, gives it a quick scan, then walks back up the tunnel.

Maxwell raises his head as he hears the man walking away. "That was close."

"Damn it," Jenkins complains, sliding his soggy rifle out of the mud and looks at it disappointedly. "We just ruined these guns by throwing them in the mud."

"Oh, my poor, simple-minded friend," Tim says as he pulls his rifle from the mud and smiles at it. "This is a Soviet-made AK-47. It's extremely durable and reliable. You could throw it off the roof into the mud, run it over with a truck, pick it up, chamber a round, and fire away like nothing ever happened."

Just then, loud pops and yelling echo off of the walls up the tunnel.

Tim stands up and looks at the exit. "Sounds like our friends are right on time. You guys ready for a fight?"

"Hell yes, we are," replies Maxwell.

Tim points to the crates on the other side of the room. "Ok, you three, go and get behind those crates and wait for my signal. JJ, get inside that old mine car. You know what to do."

The three soldiers quickly run across the room and take cover behind the crates. JJ leaves the cage, jumps inside the old metal mine car, and ducks below the rim. Inside the cage, Tim positions himself with his back to the door and his rifle resting in front of him, ready to fire.

A few moments later, three men come running down the tunnel

with their rifles ready to execute the prisoners. When they reach the cage, they stop and seem surprised to see that the door is open with only one prisoner lying dead, and the rest missing. They stand there momentarily confused until they hear a whistle coming from deeper in the room. All three men turn suddenly and look at the mine car. Tim quickly rolls over and shoots one of the men twice in the chest through the bars. JJ then pops up from his hiding place and shoots the other two before they can react. The men fall on top of each other like sacks of potatoes on the muddy floor.

Tim jumps to his feet and leaves the cell, kicking the rifles away from the dead captors as he passes. With a focused expression, JJ jumps from his mine car and keeps an eye his now lifeless captures. He stops just before one of the bodies and lines up for the kick. With two long strides and a strong swing of his leg, he strikes one of them right in the groin with his combat boot.

"What was that for?" Tim asks with a painful grin.

"Just making sure he's dead," JJ replies. He looks down at the bloody captives face for a second. "Yup, he's dead."

"Come on, you three. Keep low and keep quiet," Tim says, waving to the soldiers behind the crates.

The pounding of gunfire and shouting gets louder the further they walk up the tunnel. The light of day begins to illuminate the way as they reach the entrance. A fierce firefight between US soldiers and about ten insurgents rages on through the entrance to the mine. Lucky for them, the insurgents were too occupied with the soldiers to notice their captives coming up from behind. Tim motions to JJ and the others to spread out to the side of the tunnel and stay low. They slowly close in behind what remains of the insurgents and take cover behind a line of boxes.

Tim looks over at JJ and counts down with his fingers. "Three... Two... One... NOW!"

As the Northern Texas sky begins to change from a star-filled black to a light blue, Tim and Garrett speed down the old dirt road toward the O'Connell's family farm. The sound of the crickets chirping is almost louder than the tires crunching on the dirt road. As they reach the property line, a nice white plank fence appears running along the roadside that seems to go on for miles. Off in the field, a large herd of colorful horses gallop freely around the property. The fence leads them all the way to the turnoff leading to the farm.

Garrett clears his throat and nervously speaks, "Not far now."

Tim could sense a slight hesitation in his voice. It was probably because Garrett had been working with this militia while they were stealing crops and livestock from his family. It's doubtful that his father will greet him with open arms.

They make a right turn, and suddenly everything goes quiet as the truck tires hit a perfectly smooth blacktop road. Lining the road are dozens of old tractors and rusty antique farm equipment. In the distance stands a massive four-story house painted in pearl white, with a four-car garage attached to the right side. In the back, to the left, is an enormous warehouse with four sets of barn doors on the front. It's also painted in white and surrounded by bright white plank fencing. On the edge of a freshly cropped field to the right, sit three tall, silver grain silos next to another smaller white building. Two enormous green combine tractors are parked under a shed beside the silos. Lots of smaller tractors and vehicles are scattered all around the farm, with men walking around and working.

Tim looks around with wide eyes. "Impressive. So this is how the other half lives."

Garrett rolls his eyes and grips the steering wheel tightly. They pull up to the main house and follow the driveway around the wide circle, with a large marble fountain in the center. As they approach the house, a shotgun blast rings out, forcing Garrett to slam on the brakes and come to a screeching halt on the blacktop. Suddenly, a man comes out from behind a large dually truck, aiming a double-barrel shotgun at them.

An angry-looking snarl curls his lips behind a neatly trimmed white beard and matching white hair, covered by a big grey cowboy hat. He stands with his legs wide, wearing a white long-sleeve button-up shirt, with blue jeans and nice boots.

Garrett jumps out of the truck with his hands in the air. "Whoa, whoa, whoa, put the gun down, Dad! It's me."

"What do you want, Boy?" He yells, still aiming the shotgun at Garrett. "We're not giving anything else to those bullies. We've already given them enough for *two* armies!"

"Calm down, Dad. We're not here to take anything from you. We just want to talk."

"How could you let that group of thieves take your town and tell you what to do? O'Connell's own and lead armies. We don't take orders from anyone," he yells, waving his shotgun around wildly. "Now, you can go back to your new *friends* and tell them that we're not giving up a single ear of corn until we're fully paid for everything they've already taken. They also owe me for the twenty head of cattle they shot up for no reason."

Garrett stands in front of his dad with his hands still in the air. "I'm not working with those guys anymore, Dad. I realized they're a bunch of crazy assholes that can't be trusted."

"Ooohhh, *now* you finally realize this. I knew that from the *start!*" He points at the truck with his shotgun. "Who's that with you?"

"That's Tim. He's a friend. We think we can put together a plan to get rid of those guys, with your help, of course."

"Well, it's about damn time someone grew some balls around here," he says, turning around and throwing his shotgun over his shoulder. "Come on inside boys, and I'll get the chef to cook up some breakfast."

Tim gets out of the truck, slightly dumbfounded by what just happened. He follows Garrett through the massive white double doors, engraved with flowers and swirls of vines. As he walks over the threshold, the sheer size of the room takes him by surprise.

Hanging high above on the ceiling is a crystal chandelier with what looks like clear deer antlers laced throughout. The floors are all white marble, with black tiles lining the walls. Directly in front of them stands the most elaborate staircase he'd ever seen. It has to be twenty feet wide and splits at the top, going in both directions. The handrails are made of dark, expensive-looking wood that spirals at the bottom into miniature, hand-carved horses. Garrett's dad passes his shotgun to a sharply dressed man standing next to the door.

"Thank you, Sir," he says obediently.

As he takes a white cloth from a table to wipe his hands, he looks at his son. "Have Chef Luke make us up some breakfast, and tell Celia that Garrett's here," a smirk spreads across his bearded face. "She'll be happy to know that her baby boy has finally come home."

"Right away, Sir," he replies, and immediately walks away.

Garrett puts his hand on his forehead as his cheeks turn red. "Really, Dad? Just because I'm the youngest doesn't make me the baby. I'm a grown-ass man."

"Tell her that. She's been worrying non-stop ever since those fellas came to town. She thinks they're some kind of cult looking to bring back the Devil." He turns to Tim and offers his hand, covered in gold rings, for a handshake. "Now, this looks like a man who's been there and done that a couple of times. The name's Samuel Josiah O'Connell. My friends call me Sammy."

Tim shakes his tightly gripped hand. "Wish we could have met under better circumstances. My name's Tim Walker."

Sammy releases his grip and waves for them to follow him down the hall. "Follow me, boys. Let's get some coffee and food in ya."

Tim looks at Garrett and whispers, "Should I take my shoes off?"

Garrett just laughs and walks after his father. The house, or mansion as some would call it, is much bigger on the inside. Paintings of dead relatives cover the walls, surrounded by all sorts of antique shields, muskets, and pistols. There's even one whole section dedicated to old knives and swords. The long hallway is lined with small tables with spiraled cast-iron legs, holding antique vases and old flower pots. Moving quickly in the opposite direction, a lady carrying a big silver tray with a teapot and cup walks by.

Tim follows them through to the enormous dining room, where fancy silver light fixtures are attached to the walls surrounding a massive table with about fifteen chairs. Sammy sits at the far end of the table, while Garrett and Tim take seats on either side next to him.

Without a sound, a man dressed in a white shirt with black buttons enters through a door and sets a placemat and silverware in front of each of them with exceptional speed and precision. He then backs away and disappears through the door again. A second later, three more men dressed the same come through the door, one after another, carrying silver trays. They quickly place a plate of food in front of each of them, followed by a little gravy boat filled with white sausage gravy, and abruptly disappear.

The plate is filled with two freshly cooked sunny-side-up eggs, bacon, a piece of ham, and a biscuit. Tim looks around, wondering what to do, as the men return with glasses of fresh-squeezed orange juice, a coffee cup, and a little plate with sugar cubes for each person. Without making eye contact, or even breathing as far as Tim could tell, they vanish again. A woman then comes by, filling each coffee cup with freshly brewed coffee. Tim could smell that it wasn't the coffee that he usually had from a can. It smelled fresher and a little fruity.

After it was all over, Tim looks around like he had just survived a tornado and didn't know what to do. He looks up at Garrett and Sammy as they begin eating as if nothing had happened. They were used to this and didn't even see the help bringing things into the room. They just begin eating as if it magically appeared in front of them. Tim looks down at the fully loaded table of food in front of him, shakes his head smiling, then digs in.

He gets about halfway through dumping a whole load of gravy all over his biscuit when he hears a loud banging coming in from the hallway. He looks up to see a woman wrapped in a long white fur coat and high heels clambering toward the dining room with her arms stretched out. Her short, white hair and long, colorful fingernails tremble as she clomps closer.

She runs up to Garrett and hugs him tightly. "Garrett, my baby boy, thank God you're alive." She releases him and grabs his head, turning it back and forth quickly to check him out. "Did those evil men hurt you?"

"I'm not a baby, Mom!" Garrett complains, struggling to free himself. "Let go of my head!"

"You're my baby damn it, and nothing will change that. All of your brothers left to go live their lives somewhere else, and you're all I have left," she says, before slapping the back of his head. "Now, why did you go join that cult of devil worshipers?"

Garrett huffs loudly, sounding annoyed. "They're not a *cult*, Mom. Do you watch TV or listen to the radio? They killed the president, and now they're trying to take over America."

"Oh, is that all? Well, I didn't like that skinny little Democrat anyway, or his Mexican VP."

"Really, Mom? Have a heart. The man's dead, and now America is under attack by terrorists, or hillbillies, or someone. I don't really know. Still, have a heart. And go put on some clothes. We have company."

She quickly looks over at Tim and pushes up her hair. "Oh, where are my manners?"

In an extravagant manner, she casually walks around the table, giving Sammy a tap on the shoulder as she passes. Sammy shrugs and continues eating as Tim pushes his chair back and stands up to greet her.

She extends her hand toward him as if he was supposed to kiss it or something. "Good morning, Dear. My name's Celia. How do you do?"

Tim reaches for her slender hand, covered in gold rings and bracelets. "Hello ma'am, I'm Tim."

He shakes her hand gently and awkwardly, as if he were handling a soft, dead fish. Her slender body shakes back and forth under the fur coat.

She pulls her hand away and fluffs the fur around her neck. "Easy tiger, I'm not as tough as I look. Are you here for the lumberjack job?" She asks in a flirtatious tone. "You look like you can handle an axe."

Tim laughs. "No, ma'am. I'm here to talk to your husband about dealing with this militia…. I mean, cult in town."

"Good, it's about time someone dealt with those heathens. Just promise me you won't let them near my baby boy again. They'll fill his head with all sorts of evil notions. Before you know it, he'll be getting tattoos and playing in a band."

Tim looks over at Garrett, who is turning bright red and trying to hide on the other side of the table. "Don't worry, ma'am. I'll do my best."

"Very well then, I shall return to my room and freshen up a little bit. Samuel, be a dear and send up the masseuse. My back is killing me, and I could use a good rubdown," she says, winking at Tim as she turns and walks back down the hallway.

Tim turns back to Garrett and Sammy, confused about what just happened. They both look at him for a second, then start attacking their breakfast again without a word. So, Tim sits back down and follows suit.

After the glorious breakfast is finished, Tim takes a big sip of the strangely tasty coffee and looks at Sammy. "This coffee is excellent. Not to sound disrespectful, but this isn't that jungle cat shit coffee, is it?"

"Nope, it's from a coffee plantation I own in Columbia. They harvested this batch two weeks ago. I do have some Kopi Luwak in the kitchen if you want to give it a try," Sammy proudly replies.

"No thanks, I'm fine with this. Do you mind if we get down to business about this militia in town?"

Sammy looks at his watch and shakes his head. "Look at the time. It's not even eight o'clock yet. No business until nine in this house. Let's take a walk out to the barn and let this food settle. Come this way, boys. It's quicker through the kitchen."

"Sure," Tim replies as if he had a choice.

They leave their breakfast dunnage on the table and walk through the door to the kitchen. A couple of workers snap to attention as Sammy walks past. The kitchen is set up like a five-star restaurant. It has all stainless steel equipment, big commercial ovens, and about ten people moving back and forth in white uniforms. Sammy leads them out of a rear door to what looks like a loading bay, down some stairs, and towards the warehouse across the street.

As they approach the colossal warehouse that he called a barn, Sammy pauses and looks back at Tim. "I want to show you my prize possession. If it came to something worth fighting for, this would be it."

Sammy opens a smaller door and steps inside. When Tim passes through the door, he feels like he had stepped into a different world. The inside of the barn looks like a doctor's office, but for horses. Men and women walk around wearing white lab coats and holding expensive-looking tools. To the left are large, clear glass stalls with horses tied up inside. To the right is a complete laboratory with microscopes and computers sitting on stainless steel surgical tables.

The back has a circular horse corral, with a massive stainless steel machine made of pipes and hoses sitting in the center. A young horse is inside the corral, wearing some kind of mask. The mask has clear tubes and cables coming from it and running down a metal pipe leading to the central machine. As the horse runs around the corral, the tubes follow him. Standing just outside the corral are a group of horse scientists monitoring five different screens full of lines and numbers. They talk back and forth while writing down things on their notepads.

Sammy raises his arms into the air and slowly turns around. "This, my friend, is where I breed and train thoroughbred racehorses. I sell these horses to clients all over the world. I've grown this little hobby of mine into a multi-billion dollar empire. I have over three hundred horses and a thousand head of cattle on over ten thousand acres of land on this ranch, and I will be *damned* if I'm going to lose any of it to a bunch of pistol-packing hillbillies trying to prove a point. Now son, what can *I* do to help *you?*"

Tim looks at Sammy with a smile. "I need a small army."

Sammy drops his arms and looks around. "Well, I don't know if you've noticed, but most of my workforce is made up of science geeks and shit shovelers. I might have a couple of field hands who know how to handle a rifle, but I doubt they have the stones to stand up in a firefight. Apart from a couple of hunting rifles, the only weaponry I have, you seen attached to the walls inside the house. Is there anything else you need?"

Tim puts his hands on his hips and looks up at the ceiling. "I could use a good command center."

"I've got just the thing." Sammy says, pointing at Tim with a smile. "Follow me, boys."

Sammy leads the way out of the barn and walks to a golf cart waiting nearby. They jump in, and Sammy drives deeper onto the property, past the grain silos and combine tractors. About five hundred yards behind the main house is a lonely tree sitting on top of a large hill. Sammy parks the golf cart in front of the hill next to two old, moldy gravestones and gets out.

He places his hand on one of the gravestones and looks at Tim. "My grandparents bought this small piece of land back in the thirties, and this is where they're now buried. Rest their souls. The original house was built right where you're standing now. After we tore it down, we found out that they had a storm shelter built under that hillside. I've made a few upgrades since then. Follow me."

They follow Sammy over to the hillside and watch as he pulls a stack of branches off a pair of large steel doors surrounded by concrete. He pulls a ring of keys from his pocket and opens the lock between them. Sammy motions for them to help him, and they pull the metal doors open, revealing a large, round vault door. It looks like the one you would see securing a bank vault standing seven feet tall with large pins around the edge, sealing it to the concrete frame.

Sammy goes to the door and pulls down a hidden panel covering a keypad. The keypad lights up as he enters the code. 8-6-7-5-3-0-9. The door makes a loud click and hiss. One by one the pins retract from the concrete frame. The door cracks open, and air rushes out, spraying dust into the air. Sammy effortlessly pulls the door open, revealing a square tunnel leading down a dark set of stairs. He steps one foot inside and hits a switch on the wall that sparks and hums. The lights down the staircase start to flicker and click to life.

He looks back with a smile and waves for them to follow. "I spent about three years having this bunker rebuilt. I figured if I needed a place to hide, it should be nice."

Tim looks around in amazement. "This place is huge."

"Just wait. There's more," Sammy says, leading them deeper into the tunnel.

They reach the bottom of the stairs and enter a hallway about a hundred feet long, and follow along as Sammy continues his tour.

"To your right, you will find the fully operational generator that's fueled from a direct line to a ten-thousand-gallon tank located under my barn. It also has a six-month reserve battery storage capacity, with solar panels buried in the next field that'll deploy on command to recharge. On your left, you can see the water and air treatment plant that pumps water directly from my lake. It purifies it at one hundred gallons per minute for drinking. It has a two-hundred-gallon water heater system that provides hot water throughout the bunker for the sinks, showers, and radiator heater system. The air filtration system has an activated charcoal filter capable of filtering irradiated air for ten years without needing to replace the filters. Further down here to the right, we have the living quarters for the workers. There's space for twenty people to sleep on bunk beds with showers and bathrooms in the back. The kitchen, food storage, and laundry facilities are over here to the left. Now, follow me for the grand finale. The family living quarters are straight ahead."

The tunnel opens up to a circular room that's at least a hundred feet wide, with a twenty-foot-tall ceiling. It's divided into four quarters. The closest section is the dining room, with a large wooden table surrounded by fifteen chairs. The left section is set up like a fancy study with carpet, tall shelves fully stocked with books, a massive wooden desk, and stylish, dark brown leather couches.

The far section has a fully stocked gym with fifteen different workout machines and treadmills. The last section to the right has a pool table, foosball table, and two old pinball machines. Along with a large white sofa facing a flat-screen TV with an Xbox and a ton of DVDs and video games stacked up on a shelf. On the main room's outer wall, there are five metal doors leading outward. Two on either side of the room, and one at the far end.

"Ok, let's continue the tour, shall we? As you can see, the main room has everything we'll need to keep us occupied during a long stay. There are four bedrooms equipped with king-sized beds and full bathrooms with showers and bathtubs. But wait, there's more!"

Sammy leads them to the other side of the room and opens the door, leading out into another hallway.

He turns immediately to the right and opens another door. "This is our communications room, fully stocked with a long-range radio. The antenna is installed discreetly inside the tree on top of the hill outside. If we're ever stuck down here, I want to be able to find any survivors. One last thing is out here." He leads them out to the main tunnel and points to the right. "This way leads to a system of tunnels reaching out to every side of the farm, including the main house. One tunnel even leads all the way to Chesterfield, just in case I'm not able to reach the main entrance in time. Each has a hidden door like the one we came through, with the same passcode. You're welcome to use this as you need. Save two rooms for my family, just in case the apocalypse happens in the meantime."

Tim looks around with wide eyes and is almost speechless. "I think this will work for what we need. Thank you very much, Sammy. Garrett, we have some planning to do."

Sammy shakes Tim's hand and slaps Garrett on the back. "Then I'll be leaving you now. Feel free to come and see us at the main house when you're hungry or if you need anything else. Someone will always be around to help you if you need it."

Sammy turns and walks back out the way they came in, as Tim sits down on the couch in the study portion of the big room to let things sink in for a minute. He spots a giant world globe sitting next to the couch, and gets to thinking.

He reaches out and touches the globe, and thinks to himself. "Could it be?"

Sure enough, the top half of the globe opens, revealing a secret alcohol compartment inside.

Tim looks over at Garrett, who is standing at the desk, and asks in his most fancy English accent. "Would you care to partake in a glass of Scotch, old boy?"

Garrett looks over and raises his chin. "By George, I think I would."

Tim pours each of them a glass of twenty-year-old scotch, and they raise their glasses for a toast.

"To new beginnings," says Tim.

"To rich-ass parents," replies Garrett.

Tim finishes his scotch and sits down on the fancy couch. He can feel his eyelids getting heavy after a long night of mayhem. Before he can fight back, his eyes involuntarily close, and he's fast asleep.

Back in the sheriff's station, Colonel Wallace arrives and sits at his desk. "Jenkins! Where's my coffee?"

A skinny, awkward looking man wearing an oversized R.R. uniform comes running around the corner with a black coffee mug in his hands. "Here it is, Sir. And I also have a confidential letter from Command here for you."

Wallace takes the coffee mug and points to the next room. "Go get our super soldier out of lock up. I want to have another word with him. We could really use a man like that on our side."

"Right away, Sir." Jenkins rushes out of the office and heads for the back of the station where the holding cells are.

As he passes the guard desk, he looks around suspiciously because no one was manning the post. He walks quickly down the hallway toward the holding cells and stops, putting his hands over his wide-open mouth.

He turns back, then around again, hoping his eyes were playing tricks on him. "Oh shit! He's going to kill me for this."

Jenkins walks slowly through the door to Wallace's office and stands in front of his desk. "Sir, we have a small problem."

"What is it, Jenkins? If he's still sleeping, wake him up, for Christ's sake."

"That's not the problem. Sir, the man is no longer with us."

Wallace looks up, shocked. "He's dead?!"

"Not exactly, Sir. He's no longer with us, in the holding cell. He's gone, Sir."

"Who let him out? I swear, I'm working with a bunch of imbeciles. Send a team to his farm and bring him back. Bring his whole family back if you have to. And where is that damn sheriff?"

"I haven't seen him yet this morning, Sir."

"When he gets in, I want to see him. I need to get to know the surrounding area better. We're quickly running out of space in this tiny town. We might need to find a bigger place to set up soon."

Jenkins swiftly leaves the room. "Right away, Sir."

Four trucks with machine guns mounted on top kick up dust as they turn into the Walkers' farm. They come to a sliding halt in the driveway. Without saying a word, the men jump out and surround the house, looking in the windows.

One of the men makes a go signal with his hand, and another kicks the back door in, shattering the glass center. They sweep through the house, checking every room as they go.

After they look through all of the rooms, a man yells, "All clear!"

They make their way back outside to their trucks and report to the officer in charge. "Sir, the house looks deserted. There's trash all over, and all of their belongings are gone. Looks like they left in a hurry."

The lieutenant looks over his shoulder at the farm. "Search the barn and that shed. If they're hiding here, I want them found."

As the Walker family takes refuge inside their underground shelter, Marco hears the rumbling of vehicles on the driveway and points to back of the room. "Get in the storage room, quick."

Mary grabs the baby, and Nancy follows as they rush into the next room. Marco grabs a shotgun off of the wall and sets up his position in the living room, aiming at the ladder.

The R.R. team spreads out across the farm, checking the barn and the tool shed. But they pay no attention to the bale of hay casually sitting behind the shed. One man tries to enter the boathouse, but the door is locked. He peeks in through a crack in the wall and turns away.

The men return to the lieutenant empty-handed. "All clear, Sir."

The lieutenant huffs and waves for them to get back in the trucks. "All right, load up. They must have packed up and left town."

The men return to Chesterfield, and the lieutenant walks into the sheriff's station, still wearing his full combat gear. He walks past Jenkins sitting at the clerk's desk, and knocks on Colonel Wallace's door.

"Enter." Wallace commands from inside.

"Sir, the farm was empty. It looked like they left in a hurry."

Wallace slams his fist down on his desk. "Damn it. Are you sure they weren't hiding somewhere on the farm?"

"Yes, Sir. We checked the whole place. No sign of them."

"He better not pop up out of nowhere and cause a mess, or it's going to be your ass on the line, lieutenant. Dismissed."

Tim wakes up abruptly as he hears a metal door slamming shut. The sound echoes around the concrete room like an old auditorium. He sits up and looks at his watch, seeing that it's almost three in the afternoon.

Garrett comes walking from one of the bedrooms, buckling his pants back up. "The toilets work."

"Shit, I need to call the farm." Tim says, standing up and rubbing the sleep from his eyes.

The two of them walk toward the communications room, and Tim looks around, still in amazement. "Did you know your dad had this place?"

Garrett huffs and shrugs his shoulders. "Nope. My dad is slightly eccentric, if you didn't notice. He often had heavy equipment building stuff on the farm when I was a kid. I never knew what was going on."

Tim opens the door to the radio room and pulls the small radio from his pocket. He places it on the counter and looks at the frequency for the farm. Then he finds the power switch on the big radio and turns it on. Lights and gauges flicker and come to life on the large panel as the power flows through it. After a couple of seconds, Tim finds the dial to set the frequency and turns it to match the radio in the bunker.

He grabs the microphone sitting on the counter and hits the call button. "Homestead, Homestead, this is Toolman. Do you read? Homestead, Homestead, are you there?"

The speakers are silent for a second, then a familiar woman's voice speaks. "This is Homestead, Toolman. Can you hear me?"

"Read you loud and clear, Homestead."

"Where have you been? We've been trying to get a hold of you for an hour." Mary replies angrily.

"You wouldn't believe me if I told you. Did the men come looking for me at the farm?"

"Yes, they did. We heard a lot of noise outside, but they didn't find us."

"Don't worry. I have somewhere safe for us to hide. I'll come and get you. Hang tight."

"Ok. We're not going anywhere. Homestead out."

Tim grabs the radio off the counter and switches it to channel two. He checks the frequency and sets the big radio to speak to Randy.

"Whiskey, Tango, Foxtrot, this is Toolman. Are you there?"

"Whiskey, Tango Foxtrot, can you hear me?"

The radio sits quiet for a few seconds. Then, an excited voice comes through the speakers.

"Hey, hi! This is Whiskey, Tangerine, Fox-something. Yeah, I'm here. What's up? Over."

"How's the situation at Ground Zero?"

"Everything's normalish. I'm setting up for tonight's shenanigans," he replies with an excited giggle. "It's gonna be a bikini motor oil wrestling competition. Over."

Tim looks up at Garrett awkwardly, "Excellent, keep it up. I'll be coming to you tonight. Keep the back door unlocked."

"Roger, Roger! Always is. Over and out."

Tim puts the microphone down and turns to Garrett with a confused smile. "Did he just say... bikini motor oil wrestling?"

Garrett shrugs his shoulders. "I think so?"

They walk out of the radio room, and as they make their way to the main chamber, Tim looks around and turns to Garrett. "Okay, here's the plan. We need weapons and ammunition. Take my truck back to the farm and pick up my family. Tell my dad to bring all of the guns and ammo he can fit in the bed. Meanwhile, I'll sneak into town, have a chat with Randy, and try to get a feel for how this R.R. is running things. I'll meet you all back here tonight. Stay next to the radio in case I need a quick ride out of there."

"Ok, I can do that," Garrett replies hesitantly.

Tim reaches out and puts his hand on Garrett's shoulder. "Hey, make sure my family gets back here safely. I know you can do this. I'm counting on you."

Garrett straightens his back and looks at Tim confidently. "Thanks, I got this." He replies and starts jogging towards the main entrance.

Tim watches as Garrett runs off then he turns back to the dark tunnel leading the other way. "Now, it's time to make it through these tunnels without getting lost."

CHAPTER 5

FIRST STRIKE

"Get a move on, *PSYOPS*. The Colonel wants to see you in the command center ASAP," grumbles an infantry soldier as he sticks his head through the flap of Tim's tent.

"We're coming, and you'll watch your tone, or I'll slap that sham shield off of your collar before you know what hit you," Tim replies, pointing to the higher rank on his collar.

"Yes, Sergeant," he quickly replies, and pulls his head back out of the flap.

"Bet you won't! No balls!" JJ taunts, sitting back in his chair, laughing.

Tim throws a pad of paper at him and stands up from his makeshift desk made out of black tough boxes and a piece of wood. "Let's get going before the Colonel has a heart attack and dies on us. I want to get out of this damn country sometime this year."

Tim pushes JJ through the tent's door, and they are immediately blasted by the hot desert sun. Today is a blistering 125-degree day in Iraq. Not even the wind can cool the air. It only makes it hotter. It feels like sitting in front of a hairdryer on full blast, except this hairdryer is also full of sand.

They've been in-country for three months but haven't seen any real action yet. Mostly just working on deciphering Al Qaeda propaganda posters or hiding from the occasional incoming mortar attacks. When a mission opportunity finally came their way, Tim and JJ were ready to get their hands dirty.

They walk through the seemingly endless line of green tents. Aside from their footsteps, all they can hear is the constant hum of generators and the flapping of loose tent straps in the wind.

Eventually they make it to the only hard structure in the camp, if you want to call it that. It's barely held together by loosely laid brick and mud, but these infantry guys take what they can get. They step through the front door and make their way to the back where the Colonel's office is.

His door is open, so the CO waves them in and motions for them to take a seat in front of his desk. "Afternoon, men. I was looking over your mission brief this morning, and frankly, I'm skeptical about it. Do you think you can pull all of this off? You're aware that we don't have the heavy assets available to back you up if things go sideways."

Tim sits tall and confidently responds. "Yes, we understand, Sir."

"Do you guys really have all of this crap on station? Did you seriously haul a bunch of speakers all the way out here?"

"Yes, we did, Sir."

The Colonel looks at the mission brief in his hands and raises his eyes to Tim and JJ, who are waiting patiently for his decision. "Okay, our teams are briefed and will be ready. Your mission kicks off at zero five hundred tomorrow morning. Good luck, men," he nods his head and turns back to his computer.

Tim and JJ excitedly leave the command center and quickly return to their tent.

With a nervous yet excited look on his face, JJ scrambles to the back of the tent to gather his gear. "Finally, we have a mission outside the wire. I'll go get everything ready."

Tim waves his hand at him calmly and smiles. "Slow down, JJ. Let's make sure to do this right. These guys don't trust us already. Let's show them what two properly trained guys and a bunch of cool tech can do."

At zero five hundred the next morning, Tim and JJ are all loaded up in their Humvee and ready to roll. Attached to their mission are two squads of infantry soldiers and two sniper teams, following in five additional Humvees. Their objective is a small village about twenty kilometers south of Baghdad. The Tactical PSYOP Team was called in for this mission because this village is a known Al Qaeda hideout, but is also heavily populated with civilians. The infantry can't just go in guns blazing and kill a lot of innocent civilians. Lucky for them, the TPT was ready and willing to help.

After a long, slow convoy march from the FOB, the trucks circle up at the initial rendezvous point about three hundred meters south of the village. They chose this location specifically because it was in a low valley just out of view of the village ahead.

Tim takes a quick look out of the window to ensure everyone's still accounted for, then calls out over the radio. "All teams, this is Phantom One. Radio check in sequence, over."

"Alpha One, check. Alpha Two, check. Bravo One, check. Bravo Two, check. Bullseye One, check. Bullseye Two, check."

"Ok, you know where you need to be. Keep it slow and quiet. We don't want to spook them out just yet. Do not engage unless you are fired upon first. Move out!"

Four trucks slowly peel away from the circle. Two of them head toward the village's west side, and two go for the east. The sniper teams dismount and spread out on either side of the TPT's Humvee. Tim maneuvers the Humvee and parks it with the tailgate facing the hill at the edge of the village.

Soon after the others are set up, he hears them call over the radio.

"Alpha One and Two are in position. Bravo One and Two are in position."

As everyone gets arranged, they jump from their truck, and Tim checks the speakers mounted on the roof. These are no ordinary speakers. They're military-grade, high-voltage speakers lined up in two rows of four. After confirming everything is still in working order, Tim takes out a laptop and places it on the hood. He grabs a cable running from the speakers and plugs it into the laptop. At the same time, JJ runs to the back of the truck and pulls out two large rolled-up fire hoses, setting one of them on the ground behind the truck. With the other hose spun around his arm, he takes off running to the left side of the truck. The hose unravels and lays out about fifty yards long. As he reaches the end of the hose, JJ stops for a second to catch his breath, then runs back for the other one.

As JJ comes running back, Tim finishes loading the computer and looks up. "Are you ready with the smoke generator yet?"

JJ clomps through the dusty field and replies, breathing heavily. "Almost, one more hose, and it'll be ready."

He grabs the second hose, slides his arm through the center, then takes off to the right side of the truck, laying it out on the ground as he runs. Soon after, JJ returns out of breath, with sweat pouring from his face. He drags the ends of the two hoses up and attaches them to a special Y-pipe on the back end of the smoke generator. Earlier that week, they modified the hoses with small holes every couple of feet and a cap on the end. When the smoke generator starts pumping out, it will fill the hoses and disperse the smoke evenly over the one hundred yard span. JJ finishes his tasks by sending Tim a thumbs up from around the truck while putting on his gas mask.

Tim responds with a nod, puts his mask on, and picks up the radio mic. "All teams, stand by. Initiating smoke, time now."

JJ turns the ignition switch on the smoke generator, and the hoses on both sides begin to inflate. The smoke sprays out of the holes and fills the low valley with a thick, white cloud, completely engulfing the sniper teams and the TPT truck. Satisfied with his surroundings, Tim reaches out with a finger and presses play on the laptop. The speakers crackle to life with a prerecorded sound of tanks and large diesel trucks driving off in the distance. As the audio track plays longer, the sound of the engines gets louder. Tim can feel the Humvee vibrating as the powerful speakers belt out the sound of an M1A1 battle tank on the move. Once the audio track hits full blast, the thunderous roar makes it feel as if there really is a fleet of tanks and trucks driving at full throttle toward the village, ready to attack.

A muffled thump rings out from one of the sniper's suppressed rifles to the right. "One contact on the hill, target ran back over."

The snipers were using thermal optic sights, so they could see through the smoke. They were instructed to keep anyone away from the edge of the hill to maintain the authenticity of the illusion.

Another silenced thump comes from the left. "Got another. He limped back over the hill."

Tim grabs his radio mic. "Initiating Phase Two."

He hits the next track that makes it sound like fifty different vehicles are hitting their squeaky brakes and coming to a stop, with their engines still humming in the background. Earlier, Tim worked with an interpreter to create a message specifically tailored to Al Qaeda in Arabic.

He hits the play button, and it blasts out of the speakers. Roughly translated, the message said, "We are the United States Army. We have the village completely surrounded by tanks. We are here for the Al Qaeda soldiers hiding in this village. Drop your weapons and come out now, or we will disgrace you in front of your families by dragging you through the streets for all to see. This is your only chance to keep your dignity and live to see your families again another day."

Tim plays the message over the speakers at full blast. After it finishes, the loud humming of the engines remains as he waits for a response. A few minutes pass, and he repeats the message.

All of a sudden, Tim hears one of the teams call out over the radio. "Phantom One, this is Alpha One. I have multiple contacts coming from the village to the west. It's working. Holy shit, it's actually working. They're coming out of the village with their hands up."

"This is Bravo One. More are coming from the east. They're unarmed and walking this way. I can't believe this worked."

"This is Bullseye One. We have five unarmed men coming over the hill towards us."

"This is Phantom One. All teams, collect them up and clear the village. Let's get back to the chow hall before they stop serving breakfast. Phantom One, out."

<hr>

Deep inside the Texas bunker, Tim walks down the dark tunnel, past the communications room, and finds himself in a round chamber with four doors leading in different directions. The tunnel system for this massive bunker seemed pretty straightforward. Hanging over each door is a green street sign with the name of the destination on it. The signs read, "Lake House," "Main house," "Horse Barn," and "Chesterfield." Tim opens the door leading to town and goes through, closing it behind him.

One small light on the ceiling illuminates the entryway, and all he can see is a gray power box on the wall with green and red buttons on it. He pushes the green button, and the tunnel lights begin to flicker and come to life. The inside of the tunnel looks less finished than the main chamber. The walls are made of rock and dirt rather than concrete. Large wooden pillars line the walls like an old mine shaft.

He walks down a small set of stairs to a lower platform. The floor is concrete, but the tunnel leading out is narrow with an unfinished dirt surface. Sitting at the end of the tunnel on the concrete pad is a golf cart with four seats and a small cargo bed on the back. It's conveniently plugged into the wall with a long charging cable.

Tim unplugs the cable from the wall, stows it in the cart, and turns the key on. The battery gauge reads full, so he shifts into drive, and takes off down the underground dirt road. Every ten feet or so, lights hang from a long black cable mounted on wooden pillars. The tunnel is reasonably straight, and the elevation doesn't change much while driving along. It looks like a professional crew took their time constructing it. If he estimated correctly and drove in a straight line, the town should be about twenty miles from the O'Connell's farm. After cruising slowly through the tunnel for over an hour, another round opening resembling the other side appears.

As he drives up and parks, he finds another golf cart patiently waiting, attached to the wall. "This looks like the end of the line," he says parking it along the wall.

He turns the cart around and plugs it into the outlet while looking around. To the back is a flight of stairs leading up to a metal door. The rusty metal door leading out squeals as he pushes it open, revealing another small and narrow set of stairs leading up to a security door next to a keypad on the wall.

Tim punches in the passcode, and the door makes a metallic click, followed by a hissing noise. The security door wasn't as big as the main entrance door back at the farm, but it looks just as secure. It opens toward him and reveals a small, dark hallway leading up to the ceiling. A short metal handle hangs from the top, so he grabs it and pushes it open.

The top tilts upwards with a hydraulic hissing sound, and all he can see is a small room with shiny white walls all around. He stands up, and the door lowers itself, closing with a magnetic click. Feeling with his hands along the walls, he discovers small etchings in them. He looks closer to see that they were names. Then it dawns on him that he's inside a tomb of some sort. Small beams of blue light come through the door at the end of the room, so he pushes the door outward and finds himself in the middle of the town's cemetery. Looking back at the tomb, he sees the name "O'Connell's" etched in large, fancy, old English letters along the top of the door.

The cemetery is located on a hill about fifty yards from town, with a narrow, old cobblestone path connecting it to the back of the church. As he makes his way out of the cemetery, the sun is starting to set. Tim looks up and pauses to take in the mysterious, yet serene way the fiery orange sky looks behind the tall, chiseled gravestones. It makes him think of Halloween as a kid. They would wander through the cemetery and try to scare each other by making spooky noises. Now, it looks like a peaceful yet inevitable resting place. After taking it all in, he turns and walks down the path towards Randy's Bar.

With the sun fully set behind him, Tim follows the old cobblestone path to the back of the church, then along a fence to the back of the bar. As he gets closer, the thump of loud music pulsates from the bar. He quickly finds the back door and enters what looks like the storeroom. The place smells like week-old stale beer and vomit. Broken beer glasses lay scattered all over the floor, and a mountain of beer kegs sits stacked against the far wall. Lots of yelling and banging of glasses comes from a crowd of men in the front of the bar. He goes over to the door leading inside and cracks it open to see what's happening.

At least twenty men stand around, drinking and cheering on a couple of beautiful young girls in the center of the room. The two girls look exactly alike, with long dark hair and matching red, white, and blue bikinis. They stand knee-deep in a plastic swimming pool filled with what looks like engine oil. The girls reach for each other and grapple back and forth in the slippery oil until one of them slips and falls out of the pool onto the hardwood floor with a loud thud. Two drunken R.R. soldiers pull her to her feet, and she dives back into the pool headfirst, sending a massive splash of oil toward a group of soldiers standing on the other side.

The place erupts in laughter and cheering as Randy comes around the corner holding a bottle of tequila and a bucket of limes. He makes a spinning move to avoid being run over by a falling man, then does a quick dodge to the left, avoiding a splash of oil flying through the air. He places the bottle and limes on a table and moves quickly toward the wrestling match, just in time to stop one girl from drowning the other in the oily mess.

"And we have our winner!" Randy yells, leaning in close to ask the girl which one she was. "Jezebel! Let's give it up for the Swanson sisters!" He grabs the girl's oily arm, raises it into the air, and then helps her out of the pool.

The soldiers cheer and laugh while spilling their drinks everywhere and sliding in the oily mess. The other girl scrapes herself from the bottom of the pool and rolls out onto the floor. Two drunken soldiers help her to her feet and give her a beer. She chugs the entire beer, and throws the can to the floor while pushing her way through the crowd, and out the front door. Celebrating her victory, Jezebel attempts to bounce around joyfully but is sliding too much on the oil and almost falls over. She waves to the men one last time and follows her twin sister out the front door and into the street.

As the men follow the oily girls out the door, Randy turns towards the back of the bar and spots Tim waving for him to come over. Randy says his goodbyes and waits until the coast is clear. He then quickly walks towards the storeroom door. As he hurries past the swimming pool, he slips on a big puddle of oil on the floor and slides toward the storeroom door. Tim reacts as quickly as he can and opens the door wide, just as Randy slides through on his back and crashes into the mountain of empty beer kegs in the back. The entire stack falls over, banging and smashing everything in the room.

Randy sits up and pokes his head out of the pile of aluminum kegs with a big smile on his face. "Nailed it."

"You sure did," Tim replies, shaking his head and helping Randy to his feet. "Do you have anywhere less... *sticky* we can talk?"

"Yup, follow me. I have a basement that I keep locked," he replies, pulling a ring of keys from his pocket.

Randy slowly opens the door to the storeroom and looks around, then waves for Tim to follow. They go over behind the bar, and Randy reaches for the floor. He removes the lock and lifts a trapdoor, revealing a staircase leading to the basement. They climb down the steps, and Tim immediately regrets it.

He makes a face while ungluing his boot from the floor. "I thought I said somewhere *less* sticky."

The bottom of the staircase is lined with boxes of old, moldy fruit and extra beer glasses. Beer and oil drips from the ceiling from the evening's wrestling match. In the far-left corner, stands about a dozen mannequins dressed in festive clothing.

Tim looks at Randy with an eyebrow raised and points to the corner. "What are those for?"

"Hey, don't judge. It wasn't always bikinis and oil wrestling in this bar. It used to get pretty lonely at times, so I would put them around the bar to make it look busy. Plus, they're fun to dress up for the holidays," Randy says, grabbing a female mannequin and dipping her like they were dancing. "Come into my office."

They carefully step through the clutter to the basement's front side, while Randy leads them to a desk with a bunch of small cardboard boxes and plastic army men arranged on top.

Randy looks at Tim proudly with his hands spread out, showing his creation. "Look, see? I made you a tiny town."

Tim looks at the desk while holding back a laugh. "Very nice... What am I looking at?"

"It's a town, this town, only smaller. You can use this to plan your mission," he says as he grabs the bazooka Army man and aims it at Tim. "Pew! Pew! Pew! See what I mean?"

"Yes! I see it now. Outstanding job, Randy. It's called a sand table, and it'll work nicely."

Randy pumps his fist. "I *knew* it."

"Okay, first thing's first. Did you hear any information from the drunken guys while they were here?"

"Not really. A few of them were complaining about not having enough room for more people."

"Okay, that's something. Listen, I need one of their uniforms so I can do some recon around town without raising suspicion. Did any of them leave any clothes here?"

"Hmm... No. I don't think so. But I do have a passed-out guy lying upstairs. I can steal his shirt and hat for you." Randy runs toward the stairs, tripping over a stack of boxes on the way. "Just a sec."

Tim looks down at the cardboard boxes and G.I. Joe figurines spread out on the table as Randy makes his way across the bar to his victim. He looks up at the dripping floorboards as Randy's boots bang against the floor above.

Randy mumbles to himself as he goes. "Come on now. You don't need this. Sleep, sleep, sleep. Got it. Where's the hat? Oh, there it is." Suddenly, the floorboards shake with a loud thud as Randy slips on the oil again. "Oh, my ass! Got it."

He scrambles his way through the oil spill to the stairs behind the bar and comes back down. "Got your disguise, but it's a little oily. That'll wash right out though. Just add a can of Coke to the washer."

"I think by now, I would stand out if I *didn't* smell like motor oil." Tim looks at the black baseball cap. "This will work perfectly."

It looks like the same hat that the Colonel was wearing with the red railroad crossing sign. He puts on the oily black shirt and cap and looks down at the makeshift sand table.

"Ok Randy, let's make a plan of attack. I'll be this bazooka guy, and this box is your bar. I'll come out of the front door and walk towards the middle of town. I want to see exactly what kind of weaponry they have stacked up over there. Then I'll make my way over to Rose's and see if I can listen to anything the older guys are talking about. After that, I'll go across the street to the sheriff's station and see if I can eavesdrop on the Colonel."

Randy looks down at the table excitedly. "Where do you want me?"

"Let's see here. You'll be this guy who's half-melted and missing his gun." Tim looks up to see if he caught the reference, but Randy was still focused on the table with an excited grin on his face.

He knows that he has to send Randy off to do something, or he would show up at the exact wrong moment and blow the whole operation.

Tim sets the figurine down behind the bar. "I have a special errand I need you to run. You still have my dad's truck, right?"

"Yup, it's parked out behind the bar."

"Do you remember the way to my farm?"

"Yup, I used to deliver newspapers on that road as a kid."

"Good, I want you to take the truck and drive to my farm. Bring back all of the jugs of moonshine and hide them somewhere here, but *don't drink it.*" Tim looks Randy in the eyes. "You understand me?"

"Aww, really? Just a little for my troubles? Then I'll stash the rest here in the basement." Randy pleads.

"Ok, just a little. But you need to stash the rest. I have a feeling we'll need it later. It's locked up in the boathouse next to the lake. The key is above the door. There should be about five jugs still in there. And try not to break any of them. Got it?"

"Got it. You can count on me." Randy puts his hand out over the table like he's the quarterback in a huddle, looking up at Tim. "Ready?"

Tim shakes his head and puts his hand on Randy's. "Break!"

Tim and Randy walk back up the sticky stairs and close the basement hatch. Randy puts the padlock back on and shoves the keys into his pocket.

He turns to Tim as they part ways. "Good luck out there."

"Thanks, you too."

Randy leaves through the back as Tim walks out the front door and into the street wearing his R.R. disguise. He feels confident that no one will recognize him because he didn't meet any of the soldiers face-to-face. Keeping his hat down, he stays in the shadows just in case. He walks casually down Main Street toward the staging area where the large wooden boxes are stacked up in front of the schoolhouse.

One soldier with a clipboard watches over the supplies from his chair in the center. "Ya need something, soldier?"

"Nope, I'm just wondering when we're gonna move everything back inside, Sarge."

The soldier huffs and lowers his clipboard, staring at Tim with an annoyed look. "For the thousandth time, when they fix the broken water pipe in the schoolhouse. It should be done by tomorrow. Then you guys will haul all of this stuff back inside."

Tim waves and smiles. "Alrighty then. See ya later."

He glances at the boxes as he walks away. There are crates of M4 rifles, a box or two of grenades, and an entire box of RPG rockets.

Tim looks at the schoolhouse and decides that it would be a good idea to take a look and see if there were any other surprises inside. Walking toward the front door, he notices hand-painted pictures still hanging on the windows of the kindergarten classroom. The walls throughout the entranceway are covered in drug awareness and motivational posters. He reaches the main hallway and looks back and forth. Trash and discarded classroom furniture are stacked in piles along the dented metal lockers. He hears the sound of men talking to the right, so he turns and walks down the hallway. The classrooms are lined with military cots with gear strewn all about.

Tim shakes his head and thinks to himself. "I would tear into some asses if this were an actual barracks."

A soldier comes out of one of the classrooms and looks at Tim strangely. "Who ya lookin fur?"

Tim clears his throat and puts on his best Southern accent. "Where's Larry? He's got gate guard in ten minutes."

The man scratches his head, looking around. "Hell if I know, try the room down yonder," he replies, pointing to the end of the hall, then walks off.

These guys didn't impress Tim at all. He would be scared to give them a loaded rifle and tell them to shoot something. He peeks through the doorways as he passes, and each room is worse than the last. It looks like an army surplus store exploded everywhere. One room even has a big screen TV on the wall, with about fifteen men sitting around, yelling and watching Full Metal Jacket. Tim had to get out of this disaster quickly. The senior enlisted soldier inside of him was screaming. He makes it back to the front door without finding *Larry,* but guaranteed that at least five men would answer if he called out his name.

Walking back past the crates, he notices something new. A small box with "C-4" stenciled on the side. He makes a mental note of where it sits and moves across the street to the church.

The other side of the street is where the trucks are lined up. They have four old Dodge pickups full of dents and rust, with M60 machine guns mounted on the back. One of them even has a flat tire.

"Pfftt," Tim says as he walks by.

As he approaches the church's front doors, he can clearly hear a pastor inside giving his sermon. He cracks the door open and sees about twenty men sitting in the pews, attentively watching. The preacher is dressed in a black robe with a red scarf over his shoulders.

He stands behind the podium with his hands in the air, yelling to his audience. "Our Lord has given us the means to *be rid* of the plague upon our country. He has shown us that we must *stand up* and *take back* what is rightfully ours! He will help us *rain down* upon our enemies and *cleanse* this land in his holy name! AMEN!"

"Jesus Christ," Tim says to himself as he closes the door. "I guess every army needs a chaplain."

He casually moves down the sidewalk past Burt's grocery and notices it's still a mess inside. The R.R. tore it apart like a bunch of hippies from back in the city. Passing the other stores, he notices that the electronics and hardware store is still in pretty good shape. At least the windows are not smashed in, and the shelves are still standing. Finally, he makes it to Rose's Diner and can see a few of the same grey-haired militiamen sitting inside, having coffee and pie. Tim's hair isn't grey enough to pass through the front door without raising suspicion, so he decides to hide next to the open window behind some bushes and listen to their conversation.

Two older men sit at the booth inside, chatting. "Did you hear about what was happening over in that bar earlier?"

"Ya, they had those two pretty girls wrestling around in a big bowl of engine oil."

"Seems like a waste of good oil, if you ask me. Those old pickups blow out so much damn smoke. I doubt there's any oil left in their engines at all." The man chuckles and coughs.

"Hear anything about when we're leaving this little town yet? I reckon we've been here a while."

"Don't know. I heard the Colonel say he was cooking something up. Speaking of cooking something up, where is my blueberry pie? I ordered it twenty minutes ago."

Tim stands up and walks back into the street. "Looks like my next stop will be the Colonel's office."

While crossing the street, he gets a good look at the bus barrier at the end of town. It would take a bulletproof bulldozer to get through that wall of crap. He could probably sneak through if he's quiet enough, but definitely not while carrying anything. A couple of men stand and chat with each other in the parking lot as Tim passes by and goes around to the side of the building, then around the back. Thanks to Tim's earlier encounter, he remembered that the Colonel's office is on the building's back corner. Luckily for him, the window to his office was open and it sounded like Wallace was inside.

A man speaks franticly over the radio. "Our northern positions are being hit hard by the National Guard. We've been forced back to Oklahoma City. We're holding our ground for now, but we need reinforcements. Over."

"Copy that. Hold your ground in the city for now, Captain. Reinforcements are coming. Wallace out."

Wallace throws the mic down on the table and leans back in his chair with his hands above his head. "God damn it. Why is the National Guard so persistent? Don't they see who's giving them their commands? I wish I could fire those crooked generals and take over their troops. I could use an army that knew what the hell they were doing and took orders without hesitation."

Jenkins stands next to him with his pad of paper against his chest. "Soon enough, sir. We'll get a strong foothold and start taking states daily."

"That's what General Grant keeps saying. He came up with this big plan to split the states in half and fight on both fronts. We have enough trouble fighting on one front in Oklahoma alone."

"How does he plan on doing that, Sir."

"Grant said, that intel shows the National Guard is trying to cut Texas in half and split our troops. Divide and conquer, he says. But he wants to set a trap and ultimately do the same thing back to them. He'll be moving a complete artillery regiment here in a few days. I've been told to command our troops to fall back and allow as many National Guard troops as possible to come to Oklahoma City. Let them think they have their knife to cut us in half. Then we'll blast half of Oklahoma to dust, eliminating their defenses. Then we'll move forward and take Kansas. After we take Fort Riley and McConnell Air Force Base, we'll have all the armor and air support we need to win this fight."

"We're going to need more food and supplies from the local farms if we're going to take in that many more soldiers, Sir. Do you think this little town can handle that many more people, Sir?"

"This town is in a perfect location to make our attack to the north. We'll make room for the new men, even if we have to clear all the locals out of that trailer park. I agree with you about the food, though. Have a few men head out to the O'Connell's farm again and *talk* them into forking over another couple of truckloads of corn and livestock."

"Yes, sir. Right away, Sir."

"Did any of the checkpoints catch the Walker family as they fled the area?"

"No, sir. None of the checkpoints have reported back with any news, Sir."

"How did he get out anyway? Who helped him?"

"A couple of officers said they saw the owner of that bar and the sheriff driving off in the man's truck the night he escaped, Sir."

Wallace squints his eyes, looking at Jenkins angrily. "Do you think they had anything to do with it? Where is that wannabe cop anyway? I haven't seen him today. He must have helped him. That bar owner has been pissing me off, also. Always leaving my soldiers hungover and more useless. Bring him in first thing in the morning when *he*'s good and hungover. I want a word with him."

"Yes, Sir. Is there anything else, Sir?"

"Tell them to have my tools ready in the morning. I'll get some answers out of him, even if I have to pull out all of his teeth myself." Wallace snickers and rubs his hands together. "You're dismissed."

Jenkins nods his head and turns around. "Thank you, Sir."

"Shit," Tim says to himself. "I have to get Randy out of town tonight."

Suddenly, Tim hears someone coming around the side of the building, so he quickly stands up and unzips his pants. The man comes around the corner, looks at Tim for a second, then turns to the wall and starts to pee.

Through the window, Wallace yells at Jenkins again. "And tell them to stop pissing on the side of my building! It stinks like pee in here all damn day. It's the twenty-first century. Use a damn toilet, for Christ's sake!"

Tim smiles and waits for his fellow urinator to finish and turn away. He zips up and walks out toward the street. As it starts to get late, the soldiers begin going in to their rat's nest of a barracks. After walking around the town for a few more minutes, he notices a pair of headlights pass by the front gate, then turns off behind Randy's Bar. It looks like Randy was back from the farm, so Tim casually makes his way down the street towards the bar. He nods at a couple of guys as he passes, but no one suspects anything.

As he walks back into the bar, Randy comes through the back door carrying two jugs of moonshine under his arms. Randy spots him and starts to say hi, when he slips on the oil again, throwing the jugs up over his head. One jug flies straight toward Tim, and the other goes straight up in the air. Tim reaches out and grabs the first jug before it splashes into the pool of oil. Randy hits the ground hard on his back and looks up as the other jug falls back towards his face.

He reaches up and grabs the jug right before it makes contact with his head and looks over at Tim. "Nailed it."

"Ten points for difficulty," Tim replies, laughing and judging his maneuver like the Olympics of clumsiness.

Randy sets the jug down and lies there in the oil for a second. "I really should clean this up before I hurt myself."

Tim sets the other jug on the counter and looks back at Randy. "Sorry to say, but you don't have time. It would be best if you left town for good. Wallace is about to start pulling your teeth for information about my escape."

Randy stands up and rubs his teeth with an oiled finger, then spits. "But I like my teeth. I chew stuff with them."

"That's not the real problem. Wallace is about to bring the hurt down on a bunch of National Guard soldiers. We need to stall his plans somehow. I think I have an idea. You ready for a more dangerous mission?"

Randy looks up excitedly. "Hell yeah!"

"Okay, finish bringing in the moonshine. After that, I need you to put all of your mannequins into the back of the truck. Then load up your stereo system with speakers and all."

Randy looks at Tim funny. "Okay... Planning a kinky party later? I'm in."

"I have much bigger plans for them. I need some more supplies, though. Load up everything, and I'll meet you out back."

Tim leaves the bar and walks over to the barracks. Remembering the room in the back where the men were watching the movie, he sneaks in and looks through the movie selection. He grabs a copy of the movie "1917" from the stack while no one's watching, stuffs it in his pocket, and walks back outside. The soldier guarding the weapons outside realxes kicked back with his feet on a box and a clipboard in his hands.

Looking concerned, Tim jogs up to him and points back into the barracks. "Hey, Sarge, a couple of guys are playing catch with a grenade inside. You should go take that from them."

He grumbles and removes his feet from the box. "These idiots are going to get everyone killed. Watch the crates while I'm gone."

He hurries off through the front door of the schoolhouse, and Tim looks through the crates until he finds a box of smoke grenades. He throws a bandolier over his shoulder and takes off, running across the street toward the hardware store.

Sneaking through the shadows, he moves around the building to the back door. He tries to turn the handle but finds it locked, so he swiftly kicks the door and it flies open. Once inside, he looks through the dark room for the supplies. Luckily for him, these old stores not only have new stuff, but they also restore old electronics and label them as "retro," then sell them for a higher price. Sitting on the shelf is an old DVD player that has its own screen that flips up. Tim flips it over and checks if it still works, and smiles as the screen lights up with the colorful DVD logo. Over in the hardware section, there sits a mini generator and a small halogen floodlight.

He scoops them up and proudly says. "This place has everything."

On the way out the door, he grabs a roll of duct tape, then quickly moves around the building and down the sidewalk towards the bar. As he passes the R.R. trucks, a man walking in the opposite direction looks at Tim awkwardly and blocks his way.

As he stops, he points to the stuff in Tim's hands. "Whoa, there partner, where ya headed off to with all that stuff?"

Tim puts on his best Southern accent and answers. "Howdy, I'm helpin' the bar set up for tomorra's Wild West shindig. Are ya comin?"

The soldier looks at him for a second, then smiles. "Yer darn tootin'! See ya there, partner," he replies cheerfully, then continues walking past, whistling a tune.

Tim makes it back and sets his things on the counter next to Randy, while he sits on the bar, drinking a beer and looking around.

"I'm going to miss this place." Randy says sadly.

"Don't worry, buddy. I'm sure it'll still be here when this is all over. Come on and get in the truck. I need you to help me set this stuff up."

They load up all of the supplies and drive the truck, with the headlights off, out into the field in front of town. It was a dark and cloudy night, so it played to their advantage. Tim instructs Randy to set the mannequins up on the hill's crest, lining them up side by side. To the right of the hill, Tim sets up the stereo system and DVD player next to the generator. After unraveling the cable for the halogen lamp, he runs back behind the mannequins and sets it down.

Randy comes down the hill, out of breath, and meets up with Tim as he finishes plugging everything in. "All setup. What's next?"

"Ok, take these smoke grenades. You see that pin? When the time's right, you'll pull all out of the pins and throw the canisters in front of your mannequins. Now listen carefully. I have everything ready to go. All you need to do is start the generator, turn on the stereo to full blast, and hit play on the DVD player. After it's been playing for a minute, come over here and turn on this floodlight. Wave it back and forth behind the mannequins to make it look like a bunch of men are coming. Got it?"

"Uhh, yeah sure," Randy replies hesitantly.

"Tell me what you're gonna do."

"Throw smoke... Generator on... Stereo up... Push the play button... Then shake the light."

"Perfect. Once these hillbillies see the mannequins and lights, they'll come out shooting like crazy people, so get in the truck and drive. Meet me at the cemetery and keep your head down. Make sure you keep the lights off so they don't follow you."

Randy looks at Tim and gives a sloppy salute. "Roger, Roger."

"Give me fifteen minutes, then start the show. And don't get shot."

Tim runs back down the tree line, heading toward town, and goes into the bar's back door. The setup is about two hundred yards outside of town, so the front gate guards should see and hear it clearly. These militiamen are half-drunk and ready to shoot at anything, so Tim hopes they'll jump at the chance of a firefight.

Fifteen minutes pass, and the little generator kicks on, followed by the big battle at the end of the movie that Tim set the DVD player to. Loud explosions and gunfire pour from the speakers. Tim looks out the front window and sees the men at the front gate standing up and pointing at the field full of smoke. When Randy turns on the floodlight, it creates a perfect silhouette of the mannequins projected onto the smoke cloud from behind. It looks like a dozen men are coming out of a field, ready to attack the town.

A bell rings at the front gate as the men react to the fake assault. Just as Tim predicted, men come pouring out of the barracks with their clothes half falling off, bumping and tripping over everything in their way. The men at the front gate begin shooting at the smoke-filled group of mannequins, followed by fifty other men in the town running to the gate and opening fire. Every able-bodied person, drunk or sober, is rushing out to get a piece of the action.

Tim scoops up four jugs of moonshine and runs out the front door. He quickly makes his way to the pile of crates in the middle of town. The soldier's gone shooting at nothing, so no one was there to guard anything. He sets two jugs down next to the crates and tosses the other two through the front door of the schoolhouse. The jugs burst open, sending moonshine in all directions, covering the entrance. He then runs back and grabs the other two jugs, pouring them on the trucks parked across the street in front of the church.

Satisfied with the drenching, he runs back to the pile of munitions. Remembering the location of the C4, he opens the box and shoves four one-pound bricks into his cargo pockets. Keeping low, he moves to the other side of the pile, grabs four frag grenades out of a box, and runs back toward the Sheriff's station. Keeping low and staying in the shadows, he reaches the bushes outside the station. Tim looks back at the front gate and sees tracer rounds flying in every direction as the adrenaline-crazed hillbillies shoot at everything they can.

Tim smiles and pulls the C4 blocks from his pockets. Using the duct tape he had grabbed earlier, he tapes one block of C4 to each grenade, making sure not to tape the clip down.

He tosses one of his beautiful creations lightly in the air and catches it, smiling. "Now the party's *really* about to get started."

Tim stashes two of the creations in his pockets and looks up at the building in front of him. He pulls one of the pins and hurls the little bundle of joy on top of the Sheriff's department, right next to the antenna. Like a ninja, he jumps from the bush and pulls the next pin, tossing it under the center of the bus barricade. As the second grenade lands, the first one erupts with deadly force, sending sparks of antenna and chunks of building in every direction. The blast breaks through the ceiling, and the lights go out in the building as the roof collapses.

Tim sprints towards the center of town as the second plastic explosive-laced frag grenade explodes directly under a bus's fuel tank. The center bus erupts from the inside, sending flames fifty feet high. The buses lined up next to it catch fire and erupt in sequence as the flames get bigger.

The fireball of bus carnage warms Tim's back as he runs for his next target. He pulls the remaining two softball-sized death wishes from his pocket and pulls the pins. With his adrenaline rushing, he tosses one right into the center of the munitions pile and the last one at the line of trucks. He sprints with every bit of energy he has left to get out of the blast range and hits the ground, sliding next to the church. The crates full of ammo, weapons, and explosives blow up with the force of a five-hundred-pound bomb. A mushroom-shaped fireball lights up the entire town, sending debris through the front door of the schoolhouse. The potent moonshine ignites with ease and traps all of the soldiers' gear inside. Finally, the last grenade blows up under the center of the four trucks, sending two of them flying end over end. The moonshine burns like racing fuel, melting everything it touches.

Tim lies on the ground, enjoying the fire for a moment. Suddenly, he sees the men running towards the fire, blocking the light with their hands. He turns away to leave, but hears the men yelling. Tim looks back momentarily to see the men pointing at the ground. Apparently, the oil from tonight's wrestling match was coating the street where the men walked from the bar. Ignited by the explosion, flames slowly crawl across the brick road toward the bar as the men frantically try to put them out.

They throw their rifles to the ground and swipe at the flames with their shirts and pants, but it's useless. The flames slowly creep their way up the steps and through the door to the bar. The oil-soaked wood floor ignites like a box of matches, and the building is fully engulfed in seconds. Men fall to their knees in front of their beloved bar, yelling and cursing.

Tim can't help but smile at the foolish men as he turns and heads for the cemetery, and finds Randy waiting at the gate.

Randy jumps in the air as he's still full of adrenaline. "That was so awesome! I saw the fireball from here. Did you hear the sounds coming from those explosions? It was like *boom,* and they were like *ahhhh.* I could hear the screams from here."

Tim puts his hand on Randy's shoulder. "I got some bad news for you, Randy. Remember that super sexy oil wrestling match you had earlier? Well, the oil from that was tracked by the men to the barracks. When I blew it up, that oil caught fire and kind of... well... made it back to your bar."

Randy falls to his knees and yells. "Noooo! Not my baby!"

"Yeah, the men also looked a lot like that when it happened." Tim says laughing. "Don't worry. We'll find you a new bar. On the lighter side, they probably think you burned up inside, so they won't be looking for you anymore."

"I wish I *did* die in there," Randy says, staring at the yellow and orange glow with tears in his eyes. "The captain *always* goes down with the ship."

"Come on, let's get out of here," Tim says, lifting Randy up from his knees. "I know something that'll cheer you up."

Tim leads him to the secret tunnel entrance and stops.

"How is this going to cheer me up?" Randy says, sadly looking up at the moldy tomb. "I already *died* once today. Are you going to bury me now?"

Tim opens the tomb's door and steps inside, feeling along the walls until he finds the secret sliding panel revealing the keypad.

Randy's eyes get wide as he looks at the panel. "What's that?"

"Will you do the honors? Type these numbers into the pad. 8-6-7-5-3-0-9."

Randy punches in the numbers and steps back as he hears the hatch on the floor make a metallic clunk and hiss open. "What? Secret tomb door? Where does it go?"

"Be my guest and take a look," Tim says, motioning for him to enter the dark hole in the floor. "Careful not to trip down the stairs." As he follows Randy into the tunnel, he closes the door behind them tightly.

They make it to the tunnel system entrance to find everything right where Tim left it.

Randy looks around excitedly. "Golf carts? Where are we going?"

"You'll see. Jump in, and I'll drive," Tim says, unplugging the cart and motioning for Randy to jump into the passenger seat.

They drive down the tunnel for what seems like forever. With the adrenaline wearing off, Randy falls fast asleep, with his head bobbing back and forth with the movements of the cart.

As they reach the end of the tunnel, Tim nudges Randy with his elbow. "Wake up. We're here."

"Huh, where are we?" Randy replies, looking up with squinted eyes, still half asleep.

"The coolest and safest place you'll ever see in your life," Tim says, ushering him through the door to the main room.

As he passes through the final door, Randy looks around with his hands on the sides of his face. "Whoa, is this the Batcave? Are you Batman?"

"No, I'm not Batman. This is an underground survival bunker, courtesy of Mr. O'Connell."

Randy runs around the main room like a kid in a new arcade, yelling. "Oh, it has a gym and an Xbox! Look at that table! It's huge! There's even a fancy library! This place is *amazing!*" He finishes the full circle and stops in front of Tim again. "Are you *sure* you're not Batman?"

"I'm positive he's not Batman," Mary says with a smile as she pops her head out of a bedroom door on the left side of the room.

Garrett comes out of one of the bedrooms to the right. "You're back! And you brought Randy with you.... great."

"I had to, since I accidentally burned down his bar."

Randy plops down on the couch in front of the TV looking sad. "Yeah, still kinda bummed about that. But the Batcave makes me feel a little better."

Tim walks over to Mary and gives her a big hug. He peeks through the door to see Victoria lying in the center of a big bed, surrounded by pillows.

From the next bedroom, Marco and Nancy come out rubbing the sleep from their eyes. "Hey Son, are you alright? You've been gone all night. We were starting to get worried."

"I'm fine. The town, on the other hand. Not so much."

Randy waves his hands in the air from the couch. "We blew it all to hell!"

Marco looks at Tim and growls. "I hope you took all those bastards down with it."

"No, I wasn't trying to kill them all. They're just a bunch of hillbillies. I did take out all of their gear and trucks, along with their radio antenna," Tim replies proudly. "That won't stop them for long, though. They have reinforcements on the way. They want to set a trap for the National Guard, and I need to do something, or a lot of soldiers will die. We can't just sit here and wait it out."

Marco puts his hand on Tim's shoulder. "It sounds like you set those guys back a few days at least. Let's get some sleep and make a plan in the morning."

"Agreed," says Mary.

"Agreed," says Randy from the couch as he stretches his arms. "I could really use a nightcap though."

Tim walks past Randy and waves for him to follow. They stop at the giant globe, and he lifts the top. A look of pure happiness spreads across Randy's face as he stares down at the stash of bottles.

"Pour us a victory drink, barkeep!"

Randy looks through the bottles for the oldest bottle of Scotch in the collection and finally lifts one. He pours them both a glass, and they raise them high.

Tim looks over at Randy with a smile. "To dodging bullets."

"May the odds be ever in your favor." Randy cheerfully replies as he touches his glass to Tim's.

They down the whiskeys in one shot and put the glasses down on the desk. Satisfied with the evening, everyone returns to their rooms, and Randy plops down on the couch.

"See ya in the morning," Tim says as he closes the door to the bedroom.

It's hard to tell what time it is when you're living underground. Tim wakes up to the clock saying one PM, but without windows, it could have been four AM, and he wouldn't know the difference. He rolls out of the king-sized bed and goes to the bathroom for a quick shit, shower, and shave. He comes out of the bedroom feeling refreshed and satisfied with last night's sabotage.

As he enters the main room, he finds Randy sitting on the couch, intensely playing a fighting game on the Xbox, while Marco, Nancy, and Mary are at the table having lunch. Little Victoria is sitting in an antique wooden highchair, covered in some kind of brown yogurt. From the looks of it, Sammy must have had a few of his staff move into the bunker to make the meals, do the laundry, and clean the place.

Tim sits down at the table and smiles at Victoria. "Mornin' everybody."

One of the kitchen staff comes out, places a coffee mug on the table, then fills it with fresh, fruity coffee. "Would you like something to eat, Sir?"

"I don't know. What's on the menu?"

"Anything you want, Sir. The chef is ready to make anything you wish."

Tim scratches his chin and looks at the ceiling. "How about a BLT sandwich with extra B and less T?"

"Fine choice, Sir. Coming right up." He obediently replies, and returns to the kitchen.

Mary glares at Tim from across the table. "Smart ass. These poor people are paid pennies to do everything for this family. It's sad."

Tim raises an eyebrow and stares back. "Okay, we can go back to Dad's tiny shelter and hide out there for a few weeks."

"No, no, that's okay," Mary replies, looking away and with a smile. "This place is really safe... for the baby... you know. We should stay here for now."

"That's what I thought," Tim says, then slowly takes a sip of his coffee while keeping eye contact with Mary. "Don't get too spoiled in here through. We do need to go back to the farm someday."

"And you need to find me a new bar!" Randy yells from across the room. "The acoustics in here really carry."

Tim's attention turns to a panel above the main tunnel when a green light starts flashing on the wall. "What's that?"

Marco points up. "Oh, Garrett said that when someone punches in the code to enter the bunker, it flashes green, so you'll know that someone's in the tunnel. It'll flash red if the door is forced open or if someone enters the wrong code. The same light's over the door on the other side of the room, so you'll know which way they're coming from."

Mary looks towards the tunnel. "Garrett must be coming back from the main house. He went to talk to his parents about something."

Just then, one of the kitchen staff comes out of the hallway holding a beautifully built BLT sandwich with bacon hanging out of the sides and a little toothpick with an American flag stuck on top.

He puts the plate down on the table and steps back. "Your BLT with more B and less T, sir."

Tim looks at the sandwich and drools a little. "Glorious. Thank you."

"My pleasure, Sir," he replies, and returns to the kitchen.

Just as the server vanishes into the tunnel, Garrett and Sammy walk out towards them.

Sammy walks up with his hands in the air and a smile on his face. "Look at this man! I don't know what you did, but we can see the smoke from here. Those hillbillies got what was coming to them." He points at Tim's sandwich on the table. "That looks like an epic sandwich. Chef! Make me one of those!"

Tim stands up from the table and shakes Sammy's hand. "Sorry to burst your bubble, Sammy, but that's only going to slow them down. They have reinforcements on the way already. They're planning to set a trap and kill a lot of National Guard soldiers in Oklahoma City."

Sammy sits down at the table next to Tim. "Is there a way to get them on the radio?"

"Not without their military encryption codes. We might have to drive up there and tell them in person. I don't know if we can make it through the R.R. roadblocks though."

Randy looks over from the couch and yells. "If you're going to Oklahoma City, I want to go too. My brother's lived in the city for ten years. He might be able to give us a place to lay low if things get crazy."

Garrett raises his hand from the other side of the table. "If it's alright with you, I'd like to come too. There's nothing left for me here, and I want to make up for helping those crazy people in the first place."

Sammy looks at Tim with a crazy smile. "I have something that might help you guys get into the city. Let's finish our meal, then I'll show you."

The server emerges from the kitchen once again, holding another massive sandwich, and places it in front of Sammy. "Your BLT with more B and less T, Sir."

Sammy looks down at the sandwich with wide eyes. "This is my new favorite sandwich."

They finish their lunch, and Tim, Garrett, and Randy follow Sammy out of the bunker's main entrance. They jump into the golf cart, and Sammy drives them over to a small barn next to the combine tractor shed. The barn doesn't look normal because it has suspiciously wide doors on the front. Sammy jumps out and motions for them to help him open it up. Inside, covered in dust, sits a small single-engine Cessna airplane with a row of black parachutes hanging on the wall behind it.

Tim puts his arms over Randy's and Garrett's shoulders and smiles. "You boys know how to use a parachute?"

Chapter 6

OKLAHOMA CITY

"This is my favorite part of the job," JJ says, excitedly while standing in line in front of Tim. "I love the rush of jumping from a perfectly good airplane just to land hard on my ass in the middle of a field full of rocks and trees."

"Me too," replies Tim as they wait to get their main and reserve parachutes from the truck.

They gather up their gear and walk to the chute shed to start putting them on.

As he sets his gear down, JJ looks out the door at the trees swaying in the breeze. "Looks like it's a little windy out there today."

"A little wind never stopped the Army from training," replies Tim with a smile.

After they finish gearing up, Tim waves to the jumpmaster to come by and check them out. The inspector today is a tall, muscular female named Staff Sergeant Wright. As she walks over, JJ looks at Tim with a crazy sparkle in his eye, like he was about to do something stupid.

Tim points at him sternly. "Don't even think about it."

JJ replies with a wink and loosens his leg straps a little. As Wright arrives, JJ puts his hands on his helmet as they're supposed to when preparing for the jumpmaster inspection. She goes over the reserve chute on his chest, then turns him around to check the main on his back. Meticulously, she inspects everything, then instructs him to turn back around and crouch down to check his leg straps. Like a good jumpmaster is supposed to, she notices that they were loose and begins to tug at them. JJ looks over at Tim with his best orgasm face as she jerks him back and forth, tightening his straps. Tim can't help but let out a laugh that gets the attention of Wright.

Realizing she had been fooled, she finishes her adjustments and stands up. Wright wasn't known for being shy or letting a foolish jumper get away with anything, so she gives JJ a ginger tap to the testicles and sits him down on the bench.

"All finished. Now, don't move, or I'll have to come back and readjust those straps again. I'm watching you, Specialist," she says, giving him a wink and turns away.

JJ sits on the bench with a look of terror on his face while grasping his crotch in pain. He knows that it would be another hour before the plane was ready. He'll have to sit there helpless with throbbing testicles crammed inside of overly tight leg straps, unable to readjust or loosen anything.

"It was worth it," he wheezes out with a painful grin.

"Dumbass," Tim says, looking over at JJ and shaking his head.

Wright then turns around and approaches Tim with an evil smirk on her pretty face. "You're next!"

"Yes, Jumpmaster!" Tim yells and quickly raises his hands above his head.

The time finally comes when their chock is called to get ready to board the C-130. They jump up and shuffle toward the door of the staging shed. The airplane had just landed after dropping the last chock of paratroopers before them. They move as a group toward the flightline entrance and wait for the plane to come to a stop. Tim can feel his adrenaline begin to spike as a blast of hot air from the engine hits his face, and the smell of jet fuel exhaust fumes sting his nostrils.

Another jumpmaster waves his hand in the air. "Chock Twelve, load up."

They shuffle across the tarmac and climb up the ramp at the back of the airplane. Once on board, Tim sits down next to JJ and buckles his seatbelt. When everyone is on and situated, the plane's engines rev up, and it turns toward the runway. A few highly anticipated moments later, the airplane shoots down the runway, sending everyone leaning hard to the rear with a strong thrust from the engines. It accelerates to its maximum speed in seconds and is airborne, flying toward the drop zone.

The onboard jumpmaster at the rear of the airplane holds up a single finger and yells, "One minute!"

"One minute!" Everyone on the airplane repeats the command.

Suddenly, the plane banks hard to the left and aligns itself with the open field below.

The jumpmaster shows a small gap with his fingers. "Thirty seconds!"

"Thirty seconds!" Everyone repeats the command and unbuckles their seat belts.

The jumpmaster shows a lifting motion with both of his hands. "Stand up!"

As one, the entire load of paratroopers stand up in unison and turn toward the rear of the airplane.

The jumpmaster shows a hook with his finger, pulling it down toward his head. "Hook Up!"

With one hand, Tim grabs the metal clip attached to a yellow line leading to his parachute and attaches it to the overhead cable. With the other hand, he carefully covers the release handle of the reserve parachute on his chest.

The jumpmaster motions toward his chest with both hands. "Sound off for equipment check!"

Tim looks down at the guy standing in front of him and gives his main chute a good look, making sure everything is still properly attached. The repeated chant of "OKAY" comes closer from the front of the plane as each person taps the person standing in front of them, ensuring that their gear has been checked.

Soon after, Tim feels JJ slap his ass and yell, "OKAY!"

Tim repeats the chant, and so on toward the rear of the plane, it goes.

When the last person has been checked, he raises his hand to the jumpmaster and yells, "OKAY, Jumpmaster!"

The excited jumpmaster slaps his hand and turns to look out the side door. He does his methodical checks up and down, left and right, in and out, making sure the door is safe for his paratroopers to jump.

Once he's satisfied with his checks, he pulls the first jumper in front of the door and yells, "Get ready!"

He takes the yellow line attached to the cable running along the wall and pulls it out of the jumper's way. Above the door, a little red light flashes, signaling the quickly approaching drop zone.

Suddenly, it turns green, and the jumpmaster yells, "GO! GO! GO!"

The line of paratroopers shuffle toward the door as he ushers them out one by one, grabbing each yellow line and sliding it to the rear and out of harm's way. Tim shuffles closer and closer until he's next up. He hands off his line and turns toward the door. As the intense rush of wind swirls around him, he looks out at the ground slowly passing by. He takes one step forward and pushes off with all his might. The rotor wash throws him around like a rag doll in the air for a second. Holding on tight to his reserve chute and praying for the main to open, he hears the comforting pop of the parachute catching the air and is violently jerked back upright.

At this moment, Tim truly understands what JJ said earlier about this being the best part of the job. For two full minutes, he calmly floats freely in the breeze. The clouds are so close, he can almost touch them with his hands. For miles all around him, the beautiful countryside stretches out, full of vibrant colors. The only sound is the air passing through the parachute above him and the light hum of the departing airplane. Just then, the entire experience is ruined when JJ comes screaming past him to the right.

He glides past, kicking and yelling at the top of his lungs. "Aaahhh, Myyy Baaalllsss!"

With the Texas sun high in the sky, the guys help Sammy push the airplane out of the barn and onto the road. Hanging on the wall inside the barn are a line of dusty parachutes and helmets.

Sammy grabs one of the parachutes off the wall and dusts it off. "A while back, I was getting into skydiving until my back went out. After that, I mainly stuck to flying the plane around for fun."

"How long has this stuff been sitting here?" Tim asks, as he runs his finger through the dust on one of the helmets.

"Oh, about a year or so."

Garrett looks at his father, confused. "Why didn't you tell me you were skydiving, Dad?"

"I didn't need your permission, Son. Anyway, you were too busy off playing sheriff to come and visit. We could have gone up together."

"I don't think so. This is crazy," Garrett says, shaking his head and backing up. "You don't seriously plan on jumping out of this airplane. Do you? There's not an airfield somewhere we can land?"

Tim grabs a helmet off of the wall and tosses it to Garrett. "Not one that your dad will get out of alive. I'm sure the R.R. is occupying everything in the area. Jumping is our only option. You're not backing out now. Are you?"

"I'm in!" Randy says, jumping excitedly.

Garrett looks around nervously for a second, then finally answers. "Okay, I'm in."

"Excellent! This'll be fun, trust me," Tim says, with an evil smile. "There's one extra chute, so I'll give you guys a crash course on how to use them."

"Don't say crash!" Garrett replies sharply.

Tim opens one chute, ties a rope around the lines, and hangs it from the barn's rafters. He persuades Garrett to get into the harness, then Randy and Sammy pull him off the ground.

"Ah! My balls!" Garrett groans as his feet leave the ground.

They all get a good laugh seeing Garrett hanging there, spinning helplessly like a piñata for a few seconds.

"Okay guys, pay attention for a minute," Tim butts in, holding back another laugh. "Garrett, look up at those handles. Grab one with either hand. Those are how you'll steer in the air. Pull the right one, and you'll turn to the right, and the same goes for the left. You'll have a slight delay after pulling them, so don't wait until the last second to turn. When you get close to the ground, extend both arms all the way down to your knees. If you time it right, you'll land slowly and walk away from it. If you time it wrong, you'll hit the ground really hard. For someone inexperienced like you guys, it would be safer to aim for the trees. It's better to get hung up than to break a leg in a combat zone. I'll be watching you both closely on the way down, so don't worry. I'll find you after you land."

"This is gonna be great! I've always wanted to skydive!" Randy says, jumping up and down, holding his helmet.

Tim reaches over and unties the rope holding Garrett in the air, and he falls quickly to the ground with a dusty thud. "We won't be high enough to freefall. I'll have Sammy drop us no higher than one thousand five hundred feet, and I'll pull your ripcords as you leave the plane. All you'll have to do is hold on and steer to a safe landing zone. We need to go now and get some weapons and gear put together. Make sure to bring everything for a fight and a couple nights surviving in the city."

They grab the remaining three parachutes and head back down into the bunker. They lay all of the weapons and ammo out on the big table, along with three backpacks, food, water, flashlights, a compass, and a first aid kit. Tim shows them how to attach their backpacks to the bottom of the parachute so they won't fall off, and how to sling their rifle so it doesn't get in the way of steering in the air. They eat one last big meal, have a shot of whiskey, and gather their gear. Tim gives Mary and Victoria a kiss goodbye, and they make their way to the airplane. While Sammy starts the engine and does his pre-flight checks, the guys stuff themselves and their gear into the airplane.

Tim can see the fear on the guys' faces, so he decides to give them a little motivation. "Boys, today you become men. What we're about to do is going to save the lives of countless others. Fathers, mothers, brothers, and sisters will live another day to be with their families. The road ahead will not be easy, but I want you to know that I'll be there with you both the entire time. I give you my word that I'll do everything in my power to get us all back home safely."

Sammy pushes the throttle forward, and the small airplane lunges forward toward the makeshift runway/driveway. As he gives the engine full throttle, they bounce along for a couple of seconds, then smoothly leave the ground. When the plane gets high enough, they can see the smoke from Chesterfield still spiraling into the air. Looking out the window, their town was not the only smoke trail they could see. In all directions, little black trails rise up from the horizon.

As they near Oklahoma City, the sun had fully set. The entire city is pocketed with fires burning out of control, and the light from the flames illuminates the night sky like an artificial sun. The smoke in the air is so thick that it makes it almost impossible to fly over. All of a sudden, the sky around the tiny airplane erupts with explosions.

Tim reaches for Sammy in the cockpit. "Turn off your lights! They have anti-air defenses! Get lower! We need to jump out now!"

The anti-air guns fill the air around the airplane with black starbursts, sending small pieces of shrapnel bouncing off the fuselage.

Tim points out the window and taps Sammy. "Look to the left! Fly over that park!"

Sammy banks hard to the left and lines up with a small inner-city park. As Tim opens the side door, violent rushing wind fills the airplane all around them.

He looks over at the two scared faces staring out at the exploding night sky. "It's now or never, Men!"

Randy claps his hands together and shrugs his shoulders, psyching himself up for the jump, while Garrett holds tightly onto his seat and stares out of the open door. A loud explosion jolts the airplane hard to one side, and Garrett closes his eyes and grits his teeth.

Seeing his distress, Tim grabs his shoulder and looks him in the eyes. "You got this! Remember what I taught you, and you'll be fine!"

"Get ready!" Sammy yells from the pilot's seat. "We're almost there! GO! GO! GO!"

Randy stands up and moves to the door as Tim lines him up, grabbing his ripcord. He looks back with a big smile, and Tim gives him a tap on the head before shoving him out the door. His chute comes out immediately and opens fully, sending him floating away. Tim waves to Garrett to get up, and he slowly moves towards the door. He grabs the side of the door firmly, having second thoughts about the jump, but Tim reaches out and grabs his hands. He folds his arms across his chest and pushes him out the door, pulling his ripcord as he falls. A second later, the chute opens without a problem, and he floats away. Tim looks one last time at Sammy, gives him a thumbs up, and leaps from the plane, pulling his ripcord as he falls.

The sound of the airplane's engine fades away in the darkness, and all that's left is the air rushing all around him. Randy reaches up for his steering handles and fumbles with the cables, but finally gets a hold of them. The small green park below him slowly grows larger as he floats to the ground. He remembers what Tim said about the trees and spots a group off to the right of the park. He slowly pulls the right toggle, but he doesn't turn. He pulls a little harder, but nothing happens. The ground is fast approaching, so he pulls the right toggle all the way to his knees, and the chute darts to the right, sending him swinging high to the left. His flight path lines up with a tall tree, and Randy covers his face with one hand and his crotch with the other.

Sticks and branches smash against his body as he pierces the upper part of the tree. His parachute cables become tangled, and the canopy collapses, sending Randy falling straight towards the ground. Helplessly watching as the ground speeds toward him, Randy covers his eyes just before impact. To his surprise, he never makes it to the ground because his lines were too tangled up in the tree branches. He breathes out a sigh of relief and lets his hands fall towards the ground as he hangs upside-down, spinning with one foot caught in the lines.

Garrett screams as he falls from the plane, holding onto the front of his harness with all his strength. He hears a loud pop and is jerked upright as the chute opens and catches the air. As he swings back and forth, he opens one eye and looks out at the orange flame-filled horizon. Remembering what Tim said about the handles, he looks up and sees them hanging from the cables, and hesitantly reaches up for them. The little park is closing in fast, so Garrett pulls the right handle, causing him to turn slightly to the right. He pulls the left handle and slowly turns back to the left. Feeling confident that he could control the landing, he decides to aim for the center of the park and land safely on the grass.

As the park closes in, he aligns himself with a long patch of grass in the center. Just before he hits the ground, he gets distracted by Randy's parachute covering the top of a tree and forgets to pull down the handles until it's too late. He hits the ground running as fast as he can, but his legs aren't fast enough. His feet get tangled up with each other, causing him to trip and slide behind the chute that's now dragging his helpless body through the park grass.

Garrett desperately rolls and pulls the handles, trying to regain his footing and slow the chute, but it's too late. He slides face-first into a shallow pond at the end of the park and comes to a stop. The chute falls into the water, and he flips over onto his back in the pond. He spits out a mouthful of murky water, and takes a deep, victorious breath.

Tim watches as the other two parachutes make contact with the park. Randy takes the safe route and ends up soaring into a tree, while Garrett goes for a slide and ends up knee-deep in a pond. He follows Garrett's route to the park and aims for the long, grassy field in the center. As the ground approaches, he pulls the toggle handles all the way down, and the chute fills with air, slowing his descent. He hits the ground running and stops just before reaching the pond where Garrett was currently standing.

Tim effortlessly lays his chute on the ground and looks at Garrett in the water. "Now that wasn't so hard. Was it?"

Garrett sloshes through the water to the shore and falls on his back in the grass. "Never again."

Tim runs over to see Randy hanging three feet off the ground, half upside-down, and spinning slowly.

He swings his arms around to look at Tim and laughs. "That was awesome! Can I get a little help, please?"

"I got you. Hang in there."

Tim pulls out his knife and cuts the line holding his foot in the air, and Randy swings around to put his feet on the ground. As Garrett slowly walks over, his feet make a squishing noise with every step. Randy looks over at him, points, and laughs. With an inconvenienced scowl on his face, Garrett just stands there as water drips from his hair.

"Great job, guys," Tim says, taking a knee and looking around.

"Don't forget we're in enemy territory now. Take a couple of minutes and fix your gear, then we need to head out."

Tim cocks his pistol and checks the magazine, then does the same for his AR-15. He then quickly puts his backpack on, and pulls a compass from his pocket to get his bearings. As he finishes, he looks up to see Garrett taking off his boots, wringing out his socks, and draining the water from his backpack. Randy stands there, picking the leaves from his hair, while struggling to untangle his backpack from the spider's web of parachute cord hanging from the tree. Tim shakes his head, grabs a dry pair of socks from his bag, and tosses them to Garrett. He then goes to Randy, cuts his backpack from the parachute harness, and hands it to him.

"Time to move out. North is that way," he says, looking down at his compass and pointing towards the city.

All of the streetlights and traffic signals are powerless, so the dancing shadows from the fires light the way through the empty streets. Everything is dead quiet except for a car alarm going off in the distance. They walk down the deserted street, passing stores with their windows shattered into millions of tiny pieces all over the sidewalk.

Tim passes through what looks like a barricade made from the skeleton of a car that was burned to a crisp. "The rioters really did a number on this place."

"Yeah, I hope they got it all out of their system by now," Garrett says, looking through the blackened car window.

A noise from up the street forces them to stop in the middle of the intersection, as the buildings all around them echo with the sound of breaking glass and metal banging.

Garrett looks up with wide eyes and whispers, "Sounds like they didn't."

"Move to the side of the street and stay low," Tim says as he waves at the other two. "Randy, keep your eye our rear. Don't let anyone sneak up on us. Garrett, scan the buildings up high. Look for anyone watching us. Stay alert and follow me."

Tim takes a right through an alleyway between two tall buildings, trying to avoid the source of the noise. The three men pop out of the alleyway and continue down a side street. They soon realize that this was a colossal mistake.

Off in the distance, a group of people dressed in colorful clothing and wearing helmets and facemasks march in their direction. A few of them are carrying big pipes and baseball bats in their hands. Tim motions for them to get down just as he hears a loud pop from the opposite direction. They look up as a canister of tear gas flies over their heads and bounces in front of the mob of rioters. They turn around see a wide line of police officers, decked out in full riot gear, with shields and batons in their hands. Another tear gas canister flies over their heads, and Tim grabs Randy and Garrett by their gear and ducks through a shattered storefront window.

"Good job, Tim," Garrett says as he hides behind an empty clothes rack. "You walked us right into a huge battle."

"How was I supposed to know that? The whole damn city is a war zone." He barks back.

The rioters from the left march forward, yelling and throwing rocks towards the line of police. One of them throws a Molotov cocktail that lands just in front of the shield wall in a massive fireball. The police simultaneously bang their batons on their shields as they push forward towards the feral mob of rioters. Suddenly, a small group of men in body armor make a run for the shield wall and throw themselves at it. The impact knocks two of the policemen to the ground. Others from the back bash the suicidal rioters with their batons as they help their fallen comrades to their feet. But it was too late, and the rabid wave of rioters swarm the police in a massive clash of chaos and violence.

Garrett watches helplessly and turns to Tim. "We have to do something to help! Those police don't stand a chance."

Tim looks around for a second, weighing his options. "Ok, see that empty building across the street? When I say, aim high and unload your magazine into it. That should scare the rioters away long enough for the police to recover. Spread out along the window. Ready? Fire!"

The men aim high above the crowd, and each of them unloads thirty rounds into the building behind the fighting. The rioters immediately fall and scramble in all directions. They knew that the police wouldn't use deadly force against them, so they weren't afraid to attack. Throw a bunch of armed citizens firing their guns at them, and they crumble like paper and run back to their parent's basement. As the last rioter flees, the police pick themselves up and look at the window from where the shooting came.

One of the policemen points at the dark storefront and shouts. "You in the building, put down your firearms and come out now!"

Tim lowers his rifle and yells back out the window. "We're with the National Guard. We're not here to hurt you. We're coming out now. Don't shoot us!"

As they walk out slowly into the street, the team lowers their rifles and raises their hands. The line of riot police hide behind their shield wall as the three men crunch through the broken glass and step out into the light.

A man moves one of the shields out of the way and steps forward. "National Guard, huh? What are you doing inside the city? And why are you shooting at people?"

"You were getting your asses kicked out here." Tim says, pointing in the direction the rioters fled. "What were we supposed to do? Sit here and watch you all die? You're welcome."

"We didn't need your help." The officer snarls back. "You didn't answer my question. What are you doing inside the city? The front line is on the north. That's where the R.R.'s held up."

"We're coming back from Texas. We're a long-range recon team. We need to get past the R.R. and back to the main body of the National Guard with important information vital to stopping an attack." Tim explains, looking the man in the eyes, hoping he would buy his story.

The officer looks the three men up and down for a second and lets out a deep breath. "The city's a disaster right now, if you couldn't already see. Take the street behind us to the north. It'll eventually lead you to the front line. It's about seven miles from here. *If* you make it there, I don't know how you'll make it past the R.R. line. They're dug in deep and been fighting with the Guard for a few days now. Riot groups like this one are all over the city, wreaking havoc. Be careful. And hey! Thanks for the help back there."

"Thank you, Officer. Good luck out there."

Tim waves at the other two to follow him, and they slowly pass by the group of recovering policemen.

Once they get clear of the battlefield, Randy nudges Tim and smiles. "How can you say all of that stuff so smoothly? I almost believed you."

"The last thing we need right now is to get detained by the local police. Sometimes you need to lie to the good guys to complete the mission."

"Got it. I'm lying to everybody from now on," Randy says proudly, standing tall like he's some kind of elite soldier. With a deep voice, he holds out his hand to an imaginary civilian. "Stand back, Ma'am! Long Range Recon Team Delta coming through."

Garrett shakes his head and rolls his eyes. "Were you breastfed as a child?"

"Only when your mom came over," Randy quickly replies.

While exchanging more mom jokes, the team walks for another couple of blocks through the dark streets. The condition of the city degrades the further they go. Cars and buildings are on fire. Trash and debris litter the streets, with all of the stores smashed open and looted.

Garrett looks down at his throbbing feet and lets his arms hang low. "We've been walking *forever*. Can we find a place to take a break for a few minutes?"

"Hey look, my brother's apartment is in one of those tall buildings over there," Randy says, pointing to the left. "We can go see if he's still home."

"Sounds like a plan to me." Tim replies. "Lead the way."

They take a left off the main street and go deeper into the city towards a tall set of apartment buildings. The group of four buildings forms a square with a large open area in the center. They stand about thirty stories high and three hundred feet long. As they get closer, Tim looks up and notices the flicker of candlelight through a few of the windows.

Approaching the side of the buildings, something seems off. Large piles of trash and scrap metal block the path through the gap between the buildings. Pieces of wood and chains also block the lower entrance doors on the sides.

Tim peers at the blockages as they walk past. "Someone's made a fortress out of this place."

They continue around the complex, looking for a way inside, and find a tall metal gate with barbed wire sealing off one of the gaps. Suddenly, two bright spotlights flash to life, pointing at the men as they freeze in their tracks.

A man with a loudspeaker shouts from over the top of the gate. "Who are you? What do you want?"

"My name is Randy Morgan!" He yells as he steps forward, with his hand blocking the light from his eyes. "My brother lives here! We're trying to find him!"

Not a sound comes back from the gate for a minute, and then another voice shouts down at the team. "Randy, is that you? You crazy son of a bitch. What are you doing in the city?"

"Nash, you're still alive! Let us in. We're on a top-secret mission for the National Guard," Randy replies, then turns to Tim and winks.

"What kind of top-secret mission?"

"The secret kind… At the top level… *Open the gate!!*"

The gate makes a loud, metal scraping noise as it slides open to the side. The spotlights turn off, and four men appear standing at the top with their rifles aimed down at the team. As they walk through the center of the buildings, a skinny man wearing a blue tracksuit and sneakers walks up with his arms open, smiling at Randy.

He walks forward and gives him a hug. "What are you doing, Bro? How did you get through the city? Rioters are attacking everyone they can find out there."

"Dude, we flew in on this tiny airplane, and then my parachute got stuck in a tree. Then Garrett there landed in a pond, and we were attacked by a bunch of crazy people. We almost died, but my friend here, Tim saved the day," Randy explains, almost running out of breath.

"Wow, thank you, Tim. Come inside, guys. Take a load off. Welcome to our little sanctuary."

They follow Nash into the center of the buildings, and the weight of the world immediately comes crashing down upon them. The survivors of the devastation had fled their homes and turned the courtyard into a refugee camp for anyone who could get away. Families with children huddle closely together on tattered couches, trying to stay warm. Makeshift tents are propped up using streetlight poles and broken bed frames. A couple of men walk back and forth with their rifles at the ready. They stare suspiciously as Nash ushers the team through to an empty picnic table in the center of the camp.

"Take a seat, fellas," Nash says, motioning for everyone to sit down. "You guys want some water?"

Randy looks around at the sad faces and plops down at the table. "Got any whiskey?"

"Sure thing, Bro. Wait here."

Tim takes a seat at the table and looks around at the dirty faces staring back at him. "These people must have lost everything. I can only imagine what it was like in the city when everything collapsed."

Nash comes back with an unlabeled bottle containing brown liquid and pours it into five dirty glasses. "To the end of the world."

The rest of the men can't think of anything positive to drink to while in the presence of all the suffering and pain around them, so they raise their glasses in silence. They drink their watered-down whiskey and put the glasses down quietly.

Tim takes another glance around the camp, then turns to Nash.

"You're doing a good thing here, helping all of these people stay safe. It really is a nightmare out there. We're coming from my farm down south. It's not much different there, either. The R.R. is making a huge mess of the country."

"We're almost at max capacity here. I don't know how much longer we can survive inside the city. Every day, we send out people to look for supplies, but sometimes they don't come back. When they do return, they find very little and say that most of the stores are already empty."

"I believe you. Listen, we need to get to the National Guard up north. We have some information that could save a lot of lives. How can we get there and not get killed by the rioters?"

"What? There's no way to get there on foot. If you had a helicopter or something, you might get lucky."

Randy looks over at Nash. "There has to be a way. A lot of people depend on us."

"Come with me," Nash says, standing up from the table waving for them to follow. "I want to show you what you're up against."

Nash leads the team through a side door to one of the buildings and up a never-ending flight of stairs. After finally reaching the top floor, they drag their tired feet through the door. Breathing heavily, they look out over the city in shock.

"Holy shit," Tim says, looking out with wide eyes and a dropped jaw.

They move to the edge of the roof to get a good look off of the thirty-story building. The night sky is lit up with a bright orange glow from the fires burning everywhere, while smoke pours from every rooftop. Where the team just came from to the south, a large explosion lights up an intersection where the police clash with the rioters again. Where the front line is to the north, the R.R. and the National Guard are fighting. Tracer rounds fly through the air in all directions, while bright balls of light erupt behind the buildings. A pair of anti-air guns spew glowing lines of bullets into the air as they chase something through the night sky.

Nash raises his hand and points to the fighting. "As you can see, it's impossible to make it to the front line," he says, then sadly lowers his gaze to the street below. "Unless..."

"Unless what?" Randy asks.

"You see that entrance to the subway over there, about two blocks away?" He says, pointing down. "If you can get into that subway tunnel, you might be able to go under the riots and reach the other side of the city safely."

"That seems like a better plan than hitting the city head-on," Tim says, looking at the others. "We might even be able to take that all the way under the front line to the Guard side."

"That sounds like a good plan to me," Garrett replies.

"Agreed," says Randy.

"Then that's what we'll do," Tim says confidently, looking out over the destroyed city.

They walk back down the thirty flights of stairs to the ground floor again. Both Randy and Garrett gasp for air as they reach the bottom. They stop just before the gate and take one last look at the refugees occupying the camp.

"Thank you very much for the whiskey and the plan, Nash," Tim says as he shakes his hand. "We need to get back on the road."

"Anytime, boys. Good luck out there, Bro," Nash says, as he turns to Randy and gives him a hug. "Come back and visit when this is all over and cleaned up. I just bought myself a new seventy-inch plasma before the lights went out."

"Will do. Later, Bro," Randy replies with a tear in his eye.

"Thank you," Garrett says as he turns around and walks towards the gate.

The team walks through, and the gate slides closed behind them with a loud bang. They immediately raise their rifles and look around as they find themselves all alone in the anarchy-ridden city again.

"The subway's this way, guys," Tim says, looking down at his compass. "It's one block north, and one block east."

The streets are momentarily clear of rioters, so they pick up the pace to a slow jog. Tim knows that the less time they spend out in the open, the less chance there is of something bad happening. Ten minutes later, they turn a corner and the dark entrance to the subway comes into view.

"We made it," Garrett says, wheezing and leaning over, trying to catch his breath.

Right behind him, Randy comes jogging up, equally out of breath. "Remind me... to run... more often."

Tim looks down the stairs leading into the subway system and reaches for his backpack. "Get your flashlights out. We're gonna need them."

Randy and Garrett creep forward until they can see down the long, dark staircase. They look at each other with scared faces as Tim shines his light down the endless pit of doom. Even the bright flashlight seems to be halted by the blackness at the bottom of the stairs.

Tim looks at the other two and smiles. "Hope you're not afraid of the dark."

As he slowly walks down the concrete stairs into the subway station, Randy and Garrett turn their flashlights on and cautiously follow behind. They finally reach the bottom, and with the small beams of light, they find the platform completely empty except for a shiny metro train sitting powerless on the rails.

"This feels like we're on one of those ghost hunting shows," Randy whispers. "Are there any spirits in here with us? Knock twice on the wall if you can understand me."

Suddenly, a bang comes from near the end of the platform. All three of them turn and shine their lights at the lifeless train as a small head pops out from behind the window, then quickly ducks back inside.

"AHH!" Randy screams and hides behind Tim. "There's a ghost on the train!"

"That's not a ghost. It's a child," Tim says, detaching Randy from the back of his jacket and moves closer.

They slowly walk toward the open door to the rear of the train. Another shuffling noise comes from inside as they shine their lights through the glass windows. Randy lets out a gasp as the bright, white light illuminates the inside of the train, and countless faces turn or raise their hands to block the light. The entire train is packed from front to back with people. Refugees from the city had taken shelter in the underground station to escape what was happening on the surface at night.

"There are so many people in here," Garrett whispers, looking inside the train.

"We need to get through to the other side," Tim says, pointing at the front. "The tracks are blocked from the outside, so we need to go through the cars."

The team weaves through the people in the train car, heading toward the front. They watch the faces stare back at them as they slowly pass through. There are all types of people inside. One thing that occurred to the team as they pass, is the lack of segregation in the dark hiding place. There was no upper-class or lower-class part of the train. No one was arguing over priority, or who's rich and who's poor. There's only fear, and the primal instinct to survive.

As they creep through the rows of people to the front of the train, a man stops Tim and asks for water. He takes a bottle from his backpack and hands it to him. Garrett and Randy do the same, giving their water to a couple of families huddling together.

This is the part of war that's rarely talked about. The endless number of people who are caught in the middle of the destruction, forcing them to do unthinkable things to survive. Looking at the dirty, sad faces on the train just puts things into perspective. No matter what country you're from. No matter what social class you belong to. No matter what political party you stand for. War is hell.

They finally make it to the front of the train, and Tim pries the door open, leading to the tunnel. The team jumps out, and Tim can see Garrett wiping the tears from his eyes.

He pretends not to notice and points down the tunnel. "That's the way we're going."

As they walk through the tunnel in the dark, Randy frantically shines his light around. "I'm glad this isn't the zombie apocalypse, because you would never get me to do this."

"Oh, trust me. I would never come down here if there were zombies," Tim replies, waving his flashlight around. "And thank you for putting that thought in my head."

While walking through the dark subway tunnel, Tim keeps a rough pace count in his head, so he knows about how far they've gone. At about four kilometers through the dark, he notices something strange ahead.

"Guys?" Tim says, shining his light at the end of the tunnel. "We've got a problem."

Getting closer, all three of them shine their lights at the collapsed tunnel before them. Rocks and slabs of concrete have completely blocked it off.

"Well shit. Now, where do we go?" Garrett says, looking around.

Tim shines his light up at the walls. "Look around for a service door or something."

Randy walks further towards the collapsed tunnel and yells back. "Found something! There's a ladder here going up."

"Perfect. Let me go up and see where we are," Tim says, reaching for the ladder. "If I counted right, we should be close to the north end of the city."

Tim climbs up the metal ladder to a manhole leading to the street above. He pushes his face close to the holes and looks through. All he can make out is the side of a building with flames rising from it. The sound of crackling embers and distant gunfire echoes through.

"We're still inside the city," he whispers down the ladder.

"Which side of the front line?" Garrett asks.

"I don't know. Let me get this manhole cover open, and I'll take a look."

Tim pushes with all of his strength, and the manhole cover pops upward and slides to the side. Slowly popping his head out, he realizes that he's not in the city where the looters and rioters had smashed windows and burned things. He's on the edge of a war zone. The buildings have massive holes from high-explosive tank rounds. An overturned Humvee sits just behind the manhole, with the body of a soldier hanging out of the window. The street is littered with brass casings and large-caliber shells. Automatic gunfire echoes off the tall buildings, followed by an explosion that rattles all of the empty shell casings around him.

Tim pulls himself out of the manhole and waves to the others to climb up. He instinctively pulls his rifle up and scans the streets for anything moving.

As Randy pokes his head out of the hole, Tim helps him to his feet. "Keep quiet. Move to the alley quickly."

Looking around in shock, Randy almost pukes on himself when he sees the dead soldier in the Humvee. Tim has to smack him in his chest to get his attention, and he moves out of the street to the alley. Garrett follows closely as Tim helps him out of the manhole and points to Randy standing on the side of the street. They quickly move to the alley, and just as they leave the sidewalk, they hear a vehicle approaching.

"Get down. Don't move." Tim says, shoving them behind a dumpster and kneeling down.

A large, green five-ton Army truck rolls past, heading north. The glass is dirty, but he can see that the driver has a long beard hanging off his face.

Tim ducks back behind the dumpster and looks at the other two. "Shit, we're on the R.R. side. Let's find some higher ground and see exactly where we are."

Tim points deeper into the alley, and they move to the other side. He looks up when they reach the next street and sees a tall parking garage about a block away. He taps on Garrett's shoulder and points to it. Garrett nods and taps Randy, pointing silently. They rush across the street into the adjacent alley, keeping their rifles up and ready.

They finally reach the parking garage and walk slowly up the spiral entrance ramp, watching for any R.R. soldiers that may be occupying the garage. As they reach the sixth floor, the area seems to be abandoned. Randy and Garrett arrive breathing heavily and are barely able to hold their rifles up as they walk out onto the rooftop parking area. They keep low and move toward the north side of the building, trying to get a good look at the front line.

Reaching the edge of the parking area, they're shocked to find that the garage is backed up to a wide rail yard. About twenty sets of train tracks run alongside massive warehouses for as far as they can see in either direction. The R.R. holds the south of the yard with large barriers stacked high with sandbags, and machine gun positions aiming to the north. On the opposite side, the National Guard holds the warehouses with metal shipping containers blocking the way. The wide-open tracks are filled with burning trucks and bodies that were cut down by the crossfire.

"That's No Man's Land," Tim says disappointedly, then sits down with his back to the wall.

Randy turns and sits next to him. "What's No Man's Land?"

"That's the area that no one can cross without getting killed. Did you see how flat it is with nothing to hide behind? There's no way to make it across without being cut down by the other side. The bad thing is, we *need* to get over there."

"Is there a way to sneak across or make a distraction, or something?"

"I'm sure that both sides are using night vision, so no. They'll see us for sure."

Garrett peeks up over the wall again. "How far do you think the gap between the warehouse and the parking lot is?"

"I don't know. At least two hundred feet. Why?" Tim replies.

"Do you think there's a way to jump over it? That would be quick enough to get us there without being shot. Don't you think?"

Tim looks at Garrett with a confused smirk. "Maybe if we had a NASCAR to get up enough speed, an industrial-grade ramp, and some heavy-duty cushions to catch us on the other side. Ya, we could make it."

Randy stands up and walks away from the others. "I'm going to take a piss. This shit's getting depressing."

"Do you think we can get back into the subway tunnel through another manhole somewhere?" Garrett asks as he scoots closer to Tim and relaxes his legs, straightening them out.

"We're too close to the front line. The National Guard probably collapsed that tunnel on purpose so the R.R. can't sneak through. It's most likely caved in all the way across."

Footsteps on the concrete come pounding toward Tim and Garrett through the darkness as Randy arrives, out of breath. "You guys gotta come and see this."

Randy leads them across the parking lot to the other side of the building, where a shiny box on wheels sits in the dim moonlight.

"Look at this old shaggin' wagon. It even has a unicorn painted on the side." Randy excitedly proclaims as he runs his fingers across the paint. "I always wanted one of these."

Garrett places his hand on the hood, admiring the paint job. "Who would leave this here?"

"Someone probably stole it during the riots and parked it here, thinking it would be safe to collect later," Tim replies, looking at the van.

The old van is from the 90s and is painted gloss black. On the side is a hand-painted giant white unicorn rearing up, with rainbows shooting over it. The suspension in the front is lowered, so the oversized tires in the back make it look like it's ready to pounce on unsuspecting prey. The shiny chrome rims match the four exhaust pipes sticking out of the sides.

Randy reaches for the driver's door handle and pulls. "Oh! It's unlocked."

Inside, the interior is covered with fuzzy purple fabric from top to bottom. The seats, the dashboard, and even the ceiling is covered in purple fuzz.

Randy slides into the driver's seat and grabs the fuzzy steering wheel with both hands. "My God. This is the softest thing I've ever touched."

Tim goes around to the passenger door and jumps in. "Shaggin' wagon is about the right term for this, Randy."

He reaches up and jiggles the purple fuzzy dice hanging from the rearview mirror, then turns around. The back of the van is basically one big mattress. Purple cushions line the walls and ceiling, and a big pile of purple pillows are stacked up to the side.

This van doesn't seem like a simple show car, so Tim decides to investigate. "Randy, pop the hood. Pull that lever next to your left knee."

Randy pulls the lever, and the hood pops up, while Tim jumps out. As he lifts the hood, he's left speechless. Inside sits an enormous engine with "Chevrolet" in red letters written down the sides and a bright red "454" stamped on the top. Every pipe and hose shines with chrome. Tim notices a small blue line leading back from the engine and follows it to the cab behind the passenger seat. A large blue NOZ tank is mounted securely with 800 psi reading on the gauge. He looks up at Randy, breathing heavily, and smiles.

Randy just stares back at him with wide eyes. "You're not thinking, what it looks like you're thinking. Are you?"

Tim peeks up at Garrett through the windshield, then back at Randy, who is gripping the steering wheel tightly. "You boys up for one more flight tonight?"

"Hell yeah!" Randy replies, bouncing in the driver's seat.

Garrett shakes his head and throws his hands up. "No way! You said it yourself. We'll never make it."

Tim goes back around to the front of the van and looks at the chromed-out monster under the hood. "The engine in this thing has to have a thousand horsepower. This parking lot is about three hundred feet long. With a boost of nitro, we can get up to about a hundred miles an hour before hitting that gap. I think we can make it."

"What other options do we have?" Randy says, standing up out of the driver's door, hanging by one arm.

Garrett crosses his arms and looks at the opposite side of the parking lot. "Okay, how do we get over that ledge? It has to be three feet tall."

"You two, go down and look for something we can use as a ramp," Tim says, closing the hood. "I'll work on hotwiring this bad boy."

Randy jumps out of the van excitedly. "I'm on it!" He says, grabbing Garrett by the shirt and pulling him away before he can complain anymore.

Tim slides into the driver's seat and grabs the steering wheel. "What in the hell am I doing?"

He reaches up for the sun visor, thinking no idiot would leave the keys there, and a tiny, fuzzy, purple unicorn with a single key attached falls into his lap. Tim smiles, inserts the key into the ignition, and turns the engine over. The massive engine roars to life, shaking the whole chassis like an earthquake. He quickly turns the loud engine off so as not to attract any unwanted attention.

Looking out the windshield and rubbing the fuzzy steering wheel, he says to himself. "Poor, poor, pony. It's a shame I have to ruin you. Someone is going to be *pissed.*"

On the next floor down, Randy and Garrett search for something to use as a ramp.

Garrett sifts through a small pile of trash with his foot and looks up at Randy. "You really think we'll make that gap in one piece?"

"Probably not. But if we survive, it'll be an awesome story to tell later."

They both look to the ceiling as the rumble of the van shakes dust from the cracks overhead.

"Looks like we're about to find out," Randy says, looking at Garrett with a big smile. "We just need to find a good ramp. Go look over there."

Garrett huffs and turns towards the elevator at the back of the parking lot. He slowly looks around the corners, hoping not to find anything to aid in this suicidal stunt. Next to the elevator is a set of tall, grey security doors, probably leading to the stairs. He grabs the handle and pulls the heavy metal door open, just as Randy comes up behind him, and eyeballs what he found.

"Good find. These should work," Randy says, hitting the door with his hand to see how hard it is. "Solid metal. I got a screwdriver in my backpack. It should come right off."

Garrett looks at his accidental discovery with disappointment. "Great... Just what we were looking for... *Idiot.*"

Randy pulls out his screwdriver and starts to remove the door's hinges. As the last screw comes loose, the door slams to the ground with a heavy thud and falls over, sending a cloud of dust outward.

"Perfect. I'll go get Tim to help us drag these upstairs," Randy says, wiping the sweat from his brow. "You get started on the other one."

Tim's heart races as he looks the van over from the driver's seat. Through the windshield, he sees Randy waving at him from the ramp. So he jumps out and follows him down one story to find Garrett standing next to a door lying on the ground.

Randy puts his foot on the door like some kind of big game he just shot. "Will these work? They're solid metal and heavy as shit."

"They'll work perfectly," Tim says nodding, and attempts to lift the heavy door.

Tim and Randy drag the first door up the ramp to the top level and lay it over the ledge. They start walking back to the ramp as they hear a heavy thud from the other door, leaving its doorframe. Breathing heavily, they return to find Garrett nervously standing over the second door. The three of them drag the last door up the ramp and set it up beside the first one on the ledge. Once they were happy with the arrangement, they stand next to the ledge and silently contemplate their life choices.

Garrett looks out over the rail yard as a barrage of glowing tracer rounds soar over the tracks at the National Guard positions. "You sure this'll work?"

"Nope," Tim replies, standing with his hands on his hips, staring at the makeshift ramp.

"Ok, let's do this already," Randy says, walking back toward the van. "I always wanted to jump something like the Duke boys."

The team jumps into the van and buckles up as tightly as possible. Randy straps into the passenger seat as Garrett clenches tightly to the back of his chair. The pillows from the back of the van are stuffed into every piece of clothing they can fit, and their backpacks are put on backward for as much protection as possible.

Tim buckles his helmet and takes one last look at Randy's and Garrett's scared and excited faces. "Any last words?"

"Thank you for letting me come with you guys," Garrett nervously replies from the back.

"Please don't kill us. You still owe me a new bar," Randy says, holding tightly to his backpack.

"I never would have made it this far without you guys. Thanks for being there for me," Tim says with a smile, as he turns the key.

The engine comes to life with a deafening growl, shaking and vibrating the entire van as it idles. He pushes the gas pedal a couple of times to get a feel for the power under the hood. The van tilts and sways as the massive engine revs up and down. Tim pulls the shifter lever down into drive and holds the brake hard as he hits the gas. The rear tires effortlessly turn and squeal on the pavement, sending up a white cloud of smoke.

He releases the brake, and the van jumps off the line. They're forced back into their seats, and Garrett is almost thrown from his firm hold on the back of Randy's chair. Tim reaches up and pushes the little red button, releasing the nitrous gas into the engine. Immediately, the van thrusts forward like a rocket, lifting the front wheels off the ground. The immense force breaks Garrett's grip, sending him tumbling over the purple cushions and hitting the back of the van.

Before anyone has time to think, the speeding van hits the metal doors and launches into the air over No Man's Land like a big black brick with a unicorn painted on the side. Like a comet, the van soars through the air for a second, reaching its peak altitude. From the back of the van, Garrett begins to weightlessly hover as their rocket ship starts its descent towards the Earth. As the warehouses across the railyard rapidly approach, Tim and Randy watch through the windshield with wide eyes.

Randy holds tightly onto his backpack and yells, "We're not going to make it!"

"Hold on!" Tim yells as the van smashes into the side of the warehouse.

The van pierces the metal wall of containers and rolls over onto its side as it lands. Tim and Randy yell and helplessly hang sideways as they slide through the warehouse, colliding with a shipping container. The van rolls again and is now upside-down, spinning across the concrete floor, destroying wooden boxes and pieces of machinery before finally coming to a stop. Everything goes quiet as the destroyed unicorn van rests upside-down, letting out puffs of smoke and steam.

Tim looks back to see Garrett leaning against the purple wall, looking like he just went through a blender. "You alright?"

"Yeah. Now I know what a pinball feels like," he replies, laughing.

Tim and Randy look at each other with their hands hanging above their heads and begin hysterically laughing at their success. Before they have time to get out of their seats, the sound of boots come stomping toward them as soldiers surround the van. Two

National Guard soldiers, wearing tan uniforms, aim their rifles through the windshield that's now missing its glass.

"Don't shoot! Don't shoot! We're friendly!" Tim yells out of the van.

"Get out of the van, or we *will* kill you!" One of the soldiers replies.

Tim looks over at Randy and laughs. "Easy killer. Getting out of this thing is easier said than done."

Randy looks back and starts laughing loudly again, as Garrett crawls from the back and pokes his head between the seats. He can barely function because he's laughing too hard, but he helps Tim and Randy from their seats. The three men emerge from the front of the van, looking like a bunch of psychopaths with their backpacks on backwards and fuzzy purple pillows sticking out of their clothes.

Despite looking ridiculous, Tim stands tall and turns to one of the soldiers. "I need to talk to your commanding officer. I have important information about an impending attack by the R.R."

The soldier huffs and aims his rifle at Tim. "Where are you coming from?"

Randy laughs and waves his arms in the air. "The moon! Didn't you see us land?"

"We're coming from Texas. Just south of the Oklahoma border," Tim replies. "I had a run-in with one of the men commanding the R.R. and learned about their plans to set a trap for you guys."

"Come with us now," he growls back at Tim.

The soldiers strip the team of their gear and pillows, then push them out of the warehouse and away from the front line. About five hundred feet north of No Man's Land is a concrete building that the National Guard had converted into their command center. They are then escorted into a makeshift holding cell and told to wait. Tim, Randy, and Garrett sit patiently, reliving the epic air they just achieved in the van for about thirty minutes, until they finally get a visitor.

A black man wearing the rank of major enters the cell and looks at them with a displeased expression. "So, you're the idiots who jumped a ghetto van over no man's land and punched a hole in my perimeter wall."

"Hell yeah, we are!" Randy replies confidently.

Tim stands up and approaches the major. "Yes, Sir. Are you the commander of this unit?"

"I'm Major Ramsey, the Executive Officer for First Battalion, Kansas National Guard. The Colonel will be returning tomorrow morning from a mission. I heard you have some information for me. What's so damn important that you felt the need to risk your lives for it?"

"We're coming from Chesterfield, Texas, where I met with a Colonel Wallace of the R.R. I overheard him making plans to set a trap for the National Guard. They'll be calling for a retreat from Oklahoma City soon and drawing you to the south. Once your units are past the city, they plan on hammering you with a regiment's worth of artillery."

"We have no intel of this. The R.R. isn't strong enough to pull off such an attack."

"I heard it from him directly. He tried to recruit me, but I told him to fuck off."

"Then we blew up the whole town with them still inside!" Randy says, waving his arms around.

"Wallace said that reinforcements are on their way to Chesterfield, and they're bringing a full artillery regiment with them. We only slowed them down enough to get the message here in time to warn you. I'm retired Army. I couldn't sit by and let my brothers-in-arms get killed by that madman."

Major Ramsey stands, staring at Tim with his arms crossed for a moment. "That was a courageous thing you did, and extremely idiotic, but quite extraordinary. I'll relay your information up to my chain of command and see what they have to say about it. In the meantime, I'll have you moved to a tent with some cots and food for the night. We'll be holding onto your weapons and gear until we can verify your intel."

"Thank you, Sir," Tim replies, and turns to the others with a satisfied grin.

A few minutes later, two soldiers escort the team to a tent near the command center and leave two armed guards outside. The soldiers give them some MREs to eat and cots to sleep on. Tim has to walk Garrett and Randy through how to open and properly eat their meals. Randy was given the chili mac, so Tim had to convince him that it was the worst of all the MREs so Randy would trade him for his tuna. After some successful negotiations, they eat their food and go to sleep on the good old, stiff-as-hell Army cots.

Tim wakes up with the sun the next morning. The smell of war still lingers in the air as gunshots pop off in the distance. He looks over and sees Randy and Garrett awkwardly sitting up on their cots.

"How'd you guys sleep?" Tim asks, stretching his arms.

Randy grabs his back and looks up in pain. "I feel like my back is twisted around backwards. How do you sleep on these things?"

"I slept like a baby," Tim replies. "I've spent many deployments sleeping on these cots. They're more comfortable than a regular bed to me."

The tent flaps covering the door open, and Major Ramsey slides through. "Morning, men. I'm sorry to say, but our higher command isn't accepting your intel as credible. They believe that the R.R. isn't capable of coordinating an attack of that scale. I'm instructed to hold you three until we can transport you back to our main command post in Kansas. There, you'll be debriefed and sentenced if they see fit."

Tim jumps up from his cot and stares at the Major. "What? This *is* a credible threat. I heard it right from the fucker myself. Do you think we would risk our lives to come here and pull a prank on you? Is your colonel back? I want to talk to him."

"He has returned and wishes to speak with you before your transport arrives."

"Good, let's go men," Tim replies, waving his hands to the others.

The major pulls down Tim's arm and points at him. "No. He wants to speak to you alone."

Tim looks at the major confused. "Okay, let's go then."

Tim slides on his boots and follows the major out of the tent and to the command center. The major leads him to the commanders office and shows him through the door. As he enters, the colonel has his back turned while looking at a map on the wall. He has a vaguely familiar posture that Tim can't quite place.

He slowly turns around to reveal himself and says, "It's been a long time, Tim."

A surprised grin spreads across Tim's face as he looks back and replies, "Damn, it's good to see you, JJ!"

Chapter 7

LONG RANGE RECON TEAM DELTA

"We're gathered here today to recognize one of our finest. After twenty-two years of service, he's decided to retire and move on from the United States Army. Give a round of applause for Master Sergeant Walker."

Standing in front of Tim, the entire Eighth Battalion claps and cheers as an administrative person steps up and starts to speak. "Attention to orders!" Everyone stops talking and goes to attention. "The Secretary of the Army has awarded Master Sergeant Timothy Walker the Bronze Star for exceptionally meritorious service while assigned to the Eighth Battalion. Master Sergeant Walker's outstanding dedication to duty, selfless service, and professionalism contributed to the success of countless missions. His service is in keeping with the highest military standards, and reflects great credit upon himself, the Eighth MISB, the Ninth MISG, and the United States Army."

Colonel Pierce reaches up and pins a Bronze Star ribbon to Tim's uniform, then shakes his hand. They turn to the cameraman and smile for a photo, while the room erupts in clapping and cheering. The Colonel releases Tim's hand and gives him a microphone.

As he brings the mic to his face, he looks out at the crowd of familiar faces. "Thank you very much, Sir. It's been an honor to have served with the outstanding soldiers of Eighth Battalion. I've fought alongside many of you in Afghanistan, Iraq, and many other countries around the globe. Not once did I see a blink of fear in the face of adversity from anyone standing here today. To those who are no longer with us, you'll never be forgotten. Special thanks go out to Bravo Company and Sergeant Jacobs. Without you at my back, I wouldn't be standing here today. Now that all the official mumbo jumbo is out of the way, get the hell out of here. I have a very important meeting with a couch and a beer to get to. Zonk!"

Tim sets the microphone on the podium as the crowd scatters in all different directions, but a select few stick around to shake his hand and congratulate him. The Army is always good at scheduling ceremonies on Friday after work. So Tim figured that this would be his last chance to stick it to the man, and free everyone to go home for the weekend, so he took it.

After the crowd disperses, Colonel Pierce walks toward Tim with a wooden box in his hands. "You've been with this battalion since before we had a name for ourselves. The hard work that you've done has paved the way for the next generation of soldiers, so the command group and I wanted to give you something special to show our appreciation."

Tim opens the highly glossed wooden box to see a polished stainless steel Colt 1911 pistol. The grip is made of the same dark wood as the box and has the battalion crest engraved on it. It sits in a custom-fitted grey felt cushion with a small gold placard on the top left corner engraved with a message.

"To one of the 8th Battalion's finest, MSG Walker. We will never forget what you have done for us. Enjoy your retirement."

Tim reaches out and shakes the Colonel's hand. "Thank you very much, Sir."

"If you ever need anything, you have my number," Colonel Pierce replies confidently. "Enjoy your retirement. You've earned it."

As Pierce turns away, JJ walks up, clapping his hands. "So, you finally decided to cut the cord. What's next?"

"I figured I would take a trip to your mom's house and hang out for a while. You should go ahead and start calling me dad." Tim replies, punching JJ in the arm. "Seriously though, first I plan on drinking for a week or two. When I get bored with that, the wife and I will pack up and move back to Texas. How do you plan on surviving without me around to save your ass all the time?"

"I have no idea. Guess I'll have to hire a new bullet shield for my next rotation. When I get back though, I plan on applying for the Green to Gold program. I might be an officer one day. Imagine that," JJ says with a laugh.

"How much time do you have left? Six more years?"

"Yup, I just signed my final re-up last week."

"Congratulations. Send me a message when you put on that butter bar. I would be proud to salute you as an officer. It's been a blast, Brother. I'll see you when I see you. Take care of yourself."

JJ reaches in for a hug. "Will do. Don't get too fat. I might need you to get me out of a jam someday."

Tim hugs him back, trying his hardest to keep the tear in his eye from dropping down his cheek in front of anyone. He lets him go and shakes JJ's hand one last time. As he picks up his things, he takes one last look around the company area. Holding back any feeling of regret, he turns his back and walks away for the last time.

"Damn, it's good to see you again, JJ. Wait! I owe you a salute." Tim stands tall and gives him the salute he promised so many years ago.

JJ salutes him back and waves at him. "Put your hand down and come give me a hug. When I heard about some crazy guys who jumped the rail yard in a ghetto van with a unicorn painted on the side, I immediately thought about you."

"You like that?" Tim replies, laughing. "It wasn't only my idea. I've got a couple of guys with me you should meet. How are you?" Tim smacks JJ on the chest over his rank. "More importantly, whose balls did you have to polish to make Lieutenant Colonel so fast?"

"I retired earlier this year as a major. Once all of this revolution crap started, I heard that the Guard needed some experienced officers to take charge, so I joined. Next thing I know, they throw a field promotion at me and put me in command here."

"Well, aren't you one lucky SOB? Congratulations. I'm sorry to use your rank in such a hurry, but we have a problem. They said that my intel about the R.R. is bogus, and now you're about to push your whole unit into a trap. You have to do something about this, or a lot of soldiers are going to die."

"I think I need to call them again and convince them that this threat is real. I trust you with my life, so they should take that into consideration. You head back to the tent, and I'll get on the horn with higher and see what I can do."

Tim throws another sarcastic salute at JJ. "Right away, *Sir.*"

"Stop calling me that, damn it. That's an order," JJ laughs while pointing at Tim with a knife hand.

Back in the tent, Randy and Garrett are putting on their clothes and stretching awkwardly from the rough night of sleeping on the cots.

Tim comes bursting through the tent flap and looks at them excitedly. "Good news, Men. I know the guy in charge. We go way back to my old Army days. He's gonna sort this out with command and keep their troops from falling into the trap. They should be releasing us soon."

"It's about time. I can't sit on this damn cot for another minute," Garrett complains.

"I second that motion!" Randy says, raising his hand.

The team finishes gathering up their things as JJ comes through the tent flap, followed by a couple of soldiers holding their bags and weapons.

JJ stands with his arms on his hips and takes a deep breath. "I got some good news and some bad news. The bad news is that they still won't take your intel as credible without proof. They tried to use one of our surveillance satellites to get some orbital photos of the area, but the R.R. is using some kind of jamming equipment that prevents the satellites from taking clear photos. The good news is that I convinced them to let me send a team into Texas and bring back proof. I volunteered you three because you guys know where the R.R. is staging for this attack. I'll be joining you along with three other soldiers. We'll wait for nightfall and take a Black Hawk over the border. From there, you'll lead us to the R.R. camp and take some photos to prove your intel. We have twenty-four hours to get in and out before I'm forced to push my unit forward and take the Texas border. You think we can make this happen?"

"Yes, we can," Tim answers confidently.

"Excellent. Here's your gear and weapons. I'll also have them bring you some tactical vests. Get some food and be ready at sunset. And Tim, it feels good to be part of your team again."

"Just like old times, JJ."

"So, you're telling me that we're now Long Range Recon Team Delta for real!" Randy says, jumping excitedly. "I'm totally getting some matching T-shirts made after this."

"JJ, this is Randy and Garrett. They were mixed up in all of this from the very beginning, and I wouldn't have made it here without them."

JJ looks at the two of them with a smirk. "Whose idea was it to jump the van over the train tracks?"

"That was me. I found the old shaggin' wagon while I was taking a piss. Then we jumped that sexy unicorn over the moon," Randy explains, simulating the arch with his hand. "I want you to know that you can count on me, Sir. I always wanted to join the Army, *but* I just never got around to it."

Garrett stands up quickly and salutes JJ. "You can count on me too, Sir."

JJ salutes him back. "Outstanding. A lot of soldiers are counting on you. Not just me. Get some food and gear up. I'll see you all tonight."

As they leave the tent, JJ and his soldiers leave the team's gear and weapons on the floor.

"I've never been on a Black Hawk before. This is going to be so sweet!" Randy says excitedly. "I wonder if they'll let me shoot the machine gun out the side."

"Easy tiger. Let's focus on the mission first," Tim says, grabbing his gear off of the floor. "If we pull this off, I'm sure they'll let you do whatever you want."

A few moments later, a soldier returns to the tent with three tan tactical vests with ceramic plates and magazine pouches. Tim shows the others how to set up the pouches for easy reloading and adjusts them to fit properly.

"These things weigh a ton," complains Garrett. "How do you walk around all day with this on?"

Tim laughs. "Try adding fifty pounds of crap in a rucksack on top of it."

Randy spins back and forth and does a few jumping jacks, followed by a somersault on the floor with his new vest on. "Just breaking the old girl in a little."

After a couple of hours of magazine change drills and simplified strategic combat instructions, Tim is confident that the two wouldn't die immediately on the battlefield. He hands out another round of MREs, and sits back at his cot. The two sit down and stare at Tim in amazement as he tears it open and digs in.

Garrett turns his MRE around and reads the nutrition label. "These things have like 5000 calories in them. How can you eat more than one of these in less than twenty-four hours?"

Randy grabs his stomach as the tuna from last night starts to dance in his gut. "Sooo, asking for a friend here. Suppose someone needed to shit their brains out on a tiny Army camp. Where would they go?"

Tim takes another bite of his food. "Well, lucky for your friend, we're not in the middle of the desert with nothing but a metal bucket to shit in. After it gets full, someone would have to burn it with diesel and stir it with a pole," he says, looking at their disgusted faces with an evil smile. "I think I saw a bathroom in the command center. Just ask around. I'm sure you'll find it."

"I'll go tell my friend really quick," Randy says standing up and awkwardly walks towards the tent opening. "Be back in a few minutes."

Later that evening, as everyone rests and anxiously waits for the mission, Tim steps outside the tent and looks around the camp. The sky is just beginning to change colors from a light blue to bright orange as the sun sets behind the rusty metal warehouses. The gunfire had stopped, and it seemed as if everything was back to normal for a brief moment. The moment passes as an explosion erupts from the front line, followed by a string of machine gunfire.

After the sun had fully set, the team gathers their gear and makes their way toward the command center where JJ was waiting for them. Without saying a word, JJ waves for them to follow him to the Black Hawk waiting on the helipad behind the building.

They jump in and get situated as JJ introduces his soldiers. "Men, up front is our pilot, Chief Lizardo. And these two are Sergeant Elliott and Specialist Ackley, our tech guys."

"Welcome to the party, guys," Tim says, waving.

As the propeller blades begin to spin up, Tim grabs a headset from the wall and puts it on. "JJ, we need to fly around the city. They hit us with air defense batteries the last time we flew over. When we get near, it'll be safe to land at Garrett's family farm. He'll show you the way."

JJ replies with a thumbs up and motions to the pilot to take off from the front line, flying westerly around the city and south towards the O'Connell's farm. The flames from the city shine as bright as ever. As Tim looks out the window, he thinks that it's such a shame to see things being destroyed only because one person doesn't agree with another. It's human nature to destroy itself one day. He just hopes that he and his family have a chance to grow old and enjoy life before that happens.

Randy enjoys every minute onboard the helicopter as he hangs his head out the window, waving his hand around in the rushing wind. On the other side of the chopper, Garrett sits stiffly with both hands tightly grasping the seat beneath him. Tim waves to Garrett and points to the headset hanging on the wall behind him.

Garrett slowly reaches for the headset and puts it on. "Is this thing working? What's up?"

"How are you doing, Garrett?"

"I hate flying. One bullet in the wrong place, and this helicopter is a spinning fireball falling to the ground."

"I'll give you a little secret that always helped me when I was new to the Army and nervous about flying. I would close my eyes and picture myself riding in the back of an armored truck down a bumpy road. If you concentrate hard enough, they feel much like the same thing. Can you feel it?"

"Yes. It does feel about the same." Garrett replies with his eyes closed.

"Good. Now imagine that truck exploding from underneath you after running over an IED. The point is that it doesn't matter what you're riding in. If it's time for you to explode in a ball of fire, nothing's going to stop it. You're along for the ride regardless. So, sit back and enjoy the ride while it lasts."

Garrett opens his eyes and glares at Tim as he stretches his legs out and puts his hands behind his head. "Thanks for the advice."

"Works for me every time," JJ says as he turns around and smiles at Garrett. "If your number's up, you might as well relax and accept it."

"Amen," Lizardo comments from up front.

Garrett rolls his eyes and looks away. When he thinks no one's watching, he crosses his arms and slides down in his seat a little to a more comfortable position. After a few more minutes, Garrett spots the blinking lights that are mounted on top of his parents' grain silos through the window.

He waves at JJ and points. "Those green lights are the farm. Set it down behind the main house near the big barn!"

As he relaxes in his leather armchair with a glass of whiskey, Sammy hears the chopping of the helicopter in the distance. Expecting the worst, he runs from the back door of the house with his shotgun in hand. Thinking that the R.R. was sending some more muscle to take his farm, he prepares himself for a fight. To his surprise, when the chopper touches the ground behind his house, a familiar face comes to greet him.

Tim waves his arms at Sammy as he walks forward. "Don't shoot. It's us. We need this chopper to get out of here later. Can we store it in your barn for the night?"

"Good to see ya, Boy. Welcome back!" Sammy says, throwing his shotgun over his shoulder. "Yeah, I'll have the workers pull it in with a tractor. Are Randy and Garrett alright?"

"Yeah, they're fine. They have some good stories for you."

Tim waves at the pilot to cut the engines, and the rest of the men jump from the chopper. They all walk toward Sammy and Tim, except for Randy, who is skipping like a schoolboy.

"Sammy, you'll never believe what we did." Randy explains excitedly. "Spoiler alert: there was a flying unicorn."

Garrett walks up confidently to his father. "Good to see you, Dad. I'm glad you got out of there without getting shot down."

"I almost didn't," Sammy laughs. "The plane took a hard hit after you guys jumped out. I tell you what, trying to land with holes in your ass isn't easy."

"Sammy, this is Lieutenant Colonel Jacobs of the Kansas National Guard and his men. JJ, this is Sammy, Garrett's dad. He owns this farm and everything as far as you can see," Tim explains. "Sammy, we need to get to town and take some photos of the additional troops and equipment the R.R. is bringing in."

"I think you might be a little too late. A small group of R.R. came through here yesterday and took a trailer of livestock at gunpoint. They left out the opposite direction of town, to the east. I think you cooked Chesterfield a little too well-done for their liking," Sammy says, with a snort.

"Do you have any idea where they were going?" JJ asks.

"No idea. There might be someone back in town who knows. You should check there first."

"Thanks, Sammy. Okay JJ, are you ready to see the nicest bunker that you'll ever see in your entire life?" Tim asks, with a big grin.

"It's the Batcave," Randy says, looking at him with wide eyes.

Sammy's workers bring a small tractor, push the helicopter inside the massive horse barn/laboratory, and close the doors. Everyone else walks toward the bunker as Sammy rides ahead in his golf cart to open the vault door. Nancy, Marco, and Mary are waiting in the main room as they exit the tunnel.

Nancy runs toward Tim with open arms to give him a hug. "Oh, thank God, you're alive."

Mary follows her with the baby in her arms. "Why do you have to go jump from every airplane you get into? Did you land safely?"

"I landed in a tree, and Garrett landed in a pond," Randy says, laughing and looking at Garrett.

"Yes, I landed fine," Tim says, motioning to JJ. "Everyone, this is Colonel Jacobs and his men. They're from the Kansas National Guard."

"Unbelievable. Good to see you again, JJ. It's been so long," Mary says, giving him a hug. "Welcome to our happy little fallout shelter."

"Good to see you again, Mary. Look at this cute little lady. What's your name, sweetie?" JJ asks, pinching her cheek as she smiles back.

"This is Victoria. She'll be two in November."

JJ looks around the elaborate bunker. "This place is amazing, Sammy."

Randy drops his gear and moves quickly for the couch. "Oh, my beautiful Xbox. I missed you the most."

"There's a radio room over there that you guys are welcome to use," Tim says, pointing to the opposite side of the room. "You and I can take a tunnel to town and ask some questions. Everyone else can hang out here until we get back."

JJ points to his men and motions for the radio room. "Elliott, Ackley, you two get command on the radio. Lizardo, stay with the chopper. Have it ready to fly at a moment's notice." He turns to Sammy with a serious, official look on his face. "Looks like this will be our new command center for Northern Texas. Sammy, I'm sorry to say this, but we need to use this bunker for the foreseeable future. I understand if you don't want that, but we can pay you for the stolen livestock in return."

Sammy looks around and huffs. "No need. It's not about the money. It's about the principle of the whole thing. Those men have no manners or respect. You're welcome to use the bunker as you see fit. It's good to see someone getting some use out of it."

JJ shakes Sammy's hand and turns to Tim. "Ok Tim, lead the way to town. Let's see what they have to say about the R.R."

"This way, Sir," Tim replies mockingly.

"Stop calling me sir, damn it," JJ replies as he follows Tim into the tunnel.

They take off in the golf cart down the tunnel to the cemetery entrance, and Tim shows JJ through the secret door. They exit the cemetery quietly and sneak up behind the old church on the side of town. The smell of burning wood and plastic fills the air. Accompanied by the crackling of embers from the charred remains. Peeking out from behind the church, what was left of the town seemed vacant of any militia.

"Looks like Sammy was right. I don't see any men or equipment," Tim says, waving to JJ. "Follow me."

Most of the streetlights still work and illuminate the destruction that was left behind. Four charred skeletons that used to be trucks are piled up in front of the church. A massive crater occupies the center of the street, with a black, smoking pile of a schoolhouse sitting behind it. To the right, Randy's Bar had been reduced to nothing but ashes due to the amount of oil left inside. Someone had left a homemade wreath made of flowers on the front step with a little sign saying "RIP" next to it.

The two men walk toward the sheriff's station to find that it has a giant hole in the roof, which rained down bricks and support beams into the lower floors. Tim can make out one or two crushed bodies under the bricks while looking through the windows, but there's no sign of Wallace. The line of buses that were blocking the back end of town are now a line of charred, bus-shaped shrapnel with an opening big enough to drive a truck through.

JJ nods approvingly at the destruction. "You really had some fun out here, didn't you?"

"Just another day in the country," Tim replies proudly. "If anyone's still here, they'll be in the trailer park for sure. Follow me this way."

They maneuver through the hole in the bus carcasses and walk toward the trailer park on the north end of town. The trailer park is lined with dull yellow streetlights, spread out over about twenty old, tan, and rusty white mobile homes. Bright-colored plastic lawn chairs sit on carpets of fake grass, with pink flamingos and lawn gnomes outlining each property. Walking by the main office at the edge of the park, Tim notices a white sign saying "No Vacancy" propped up in the window.

They slowly proceed down the center of the trailer park, and Tim calls out to whoever might still be hiding inside. "Is anyone still here? We're with the Kansas National Guard. Please come out. We only want to talk to you."

The only sound is the gravel beneath their feet as they slowly walk deeper among the trailers. Tim sees the silhouette of a person through the window of a trailer out of the corner of his eye. He instinctively reaches for his pistol and readies himself for an ambush.

Suddenly, the silhouette speaks with a woman's voice. "Tim? Is that you?"

He vaguely recognizes the voice and replies. "Yes, it's me. You can come out."

The shadow ducks back into the trailer, and a few seconds later, the front door swings open. Kari Miller from the grocery store comes out wearing colorful pajamas and holding her baby in her arms.

She walks up to the men cautiously. "Is it true? Did *you* blow up the whole town to get rid of those guys?"

"I'm sorry, but I did. There was nothing else I could do. If I didn't do something, there would be a thousand more of them here."

"I understand. Thank you." Kari turns to the trailer park and yells. "Hey everyone! It's Tim! It's the guy who got rid of those bastards in town! Everybody, come outside!"

Screen doors begin creaking open all around them as people slowly walk out of their trailers. People of all sorts, old and young, walk towards them. Most are wearing their pajamas or underwear because it was late in the evening.

An old woman with a walker, wearing a white nightgown, waves at them with a fly swatter in her hand. "Thank God you got rid of those men. Thank you!"

Next to her, an old man wearing a sleeveless shirt and short boxer shorts, waves his cane in the air. "Are they gone for good? Did we win the war?"

"No, the war isn't over yet," JJ says, stepping forward. "We need to know if anyone heard anything about where the R.R. has moved to. I'm Colonel Jacobs, and I have a battalion of National Guard soldiers waiting to strike once we can locate them. If anyone heard anything, please come forward now."

"We heard some of them talking about the Stockton landfill before they left town." Says one of the Swanson sisters, standing next to her identical twin wearing matching blue and white striped pajamas. "They were complaining about not having anywhere to get a drink once they got there."

"Are you sure that's what they said?" Tim asks.

"Yeah, I'm pretty sure that's where they went," replies the other sister.

Tim looks at JJ and speaks softly. "That makes sense. That place is huge and already has security in place around it. If it were my decision, that's where I'd go."

"Then that's where we're going next," JJ replies, then turns back to the group of people standing in front of him. "Thank you for your cooperation, and have a safe evening."

"What about us? What do we do for food and water?" Asks Kari. "The town is completely burned down."

"You need to stay here for now where it's safe," Tim replies. "Once the National Guard takes over this area, they'll supply you with the things you need."

"Go get those bastards for killing our Randy," cries one of the Swanson twins while hugging her sister. "We know it was really your fault, but we blame them for it anyway," cries the other twin.

The crowd of trailer people starts to close in on Tim and JJ from all sides, commenting on the different ways they should kill or hurt the R.R. soldiers.

Feeling trapped, Tim raises his arms and yells. "Everybody, please! I assure you we'll do everything we can. Please go back to your homes and wait for the National Guard to arrive with supplies. In the meantime, keep close to your radios and listen for any important information."

The crowd spreads out and slowly walks back to their homes, still debating on the best ways to hurt the soldiers who took their town.

Tim looks at JJ and motions for him to go. "Let's get out of here."

As they walk back down Main Street, JJ looks past all of the destruction, and notices the buildings that were still intact.

"So, this is where you grew up? Seeing how you are as an adult, I expected worse."

"Yup, it's not much to look at right now, but it was a nice little town once. See that diner? They make the best biscuits and gravy in the state."

"If we make it through all of this, I'll gladly come back and have some with you," JJ replies, patting Tim on the back.

"That would be nice."

They take the tunnel back to the bunker and park the golf cart at the entrance. JJ goes into the radio room, as Tim heads into the main room to check on his family.

"Elliott, did you get a hold of HQ?"

"Yes, we did, Sir. They're saying that the R.R. is falling back, just like they warned us. Command is seeing this as an opportunity to attack and take back Northern Texas. They're gathering up all of the units in the area for a massive offensive. They said we have less than eighteen hours to find proof of the trap, or we'll be pushing forward."

"Shit. Tell them that we believe we've found their new base of operations, and we're heading there now to recon the area. Tell them to hold fast until I return with confirmation."

JJ rushes into the main room and walks past Randy, who was fast asleep on the couch. Tim, Garrett, and Sammy are sitting at the table having coffee as JJ eagerly approaches.

"It looks like the R.R. is setting up their trap. Their front line is falling back south of the Texas border," JJ explains. "Command is seeing this as a sign of weakness and plans on moving our troops forward. We have eighteen hours to go find the R.R. and confirm the intel."

Tim looks at Sammy and Garrett on the other side of the table. "The people in town they think that they're at the Stockton landfill."

"That's a big enough area with plenty of space for anything they want to do," Sammy comments.

"We need to find a safe way to get there. The roads will be blocked for sure."

"We're not flying again!" Garrett demands.

"I think I have an idea," Sammy says, sitting up in his chair. "You guys know how to ride a horse?"

"We sure do," JJ replies with a smile. "Horses are quiet, fast, and perfect for a recon mission."

Sammy stands up, goes over to the study section of the big room, and digs through one of the shelves. He pulls out a long tube of paper and brings it back to the table, where he rolls it out, revealing a map of the area.

He points down at the map where the farm is located. "The farm's here. The Stockton landfill is about fifty miles to the east, over here. On horseback, it should take you less than two hours to get there. The main road goes towards the border and comes back to the north of the landfill. You should be able to take the horses down this old trail between the farms to the south and through this pass in the hills. That'll put you on the southern side of the landfill. You should be able to find some high ground there and get some good pictures of their operation."

"I think that's a solid plan, Sammy," replies JJ. "I'm assuming that you have some horses we can use here on the farm?"

"I got a couple that might do the job," Sammy says, with a proud smile. "Follow me to my stables."

They gather their gear and wake Randy from his nap on the couch. JJ has Ackley stay behind and man the radio, while Elliott comes with them to operate the camera equipment. They exit the bunker and walk over to the massive barn where the helicopter is hiding, and Sammy leads them through to the holding pens on the other side.

Sammy confidently places his foot and elbow on the fence railing and looks at his horses. "This is where I keep my breeders. These stallions are as strong and fast as they come, with the endurance to match. Each one of them is worth over a million dollars, but seeing the importance of this mission, I can't think of any better horses for the job."

"You are just full of surprises, Mr. Sammy," JJ replies, looking around the laboratory in awe.

Sammy waves to his workers and points out a few horses for them to gather and prepare. Once they finish, the workers bring the horses over and line them up along the fence.

"Gentlemen, let me introduce you to your noble steeds for the evening. For the Colonel, I present the 'War Admiral,' and for your soldier, here's 'Red Rum.' For my son, I have the 'Gallant Fox.' For Randy, the most appropriate choice is obviously, 'I'll Have Another.' Last but not least, I chose my prize horse, 'Man O' War' for Mr. Tim."

The recon team mounts their horses and takes a minute to get accustomed to them. As soon as they were comfortable to their new rides, Tim pulls out his compass, and the team rides off on their eastward journey.

The O'Connell's land stretches out for almost twenty miles, so they're able to ride in safety for a while before heading down the trail to the landfill. Once in the open, they start to gallop, and Tim has an idea.

He kicks Man O War in the sides and yells to the others. "Let's see what these ponies can do!"

Tim's horse rears up and takes off like a rocket across the open field, and he looks back to see that the others were following closely. These horses were bred to run and trained to be faster than the others around them, so all five horses sprint flat-out as if their lives depended on it. It feels like riding a giant superbike with bad suspension down a bumpy road.

Garrett, who had some experience with these horses, strides up beside Tim and matches his speed. Tim looks over at him and gives his horse another kick, trying to outrun the pack. Garrett looks at him with an evil grin, then throws up a middle finger and kicks Gallant Fox in the side, pushing every bit of horsepower out that he can. Garrett takes off through the field, leaving everyone else in the dust and flying grass. The rest of the horses run like hell, without a moment of hesitation, across the O'Connell's property until they come to a gate leading out.

Once they regroup and let the horses rest for a minute, they go through and follow the narrow two-track along the neighboring farm's southern border. They keep a steady gallop down the trail to avoid kicking up too much dust as they ride along.

"Making good time now," JJ says. "We're almost halfway there."

"My ass is almost halfway from falling off," complains Randy as he bounces around in his saddle.

"Suck it up, buttercup," Garrett taunts as he passes.

They ride down the two-track for miles, passing fields full of tall, green corn stalks and pastures packed with multi-colored cows, until they come to a river and are forced to stop. The rapidly flowing river before them is about twenty feet across and looks deep.

JJ pulls out his map, then looks back at the team. "We need to cross the river here. The hill is straight ahead about another half mile, and then the landfill is on the other side."

The team failed to realize that these were spoiled racing horses, not workhorses that were used to wading across deep water. They're used to being brushed every night and bucket-fed in their fancy barn, so they start to stir a little when they get close to the riverbank.

JJ slowly approaches the water and looks back. "We better go one at a time in case someone falls off. I'll go first."

The rest of the team watches as the War Admiral pauses just before entering the river. JJ gives him a kick, and he splashes into the water and pushes across. About halfway across, the water rises enough to touch the horse's belly, and he jumps. JJ holds on, snapping the reins, and his horse lunges forward and crosses to the other bank safely.

He looks back across and yells. "It's passable, but deep in the center. Be careful and take it slow!"

Next up, Elliott starts his run and quickly enters the water as Red Rum passes through gracefully and reaches the other side without a problem.

Garrett looks at Tim and Randy as if he had done this a thousand times, and effortlessly strides towards the water. As Gallant Fox reaches the center of the river, he becomes nervous and jumps. The horse gives out a loud neigh and bucks hard, kicking its feet out and throwing Garrett to the front over its head. Garrett crashes hard into the water and disappears for a second. He resurfaces, standing hip-deep in the water, and stomps over to the sandy bank angrily.

"You chicken shit horse! Get out of the river!" He yells at the horse, still standing in the water.

His horse stands there, watching Garrett waving at him with soaking wet arms. Then, the horse gives what looks like a big horse laugh and slowly walks out of the water.

Randy almost falls off his saddle, laughing and yells over the river. "Ha! We can't go anywhere without you getting wet! Let me show you how it's done, Cowboy!"

Randy lines up I'll Have Another and prepares himself, yelling, "Hi-ho, Silver! Away!"

The horse runs full speed into the river, wildly bouncing and splashing water all over. Randy tries as hard as he can to stay straight in the saddle, but the water makes it slick. He begins to slide to one side and falls face-first into the river, while his horse continues to the other side safely.

Randy struggles to hold his balance against the current and slowly walks to the other side. "Nailed it!"

Garrett walks up to help Randy out of the water with his hand out, but when Randy reaches for it, he quickly pulls his hand back and shoves Randy in the chest, sending him falling back into the river with a splash.

"Who's the wet one now?" Garrett says, laughing and pointing.

Randy stands up in the river and shakes the water out of his hair. "I needed a bath anyway," he says, walking out of the river and stands next to his horse, patting him on the neck. "Why you gotta do me like that, Horsey? You're making me look bad in front of my friends."

All alone on the other side of the river, Tim watches as Randy gets out of the water for the second time. He gently pats Man O War on the neck. "Okay boy, let's do this nice and slow."

They enter the water cautiously and make their way across. Like the others before, the water gets deep at the center, and the horse bucks once, but he holds on. Tim kicks the horse in the side, and it jumps forward like a rocket and bounces out the other side of the river with ease.

As he passes, Tim smiles at Randy and Garrett, standing in the sand, dripping everywhere. "Alright, soggy bottom boys. Mount up, and let's get this done."

Randy and Garrett jump back up on their horses, and the recon team continues down the trail. Up ahead, the hillside looms in the night sky as they get closer. It stretches out to the sides as far as they can see in the dark. The hill acts like a giant bowl containing the landfill, and it slows the high winds coming off of the open farmland. They follow the trail until it reaches the base of the hill, revealing a narrow path leading up the hillside.

JJ stops and looks up the path. "This doesn't look stable enough for the horses to climb. We're going to have to walk from here. Tie the horses up over at those trees to the right."

They tie up the horses and begin the hike up the hillside. When they reach the top of the hill, they find a plateau about twenty feet wide, and then it drops off sharply. Ahead, a bright light illuminates the center of the bowl, down past their point of view.

Tim ducks down and motions to the others. "Get low and keep quiet. We don't want them seeing us."

They creep across the plateau toward the bright light until they reach the edge of the cliff. As they lay down on their bellies, they slide forward until their heads can barely peek over the edge. Tim's heartbeat begins to race, and his eyes widen. He turns to JJ and sees that he has the same expression on his face.

They look at each other and speak at the same time, "Holy shit!"

CHAPTER 8

THE GREAT ESCAPE

"Hey Jason, wanna play a game?" Tim asks, sounding mischievous.

"I'm thirteen now, Tim. I don't play games anymore," Jason replies, sounding annoyed.

"Just follow me outside," Tim insists, pulling Jason's sleeve. "I want to show you a game that even a *thirteen-year-old* will have fun playing."

Tim pulls his younger cousin out of the house and over to the pasture behind the barn.

"It's dark out here, Tim. What are we doing?"

"Shh, quiet, you don't want to wake them."

"Wake who? There's no one out here."

"Look, over in the field," Tim says, pointing through the fence.

"What? The cows?"

"Ssshhh. Yeah, follow me and be quiet."

The boys climb over the fence and creep out into the field, stopping about twenty feet away from one of the cows and take a knee.

Tim looks over at Jason and puts a hand on his shoulder. "Ok, here's the game. When I say go, we'll run over to that cow and push it as hard as we can," Tim explains, holding back a giggle. "If we can get it leaning before it wakes up, it'll tip over and fall to the ground."

Jason looks at Tim, confused, with an eyebrow raised. "Why would I want to do that?"

"Because it'll be funny watching it fall over!" Tim replies, holding his hands over his mouth as he snickers.

"I don't want to," Jason protests.

"Come on. You're already out here."

"What if it wakes up?"

"Then you run like hell, but don't worry, these cows can sleep through a tornado. Trust me. It'll be fun."

Jason looks over at the sleeping cow, standing peacefully in the field. "Okay, I guess it would be funny to watch it fall over."

"That's the spirit. Ready? Three... Two... One... GO!"

The two boys run at full speed, side by side, and smash into the side of the thousand-pound cow. Quickly realizing that they had underestimated the beast's sheer size, they both bounce off of it and fall flat on their backs with a thud.

Jason sits up, holding his chest. "That didn't work at all."

"Ugh, I think I landed in a big pile of cow turds," Tim says, as he rolls to the side, immediately regretting his decision.

The cow that the boys just bounced off makes a low groaning noise and lets out a huge fart. The boys look at each other and laugh, until the cow turns to them lying on the ground. Being abruptly woken from its sleep, the now angry cow lowers its head and charges towards the boys.

With a fearful gasp, they look at each other and let out high-pitched screams while scrambling to their feet. The cow misses both of them as they split and run in opposite directions. Tim makes a turn and runs for the fence as Jason follows behind. Being the older one, Tim makes it to the fence faster and quickly hurdles over it. As he lands, he turns and watches as Jason runs, screaming with his hands out in front of him. With an angry cow hot on his heels, Jason grabs the fence, attempting to climb. Unfortunately, he's not fast enough. The cow headbutts his backside, sending him flying head over heels, clearing the fence, and landing hard on his back in the yard.

Tim runs over to him as fast as he can and slides on his knees next to him. As Jason lies on the ground, he breathes frantically with tears forming in his eyes.

Tim stares down at him with a satisfied grin. "And that game's called Cow Tipping."

***

"It smells like a week-old cheese sandwich in here," Randy says, making a face.

"I know, this place is rotten and infested with cockroaches," JJ replies, holding his nose and staring down at the landfill.

From where they were lying, the landfill looked like it was crawling with millions of bugs, moving around in every direction. Surrounding the landfill is a dirt road with a tall chain-link fence running beside it. Bright lights illuminate the road every ten feet, leading to a massive main gate to the north. Past the fence is a wide-open area that looks like it used to be green grass, but now is nothing but shredded mud due to the mass amount of tanks, armored personnel carriers, and cargo trucks carrying shipping containers.

Directly in the center of the compound sits a mountain of trash, waiting to be processed. Surrounding the mountain are rows of Howitzer artillery guns and Paladin mobile artillery tanks facing outward in all directions. Hundreds of Humvees are being lined up near the main office to the north, while several fuel trucks and recovery vehicles are spread throughout the area, fueling and repairing vehicles. Along the outer rim of the landfill, sit four anti-air guns aimed at the sky. Just outside the fence, multiple mortar pits are dug in deep and circled in sandbags, with soldiers readying the rounds.

"There have to be a thousand men down there. Where did they get all of these guys?" Garrett asks.

JJ pulls out his binoculars and looks down at the complex. "Before this all started, the R.R. bribed and turned some top officials on Ft. Hood, Ft. Bliss, and the Texas National Guard. When the R.R. made their initial attack on the capital, those leaders commanded their men to either be absorbed by the R.R., or face punishment. The soldiers who didn't follow orders were detained, and the R.R. topped off the ranks with any southern hillbilly who wanted to join, creating a massive fighting force. It looks like they're staging here and waiting to spring the trap. They're hoping that we'll try to surround them, thinking that they're defenseless. With those long guns, they can take out anything within about twenty miles of here. Without satellite coverage, we would drive right up on them and get destroyed. There's no way the National Guard can stand up to that kind of firepower. Elliott, start taking photos of everything. We need to get out of here before we're seen."

"On it, Sir," Elliott replies.

Inside the main office building, Colonel Wallace stands in front of General Grant as he gets chewed out.

"What the hell happened to your town, Wallace? Can I not send you to take care of a small Podunk town in the middle of nowhere and wait for reinforcements?"

Wallace opens his mouth to respond, but is cut short.

"You had one job!" Grant yells, putting his finger in the air. "Secure the only suitable town within artillery range of the Texas border! But nooo! You have to let one man, ONE MAN! destroy the entire town and force us to move here to this stink hole fifty miles outside of optimum range. What am I to do with you, Wallace? What can I do with you and your broken arm? You're almost useless to me now. At least you can still make a CUP OF COFFEE WITH ONE ARM!"

"Sir, I can still lead your troops. I can still lead you to victory."

"Get out of my office, Wallace! Get your troops in order, or I'll be convinced that your voice doesn't work either. And if your voice doesn't work, you'll be demoted to a speed bump at the front gate! Do I make myself clear?!"

"Sir, yes Sir. Moving, Sir." Wallace grovels as he leaves the office.

He stomps down the empty hallway leading out of the offices and through the reception door. Seeing red with anger, he looks for someone to yell at. Off to the right, a group of his gray-haired lieutenants sit at a picnic table, casually chatting with each other.

Wallace stomps up with his arm in a white sling, trying to look tough. "Get off your asses and do something! This is why we keep getting outsmarted by retired fuckers while we sleep!" Wallace frantically screams and points off into the distance. "Go secure the perimeter! Go rotate the guards! Go do something productive!"

Wallace stands, breathing heavily, as his lieutenants run off in all directions. He hears the front door of the building slam and turns around to see the General walking toward him.

Grant reaches out with his hand and puts Wallace in a chokehold. "This is why I have to do everything myself. You told me that this retired guy attacked your town. Send your men to find him."

"He fled the state, Sir," Wallace chokes out a reply.

"Did one of your checkpoints stop him?"

"Chhhkkk. No."

"Then he's still here somewhere!" Grant yells while pointing to the front gate. "Send a team to tear apart his home and find out where he's hiding."

Grant shoves Wallace away, shaking his head disappointingly as he turns around and returns to the building.

From their secret observation post on the hill, Tim pulls out his binoculars and scans the landfill below. A couple of grey-haired men casually sit at a picnic table next to the main building, as others carry around boxes. The men suddenly stand up as a familiar man walks towards them shouting. Colonel Wallace seems flustered as he barks commands at the elderly men with his right arm in a sling.

Wallace points his left hand towards the front gate, and the men hurry off in all directions. He stands, watching and breathing heavily, as another man walks up behind him. He's tall with a long white beard, wearing all black under a trench coat hanging down to his ankles. Wallace straightens up and attempts to salute with his injured arm, but fails. The man grabs Wallace by the throat and pulls him close to his face.

"There's someone new here giving commands now," Tim points out. "That must be the General Grant that Wallace was talking about before."

"Where is he?" Asks JJ.

"He's standing to the right of the main building, wearing the Matrix outfit, and bullying Wallace around."

"You got him on film, Elliott?"

"I got him, Sir," he replies snickering.

The team watches through their binoculars as Grant points to the front gate and shoves Wallace back. With a shameful look, he shakes his head and returns to the main building.

"I almost feel bad for the guy," Tim says, watching the humiliation unfold.

"You let that guy boss you around, Garrett?" Randy asks.

"He's much bigger up close. I swear," Garrett replies feeling ashamed.

Just then, a noise provokes Tim to lower his binoculars and look around. He spots a pair of flashlights waving in the dark to their right on the hill.

He quickly turns and taps JJ on the arm. "Quiet. Someone's coming."

Two roaming guards patrolling the plateau talk to each other as they walk along. "How much longer do we have to hide out in this shithole? Walking the outer rim is the only place where the smell doesn't hurt my nose."

"I don't know, Man. I haven't been able to breathe through my nose for a day now."

They slowly walk toward the recon team until one of the soldiers spots something strange. He raises his flashlight and aims it right at the five men lying on the ground.

"Hey! Who are you guys?!" He shouts as he reaches for his rifle.

The other soldier pulls a whistle from his pocket, takes a deep breath, and gets ready to blow. JJ immediately rolls to his side, pulling out his pistol with a suppressor attached. He shoots the guard with the whistle just before he makes a sound, dropping him straight onto his back. His buddy watches in disbelief and raises his rifle toward the recon team. Before he can aim, JJ turns and puts two silent rounds into his chest. The soldier falls back, squeezing his trigger and letting out a long burst of automatic gunfire into the air. A couple of seconds later, loud air-raid sirens start to howl, and the entire landfill erupts like an anthill someone just stepped on.

Spotlights spark to life and begin sweeping the hill around the men as they lie completely still on the dirt. They're forced to shield their eyes as one of the spotlights falls on them, giving away their position. Flashes of gunfire sparkle from behind the spotlight, and the earth starts to jump as the bullets impact around them.

"Time to go!" JJ says, sliding back and ducking behind a pile of dirt.

All of the men push back from the edge and scramble to their feet as more rounds impact around them. As he hears a familiar thump from inside the bowl, Tim freezes in his tracks. Seconds later, his suspicions are confirmed as he hears a whistling sound from the night sky above their heads.

"Incoming! Take cover!" He yells, as a mortar round impacts the ground where they were just lying, throwing dirt high into the air.

Everyone hits the ground and instinctively covers their heads.

Seconds after, another mortar round explodes twenty feet to their left.

Tim jumps to his feet and starts to run. "Move! Move! Move!"

JJ pushes himself off the ground and sees Garrett lying face down with his hands still over his head. He grabs the back of his shirt and yanks him to his feet, shoving him towards the gap in the hill. Randy bear-crawls forward and scrambles to his feet, following JJ and Garrett closely.

While Tim runs through the dirt, he looks back to see Elliott running with the camera in his hands. Suddenly, a mortar round explodes at his feet, sending him flying through the air and landing just before him. Tim looks at the mangled body in horror as Elliott's left leg is missing, and the left side of his face is charred black. With his last bit of strength, Elliott reaches out with his hand holding the camera.

"Take… It…" he gargles out with his last breath.

Tim reaches out and grabs the camera from his limp hand. He doesn't have time to say or do anything as another mortar round explodes, throwing dirt all over him. Tim turns and runs for the trail, tucking the camera into his bag as he goes.

Two more mortar rounds impact on either side of the team as they stumble down the narrow trail. Tim turns as he hears someone yelling from the top of the hill, so he takes a knee, raises his rifle, and fires through the gap just as a soldier attempts to follow them. The bullets strike one soldier, sending him falling back as he lets out a painful cry. Tim quickly turns and continues running down the hill.

Another soldier follows closely behind and aims through the bushes and trees. He opens fire blindly at the team's back, sending bullets whizzing past them. Speeding pieces of metal pop and hiss as they tearing through the leaves around him, so Tim ducks behind a bush and turns back, aiming his rifle up the hill. The sound of heavy boots thumping against the ground gets closer, and before the soldier has time to react, Tim pops out from behind his hiding spot and puts two rounds into his chest. The soldier's momentum sends him tumbling down the hill, past him, and smashing into a tree. Tim quickly stands up and runs to the bottom of the hill.

The mortar teams persistently send round after round blindly over the hill in hopes of getting lucky. At the bottom of the hill, JJ waves to the others to hurry up and get to the horses. Out of nowhere, a mortar round explodes beside him, sending him falling backward, and the horses running off in all directions.

Tim runs up to him and reaches out his hand. "You good?"

"Yeah, I'm okay. I just twisted my ankle," JJ says, wincing from the pain as Tim helps him off the ground. As soon as JJ stands up, he points back at the hill. "Shit! The horses are gone, and we've got more trouble coming our way."

Tim turns to see two sets of headlights bouncing down a trail at the base of the hill to the north.

"Everybody, get to the river. It might slow them down enough for us to get away," yells JJ.

As Tim helps JJ get his footing, Randy and Garrett sprint past them for the river. Just as they reach the watery bank, two Humvees bounce toward the men along the hill.

"Where's Elliott?" JJ asks.

"He didn't make it. I have his camera," Tim replies.

Randy starts wading through the river. "There's no way we can outrun those trucks."

"Wait! I'll stay," Garrett says, looking back at the trucks and then at Tim.

"What?" Tim replies confused.

"I'll stay and distract them! It'll give you guys time to get away!"

"They'll kill you if they catch you!"

"I know. I have to do this. I feel horrible for trusting Wallace and letting them take over my town. I need to make things right. I want to help you guys survive this so you can take the R.R. out," Garrett replies as he turns back toward the approaching trucks.

"Garrett. I want you to know how much this means to all of us,"

Tim says, shaking his hand. "You'll always be remembered as a hero and a friend to me. Good luck, Sheriff."

Garrett turns and runs down the riverbank to the south, and yells, "Thank you. Now go!"

What remains of the team crosses the river and runs down the two-track until they hear Garrett shooting at the trucks. The headlights turn downriver and chase after him, firing as they follow. The shooting continues for a few more seconds, and suddenly, everything goes quiet. Tim looks at JJ as they both know what that meant.

"See ya in the next life, Bro," Randy says sadly.

"Later buddy," Tim replies.

With a heavy heart, JJ starts moving again down the trail. "Come on. We need to keep moving. His sacrifice will mean nothing if we're caught too."

The recon team is in the clear long enough to see a small farmhouse in the distance, with a truck parked out front. Tim runs up to the little two-door pickup and opens the door, hoping to find the keys inside. Suddenly, the driveway lights up as a woman comes out of the front door holding a shotgun in one hand and a beer in the other.

"What do you think you're doing with my truck?" She yells.

"It's okay, Ma'am," Tim says, putting his hands up as he approaches the woman. "We're with the National Guard. We need to borrow your truck. There are a lot of angry militiamen after us right now. What's your name?"

She looks at them suspiciously. "The name's Melinda. You're not with those guys in the landfill, are ya? They've been shaking the pictures off my walls with their damn cannons all day. Tell me you'll put a stop to that god-awful noise, and you can have anything you want."

"Thank you, Melinda. I promise you that we'll take care of the noise."

"Here, then," she says, throwing Randy a set of keys. "Bring it back when you're done with it."

Randy looks at her with an evil grin. *"Don't worry. We will,"* he says, knowing damn well the truck's not going to survive this. "Jump in, boys! I'm drivin!"

As Randy excitedly hops into the driver's seat, Tim turns to JJ with a look of fear on his face. JJ stares back at him, slightly confused, then runs for the passenger door as Tim jumps into the bed.

Randy starts the truck, slams it into drive, and smashes down the gas pedal. "Hold onto your titties! This might get bumpy!"

The little truck's tires spin on the gravel driveway, throwing rocks and dirt at Melinda's front door. Randy turns the wheel sharply, and they slide out onto the trail and speed down the trail. Just as they make the turn, Tim looks back to see the two Humvees splashing effortlessly through the river and accelerating toward them.

"They're coming this way! Floor it, Randy!" He yells, from the truck bed.

"I'm giving her all she's got, Captain!" he replies, smashing his foot to the floor.

The Humvees gain their lost ground quickly and are soon in range for their gunners to open fire. Bullets ping off the back of the truck and blow out the rear window, scaring Randy into veering right through a wooden fence and into a cow pasture. The Humvees follow and blast through the fence behind them, while their gunners continue to fire. Tim sits up and tries to fire back, but Randy is having too much fun bouncing around the field in the little pickup.

"Hold on!" yells Randy, as the truck rams through another fence and goes airborne over a small road separating two fields.

The truck smashes through the adjacent fence in mid-air, then lands hard in the next field. Tim looks up as they level out and fires as fast as he can at one of the trucks, putting three bullets into the driver's windshield. The driver turns sharply and hits the gap at an angle, causing it to fly through the air sideways and land hard on the front right tire. As it strikes the ground, the truck flips over on its side and comes to a stop. The other truck hits the gap straight on and soars over with ease, bouncing the gunner around a little as he continues to fire his gun.

Tim looks around and sees a large herd of cattle mindlessly grazing in the middle of the field, totally unaware of what's happening in their pasture.

He leans up to the broken back window and yells to Randy. "Drive through the cows! I got an idea!"

Randy turns hard to the right and drives right into the herd of cows, causing them to stampede. The entire herd is now running along all sides of the truck as their pursuers follow closely behind.

"We're part of the herd now, MOOOOO!" Randy yells as they drive inside the stampeding cattle.

Behind them, Tim can only see the top of the gunner and his machine gun poking out above the herd as they follow.

Knowing what he has to do, Tim slides to the back of the truck bed and aims his rifle. "I'm sorry, cow," he says as he shoots one of them in the head directly behind the truck.

The cow drops dead in its tracks, and the Humvee following closely behind doesn't see it until it's too late. The truck rams into the thousand pounds of dead meat at full speed, rocketing it straight up in the air. It rolls to the right and violently flips when it impacts the ground, throwing the gunner from his turret through the air.

Randy looks out his window just as the soldier's body goes cartwheeling past him and crashes to the ground. "What just happened?!"

"Roadkill!" Tim replies, laughing. "We're clear to get back on the trail, Randy."

He takes a left, smashing back through the fence and onto the main trail. They drive down the narrow two-track for a few more minutes until headlights from two more trucks appear down a road separating the farms.

JJ points out of his window and yells, "More of them are coming to the right!"

"I got this!" Randy says, as he plows through another fence into a field of tall, green corn stalks.

The two Humvees follow them through the fence and into the dense cornfield. Their gunners open fire blindly through the stalks, hoping to get a lucky shot off. Tim ducks as he hears the bullets cutting through the leaves all around the truck, while Randy weaves back and forth in a wide pattern, forcing the Humvees to blindly follow his trail through the field.

"Hold on, Tim. I call this maneuver the crop circle," Randy yells back.

He continues his wide, swerving back-and-forth motion as the trucks follow his pattern. Thinking the trucks should follow this pattern back and forth, Randy suddenly makes a hard right turn and ends up doing a complete circle, and driving behind his now totally lost pursuers. He follows the smashed trails of corn and speeds up until they're just about between the other trucks. When they're close enough, JJ aims his rifle out the window to the right, and Tim catches onto his plan, aiming his rifle at the truck on the left.

"Now!" JJ yells and shoots the front tire of the truck to the right.

Tim opens fire at the truck to the left and blows out the front tire as well. The heavy tactical trucks pull hard, toward their flat tires forcing them to veer straight at each other. Randy quickly slams on the brakes and watches as the two Humvees collide and roll over, causing one of their fuel tanks to ignite. Everything goes quiet as the upside-down trucks burn, with their tires still spinning.

Satisfied with the maneuver, Tim jumps up on the truck's cab to get a view over the tall corn and finds their way back to the trail. They reach the gate to the O'Connell's farm without any more obstacles and make a straight shot through the open field, bouncing over the hills as they go. As the farm finally comes into view, Randy drives straight for the barn. He pulls up, skidding to a stop, and gets out jumping like he just won the Super Bowl.

"Did you see that!" Randy yells. "Dude, Melinda is gonna be so pissed when she sees her truck."

Tim looks down at their unlucky escape vehicle that's now full of bullet holes, corn cobs, and pieces of wood. "Yup, I'd be pissed too."

JJ jumps out and immediately yells for Lizardo to prepare the helicopter for takeoff. The pilot runs past the helicopter to open the large barn doors, but stops as he sees what was coming down the driveway.

"Sir, we have incoming enemy vehicles!" he yells.

JJ grabs his rifle from the truck and runs toward the barn door. "Everybody outside now! Take up defensive positions! Lizardo, stay here and guard the helo. Close these doors behind us, and don't let anyone in."

Just as three Humvees come speeding down the blacktop driveway and screech to a stop in front of the marble fountain, the team dashes through the barn doors and sprints across the road towards the back of the house. Men pour out of the trucks and begin firing at the team as they cross the road. Bullets impact the ground all around the team as they return fire and sprint for cover behind the house. A lucky round catches one of the gunners in the shoulder, sending him rolling off the top of the Humvee. The rest of the bullets fly past and smash against the fountain, sending white marble and water splashing through the air.

Looking for a safe place to hide, two of the soldiers run for the front of the house. Just as they think they're safe, Sammy kicks open the front door and blasts them with both barrels from his shotgun. The men are launched back to the ground, but the blast attracts the attention of one of the gunners. He turns his turret towards the front door and opens fire, just as Sammy ducks back inside. The front door splinters, and the windows shatter as bullets slice through the front of the house.

Tim, JJ, and Randy finally reach the backside of the house and take cover.

"There's too many of them! We need more firepower!" yells JJ, out of breath.

As he hears an engine rev, Randy peeks around the corner of the house. "They're driving around! We need to move!"

"Fall back to the tractor shed!" Tim yells as he runs.

They sprint across the backyard towards the big red shed that houses the combine tractors. About halfway there, Tim stops and fires back at the trucks as they round the end of the house, forcing them to stop for a second. As the team reaches the barn, the soldiers on foot run around the corner behind the trucks and return fire. Out of breath, Randy ducks behind a wall and shoots at one of the gunners, hitting him in the arm. The soldier spins his gun to the left, sending bullets flying into the front tire of another truck. The tire blows out, causing the truck to veer into a tree. The two remaining trucks push forward, with the soldiers running behind.

"Move for the grain silos!" Tim yells.

"We're running out of cover fast!" replies JJ.

They sprint across the road to the three grain silos at the edge of the cornfield. The silos are the last place to hide before the team is out in the open, and the soldiers see this. Randy runs as fast as his exhausted body can move, but it's not fast enough. A bullet strikes him in the arm, sending him spinning to the ground in a cloud of dust. Tim runs over, lifting him to his feet, and they run toward the silos. JJ continues to fire back as the armored trucks move forward, but against their armor, it's futile. Exhausted and out of options, they find a place to hide on the side of one of the silos in a small shed.

Tim sets Randy down and looks at his arm. "You alright?"

"Yeah, it just hurts like hell. If we live through this, it'll be proof to back up my Recon Team Delta story," he replies with a smile.

"What now?" asks JJ.

"I don't know. I'm getting low on ammo," Tim replies, looking around the corner at six men and two trucks with guns aimed in their direction. "Only one thing left to do. Go out guns blazing and hope for the best."

JJ looks at Tim with a smile. "I always knew I'd end up dying next to you in a blaze of glory someday."

Randy leans up and checks his rifle. "I've already died once this week. Why not go for a second time?"

Tim looks at the other two and nods his head. "Okay. Ready? Three... Two..."

The countdown is halted as the sound of a large engine starting up behind the soldiers. He peeks around the corner to see a massive combine tractor ripping out from the shed. The soldiers dive out of the way as it smashes into the side of one of the Humvees. Black smoke pores from its exhaust pipes as it pushes the first truck into the other and keeps going towards the grain silos. Just before it makes impact, Sammy jumps from the tractor and rolls to the ground. The industrial-strength tractor smashes the trucks deep into the side of the two-hundred-foot-tall silo, causing it to buckle at the bottom. The silo lets out a loud creak and topples over, smashing down on top of the trucks, spilling its tons of corn in all directions. The tidal wave of corn sweeps the remaining men off their feet and buries them.

Impressed by the quick thinking, the team runs out from cover to see Sammy pushing himself off the ground.

"Alright, Sammy!" Randy yells as he grabs his injured arm.

Tim points to the backside of the property. "Now's our chance to make a run for the bunker. Move!"

JJ grabs up Sammy, and they all run for the bunker entrance as fast as they can.

As they make it to the door, Sammy looks up at JJ with wide eyes. "Where's Garrett? Where's my son?"

"I'm sorry, Sammy," JJ replies, reaching out and placing a hand on his shoulder. "He didn't make it."

Sammy stares at JJ for a second as his eyes glaze over, then he looks away, reaching for the keypad to open the door. He attempts to punch in the code, but the panel lets out a buzzing noise as he enters the wrong number.

Tim calmly reaches for Sammy's arm. "Do you need me to do that?"

"Yeah. Y-you better do it," Sammy replies sadly and turns away.

Tim punches the numbers into the keypad, and the door hisses open. They quickly walk through and seal it tightly behind them.

As Randy watches the door close, he taps it with his hand. "Will this door hold them out?"

"Not for long. Get ready for a fight," Tim answers moving quickly down the hallway.

Everyone rushes down the tunnel to the main room, and Tim motions to JJ to help him flip over the big dining table for cover. They line up behind the thick wooden table and go over their rifles, counting their ammo. Marco comes out of the bedroom with his shotgun, followed by Ackley from the radio room with his rifle. They kneel beside the men behind the table, looking nervous.

Marco looks over the table and cocks his shotgun. "The girls are locked in one of the rooms. What the hell's going on out there?"

Tim loads a fresh magazine into his rifle and turns to face the tunnel. "The R.R. followed us here from the landfill, and now they're trying to kill us for the photos we took." He grabs the camera out of his backpack, shows it to Marco, and then tucks it back inside.

Everyone gets quiet as they feel the ground rumbling, like something big was driving near the bunker. From down the tunnel, they hear a loud bang on the bunker door. A couple of seconds pass, and another massive crash erupts from the end of the tunnel, knocking out all of the lights halfway down. A wave of dust pours out towards them as the giant vault door rolls down the stairs. The light above the tunnel flashes, illuminating the dust in the air with an eerie red glow. The distinctive beeping of a tractor backing up echoes down the hall confirming that the soldiers used one of the tractors to smash in the door.

"Get ready!" Tim says raising his rifle over the table and aims down the tunnel. "They're coming through!"

The rest of the men follow suit as they aim blindly through the dust in the darkness. From deep in the tunnel, gunshots ring out, but they don't see any muzzle flashes, and none of the bullets were impacting around them. For a few seconds, multiple gunshots continue to echo through the bunker. Then everything goes quiet. A few more nervous moments pass, and the sound of a single pair of footsteps tapping on the concrete floor approach them from the dark hallway. As Randy aims his rifle toward the entrance, the shadow of a single man starts to form in the darkness. The thick dust in the air fogs his vision, but he takes a shot anyway.

The shadow ducks to the side and yells out, "Randy, goddamn it, stop shooting at me!"

Suddenly, the silhouette steps forward out of the hallway, and Garrett emerges from the shadows, walking tall with his rifle on his shoulder and a proud look on his face.

Randy stands up confused, and yells back at Garrett. "Why do you think it was me shooting at you?"

"Because you missed!" Garrett says, looking at him with a smug grin.

Tim stands up in surprise. "We thought you were dead."

"Me too, when I saw those Humvees coming for me."

Sammy stands up and walks around the table with tears in his eyes. "I thought I lost you, Son."

"I'm here now, Dad," Garrett says, dropping his rifle on the floor and hugging his father.

"How are you alive?" Randy asks, still confused.

Garrett lets go of his father and wipes a tear from his eye. "I ran into one of the horses down the river. When the trucks showed up, I shot at them, and they chased me. When they got close, I jumped on Man O War, and we outran the trucks down the riverbank. Once I was clear, we ran like hell to get back here. Don't get too cozy yet. I saw a bunch of trucks heading down the road. We need to get out of here fast."

JJ points at Tim's bag. "We need to get that camera to the chopper now!"

Tim hands the bag to JJ and looks at the others. "Randy and Garrett, you guys take my family down the tunnel to town. Dad's truck should still be hidden next to the cemetery. Take them back to my farm and hide in the shelter. JJ, we can take a different tunnel to the barn where the chopper is and get out of here."

JJ goes over to Sammy and shakes his hand. "Sammy, thank you so much for your help. You should get your family to a safe location. The R.R. will come back, and they won't be happy."

Sammy huffs and shakes JJ's hand. "My family has never run from a fight. We'll stay here and do what we can to help."

"Good luck then. I'll come back through and check on you when this is all over. Your bunker is still salvageable and can be useful to the National Guard." JJ replies, turning around. "Ackley, wipe the radio encryption and meet us at the tunnel entrance. Randy and Garrett, thank you for everything you've done for us. Take care of yourself and Tim's family. We need to get out of here before more men show up."

Tim kisses Mary goodbye and waves to Marco before leaving with JJ for the tunnel. They meet Ackley at the radio room and run down the tunnel to the barn entrance. As they reach the end, Tim finds the keypad and enters the code to open the door. They climb out of a secret hatch in a backroom and run for the helicopter, where Lizardo is waiting with his rifle.

"Chief, get this chopper airborne now!" JJ commands urgently.

Ackley pushes the large barn doors open and drives the tractor, pulling the chopper out of the barn. Everyone else jumps in as Lizardo quickly hits a few buttons, and the engine begins to hum, and the rotors start to spin. Within seconds, they lift off in a cloud of dust and smoke. As they clear the house, Tim looks out of the side door to see five more Humvees coming down the long driveway towards the farm.

He grabs JJ's arm and points. "We have to do something to buy my family some time to escape!"

JJ looks at Tim with a smile and pulls a tarp off of the door gun. He reveals a full-size minigun with six barrels and a chain of ammo leading into the floor board.

He swings the back end toward Tim. "See if you can buy some time with that!"

Tim grabs the handles with both hands and can't help but smile as if he was just given a new toy at Christmas. The chopper turns toward the driveway and lines up Tim's field of fire. He squeezes the trigger, and the barrels start to spin. Suddenly, a roar of bullets comes screaming out of the minigun, sending a yellow line of tracer rounds hitting the concrete in front of the first truck. He tilts slightly to the right and watches as the steady stream of bullets impact the first Humvee, turning it into fiery Swiss cheese.

The truck explodes as the following truck rams into it and becomes his next target. He holds down the trigger without a care in the world. These guys wanted to play with the big boys, so he needed to show them the consequences. The second truck erupts in a fireball as the bullets cut a line straight through it. Tim keeps up the dirty work as the bullets pound holes through the following two trucks with ease.

As the spinning barrels begin to glow bright red, the last truck turns sharply into the field, avoiding the steady stream of hellfire. He stops firing for a second and looks at JJ in the front of the chopper. JJ gives a spinning signal with his hand to the pilot, and Lizardo turns to the right and back around to follow the last truck. As they approach, the gunner on top of the truck frantically tries to shoot them out of the sky, but his efforts are short lived. Tim aligns his barrels and opens the can of whoop-ass one last time, decimating the truck in seconds with a thousand rounds.

When the deed is done, he lets go of the minigun and can still feel the vibrations in his fingers. He shakes his hands out and gives his best friend a thumbs up. JJ gives the pilot the go-ahead to return to base with a satisfied grin, and the helicopter turns north towards Oklahoma City.

Chapter 9

MAKING A MESS

"Lots of people on the streets. Keep your eyes open," Tim calls out over the radio.

He hooks the handset back onto the radio mount of the Humvee as they drive through the crowded Iraqi village. The bustling market is overflowing with people staring at the four-truck convoy as they drive through Eastern Baghdad.

"I have a car blocking the way ahead," JJ calls out from the lead vehicle.

"Make a hole. We can't stop here," Tim replies.

JJ makes a sharp left and bumps into a small car, forcing it to veer off to the side of the street.

"All clear," JJ says with a laugh.

It's as hot as it can be in July, and the team was enroute to the Green Zone in Northern Baghdad to meet with some VIPs from the State Department. Before they reach the city center, the convoy must cross the Tigris River. Anyone who ever had the displeasure of crossing this river would remember the foul odor. The river was the primary source of trash and waste disposal for most of the city. Whenever they had to cross the sewage-filled waterway, everyone in the trucks would quickly strap on their gas masks for training purposes. On this particular day, it was hotter than ever, and Tim could feel his nose starting to burn from the fumes wafting in the air from over a mile away.

He reaches for his mask and the radio mic inside the truck. "Phantom Two, this is Phantom One. I smell a disturbance in the Force. I think it's time to don our masks, so that we can pass over Shit Creek unharmed."

JJ replies, already wearing his mask and speaking with his best Bane impersonation. "I was born wearing this mask. You merely adopted it. I didn't smell fresh air until I was already a man. By then, it was nothing to me but suffocating."

"Hahaha," Tim replies over the radio. "How long did you practice that?"

"Three whole days after I found out about this mission."

"Epic."

Periodically along the river, ropes were stretched across to catch floating particles of trash and human waste, which were then left to bake in the blistering sun. The true purpose of these ropes remains a mystery to this day. As the smell reaches its strongest, the convoy approaches one of the only bridges crossing the river that was still intact after the initial invasion.

Intact was a generous depiction of the rough condition of this bridge. Pieces of concrete were broken off from the sides and underbelly. A tall chain link fence lines the edges with large chunks of dirty fabric and trash hanging loosely throughout. The sound of crunching rubble and random pops echo from under the heavy trucks as they pass over.

Once the team crosses the bridge, they needed to turn right and follow the river for another couple of miles before entering the Green

Zone. As the lead truck makes it over, it makes a sharp right turn around a blind corner and disappears. Tim's truck is third in the convoy, and as he reaches the top of the bridge, the entire convoy comes to an abrupt stop.

"Halt! Halt! Halt! This is Phantom Two. Some cars are blocking the road just after the bridge to the right. It looks like they broke down or something. Give me a minute to push them out of the way."

JJ motions for his driver to drive toward the stalled cars, and he hits the siren attached to the front bumper, emitting a frightening wail. His gunner stands up from behind his machine gun and waves his arms at the local men who were blocking the way.

Just in front of the Humvee, four bearded men look up at the noisy American truck from behind their cars, as if they were anticipating its arrival. One man wearing a long blue man dress waves his hands in the air and gestures towards the broken car, while the other three lean over and reach for something on the ground.

They reemerge with rifles in their hands and open fire at the Humvee. Caught by surprise, JJ's gunner ducks down into the turret as bullets ricochet off the metal shield. He loses his balance and falls behind one of the seats, getting wedged upside-down. The rest of the convoy sits on the bridge at an angle that prevents the gunners from defending the lone truck under attack.

Tim pulls off his mask and grabs the radio mic. "What's happening up there, JJ! Can anyone see anything?"

Bullets tear through the fiberglass hood and smash against the bulletproof windshield. JJ tears off his mask and watches as the armed men move in closer, continuing to fire everything they have.

JJ looks at his scared driver and makes a split-second decision. "Ram them! Drive now!"

The driver slams on the gas pedal, causing the Humvee to rev up as it speeds towards the disabled cars. The military truck effortlessly pushes one of the cars back into the other. The determined gunmen jump to the side, narrowly avoiding being crushed between the cars as they slam together. JJ's driver keeps his foot on the gas, pushing both cars closer to the sandy bank of the river. Now realizing that their cover had been compromised, the gunmen retreat towards the river and continue to recklessly fire at the armored truck.

Finally regaining his footing, JJ's gunner pulls himself back up into the turret. He jerks the charging handle back on his machine gun and unleashes a barrage of bullets at the gunmen who are now exposed without cover. Their cars slide down the bank and plunge into the green river. Now, with nothing to hide behind and outgunned, the men look back at the cesspool slowly flowing behind them, realizing it's their last chance for escape.

"No, no, no! Don't do it!" JJ yells through the remaining clear spots in his windshield, as the four men dive into the river and float away.

Tim watches as the foamy river splashes beneath the bridge while the men swim past. "Ohhh nooo! Did they just do what I think they did?"

"Yes, they did," JJ replies, gagging. "I hope they enjoy their dysentery."

"That's just nasty," Tim replies, holding his nose.

JJ gets out of his truck and walks to the edge of the river as the men float away down the murky, green river. He turns back to his gunner, shrugs his shoulders, and jumps back into his truck.

"Allll righty then. The road's clear now. Moving on. Phantom Two out."

* * *

"Wallace!! Report to my office, immediately!" Screams General Grant over the landfill's intercom system.

Colonel Wallace takes a deep breath and looks up at the morning sky while standing on the outer rim of the landfill. He had just finished searching the blown-up National Guard soldier who was been left behind by a recon team taking pictures of their new command center.

Another soldier runs up the path leading away from the landfill and stops in front of him, out of breath. "There's one more body about halfway down the hill, but it's one of ours, Sir."

"Damn it. How did they manage to get all the way in here without anyone seeing them? Why do we have patrols if all they do is get shot?"

"There are a few horses running around down by the river, Sir. Maybe they rode them here."

"Of course, they rode them here. That's how they snuck in so quietly. What I want to know is, where did they get their getaway vehicle, and how many men did we lose?"

"Sir, the teams are reporting nearly fifty men are either missing or dead, and twelve Humvees were destroyed."

"This is such a damn mess. Have you heard back from the team that went to Walker's farm yet?"

"No, not yet, Sir. They should be reporting back any time now."

"Good. They better have some good news for me. I need to go brief the General. Clean up this mess and report back to me the very second you hear from them."

The soldier salutes Wallace, but the Colonel just stares at him and turns towards the landfill.

Lost out on the back roads of Northern Texas, a team of men cluelessly searches for Tim's farm as the sun begins to rise.

"Where the hell are we? I thought you knew where this farm was."

"I thought so too, but all these damn roads look the same," the driver says, looking out the window at the endless rows of corn. "I'll turn right down this one. It looks kinda familiar."

"This looks exactly like the last road. What in the hell are you talking about? Is that a farm up there? That better be a farm up there, or you'll be on tower guard for the next week."

The soldiers in the R.R. truck drive down the dusty road towards

Tim's farm, just as Randy, Garrett, and Tim's family turn into the driveway.

Garrett pushes Marco's old truck to its limit as he turns into the driveway, sliding Randy and Marco to the side of the truck bed.

As a truck approaches, Nancy looks out of the window and points to the main road. "There's someone coming down the road. Maybe it's Tim."

"Tim's in Oklahoma City with JJ," Garrett replies. "That's most likely another R.R. truck looking for us. We need to get into the bunker now."

Garrett slams on the brakes, coming to a sliding stop next to the shed, and jumps out. He rushes over to the passenger door to help Mary and Nancy with the baby out of the cab. Marco helps Randy with his injured arm out of the truck's bed, and they all quickly move towards the entrance of the secret shelter.

Garrett pulls off the fake hay bale and opens the security door. "Quickly, get inside and stay quiet."

One by one, they climb down the ladder into the shelter. Garrett is the last to enter, and he pulls the hay bale over the top. However, as he rushes to enter, he fails to notice that the disguise wasn't fully lowered over the entrance.

"Yeah Sarge, this is it. That's the same farm as last time. We searched the whole place but didn't find anything, though. What are we looking for this time?"

"The Colonel said that they have to be hiding here somewhere, because none of our men stopped them on the roads leaving town."

The truck full of men turns into the driveway and comes to a stop behind the house.

As the driver gets out and looks around, he spots Marco's truck. "Sarge! That wasn't here last time."

"Spread out and find them. They have to be hiding here somewhere."

The men search the house again and look through the barn and shed. One man kicks in the door of the lake house and discovers the moonshine still, but is disappointed when he doesn't find any extra lying around. Next to Marco's truck, a man looks down at the ground and notices fresh tracks and a few drops of blood leading towards the shed. He follows the tracks across the grass and arrives at a hay bale resting on the ground. Something doesn't look right about this hay bale because it wasn't sitting flat on the ground. He pushes it with one hand and is surprised at how light it is.

The man flips it over and discovers the entrance to the bunker. "Guys! I found something!"

From inside the bunker, Marco stands at the base of the ladder, nervously looking up at the hatch. He hears the sound of a truck pulling up and men talking above. The sound of heavy footsteps pound the ground around the opening as they spread out across the farm. He looks back at the others in the shelter as they silently wait for the R.R. soldiers to leave.

Garrett quickly bandages Randy's arm and heads into the pantry to the left of the living room. He pulls two shotguns off the rack and runs back out to see Marco waving for him to stay quiet. He hands one to Randy, then looks at Mary. She immediately holds out her hand and gives Garrett a mean stare. Feeling slightly emasculated, he pauses for a second, then huffs and hands over the shotgun.

At the entrance, Marco looks up and hears the rustling of the hay bale. Then a man yelling to the others.

He turns back to the main room in a panic. "They found the entrance! Go get in the pantry room now!"

Marco runs back to the main room, grabs Nancy and Victoria, and guides them through the door to the pantry. As Garrett follows him inside, he grabs a rifle from the rack and kneels just inside the door. Randy and Mary stand in the main room, each holding a shotgun and staring at the entrance. No words needed to be said, because they knew exactly what must happen from here, and they were ready to fight.

Mary points at Marco with hatred in her eyes. "Close and lock the door! Those men are not getting to my baby!"

Marco nods his head and pulls the heavy steel door shut, locking it from the inside. A loud bang at the entrance startles Randy and Mary, causing them to quickly take cover behind the couch. Thinking he could catch them off guard, Randy sneaks forward and positions himself next to the ladder, aiming his shotgun towards the entrance above.

As he waits, he hears something metallic clanging against the hatch, followed by the sound of a truck revving up. Before he has time to think about it, a loud bang followed by bright light pours through the entrance as the hatch is ripped from its base. Randy falls back onto his ass as dust and debris cascades down the ladder. As a head appears over the edge, he shakes off the surprise and grabs his shotgun, aiming it up the hole.

He fires and strikes the man directly in the face, causing his lifeless body to tumble down the hole. Narrowly avoiding the falling body, he runs back just as the bloody, black uniform lands hard at the bottom of the ladder. Yelling echoes down the hole as more men prepare to enter. Randy and Mary move the couch back and turn it towards the entrance, then they wait.

A few seconds pass without a sound, then something drops down the hole, bouncing off the body at the bottom. As it rolls into the kitchen and comes to a stop, Randy realizes what it is and grabs Mary.

"Grenade!" He yells as they dive backwards into the bedroom.

The concussive force of the grenade cracks the walls and shatters the lights. With their ears ringing and vision blurred, they lay on the bedroom floor for a few seconds, attempting to recover. The sound of footsteps coming down the ladder brings Mary out of her daze, and she pushes herself up onto her hands and knees. She quickly grabs her shotgun from the floor and fires blindly through the door into the living room, grazing one man as he approaches the couch.

Her shotgun clicks as the shells are spent, and she looks at Randy, who's starting to come to. "Randy! Get up and shoot someone!"

As his vision slowly returns, he blinks a couple of times before jumping to his feet with his shotgun in hand. Without saying a word, he bursts through the door to the living room, blindly firing round after round at the men as they enter through the kitchen. Mary follows him through the door, grabs the TV from the stand, and smashes a man over the head with it.

Randy pulls the trigger of his shotgun until it clicks instead of bangs. He looks down at the shotgun with surprise as the man dressed in all black stands in front of him, grabbing his chest with a smile. The man quickly grabs his pistol, forcing Randy to dive back through the bedroom door grabbing Mary as he goes. They slam the damaged door shut and wait as more men come down the entrance.

Mary looks over at Randy with fear in her eyes. "What do we do now?"

"I don't know!" He replies, frantically looking around the room for something to fight with, but comes up empty-handed. "We can't let them find the others."

They both look at the door as it flies off its hinges and lands against the wall. Two men rush through the door and grab for Mary, but she struggles and throws the first one over the bed. As he bounces forward, Randy quickly punches the man in the face and stomps on his head.

Before Mary has time to recover, the other man grabs hold of her and throws her onto the hard concrete floor. Randy watches in horror as Mary falls to the ground. Immediately after, another man bursts into the room and punches him in the face. Stars spin around Randy's eyes as he and Mary are forcefully pinned to the ground and handcuffs are placed on their wrists.

As they lie on the cold floor, breathing heavily, their sergeant walks in and looks around. "Nice little bunker you have here. Very cozy."

"What do you want, asshole?" Randy says, as he tries to kick the man, but misses.

The Sergeant sits on the bed and bounces up and down. "Where is that retired Army fucker who burned down Chesterfield? My boss *really* wants to talk him."

Mary looks up at the hillbilly and spits in his face. "My husband will kill all of you."

"Oh, you're the guy's wife? Well, aren't you a nice little consolation prize? I'm sure he'll go to the ends of the earth to get you back. And who is this guy? Wait, I know you. You're the owner of the bar in town. Well, isn't this just the best little discovery? I'm just waiting to see what's behind Door Number Two."

The Sergeant gets up and walks out into the living room, looking at the closed door to the pantry.

He motions for another soldier to kick the door in, just as his radio crackles. "Rebel One! Come in!"

"This is Rebel One," he says, grabbing the radio from his waist. "I'm kinda busy right now. Call back later."

"Rebel One, return to base immediately. We have bombers incoming. The command center is under ssskkhhhh."

With a dumbfounded expression, the Sergeant points to Randy and Mary, yelling. "Grab those two, and let's get out of here! Now!"

High above the war torn landscape, the National Guard helicopter flies as fast as possible back to their FOB just north of Oklahoma City. As the sun rises in the east, it illuminates the smoke billowing from the city like a massive black cloud. Down on the streets, tan National Guard vehicles rush around the city, aiding the disaster relief crews. Now that the R.R. had fallen back, the fire trucks and other emergency response teams were allowed back into the city to extinguish some of the larger fires. Tim watches out the window at the recovering city, but he knows the dark truth about why the R.R. fell back. JJ jumps from the chopper as it lands behind the command center and runs towards the building.

He hands the dusty camera off to another soldier and barks out his orders. "You! Get the pictures off of this camera and send them to command immediately!"

Soldiers are rushing all around the command center, preparing for the upcoming movement. The ground vibrates as a train approaching on the recently cleared tracks. It's loaded down with military vehicles and tan cargo containers full of much-needed supplies for the National Guard.

JJ waves at Tim through the busy entrance. "Tim, follow me to the conference room."

They walk through into a room with a large TV that has a camera mounted on it. The TV flashes to life as an angry-looking, grey-haired man appears behind his desk. He's wearing a freshly pressed green camouflage uniform with a four-star rank on his chest.

"Report!" He barks.

JJ stands tall, facing the TV. "Sir, we located the R.R. stronghold and took photos of the troops and equipment they have assembled in preparation for an attack. This confirms the intel that was given to us earlier. You should be receiving the pictures now."

The General turns to his computer for a minute, then looks back at JJ with wide eyes. "Outstanding work, Colonel! You just saved the lives of countless men and women. I'll send out the order to delay the movement. What are you going to do about this new threat?"

"Sir, we don't know yet. We'll have a plan of action for you by the end of the day."

"How about you go and find the biggest bomb you have in your arsenal and drop it right in the center of that compound?" snaps the General.

Tim steps forward into the camera's view and looks at the General. "Sir, these men were once US soldiers, just like you and me. They don't deserve to die for simply following orders from their corrupt leadership."

The General stares down at his desk and sighs. "I'll give you six hours to figure out what you're going to do. After that, I'll give the command myself to drop a bomb and be rid of that rat's nest once and for all. Make it happen, Colonel."

The TV goes black, and JJ turns to Tim, looking concerned. "I'm not going to kill every man inside that landfill. They deserve better than that. There has to be something we can do to persuade them to leave willingly."

"I know we'll think of something," Tim replies, patting him on the back.

"Send for the Air Guard commander and have him meet us in the war room, ASAP," JJ says to one of the soldiers sitting at the radio. "Come on, Tim, we have some planning to do."

JJ leaves the conference room, and Tim follows him down the hall to a small, windowless room at the back of the warehouse. The war room has two tall, whiteboards positioned on the right side of the room, and a table to the left covered with computers, TV screens, and a large printer. In the center sits a table with a large map of Texas spread across it. Strategically placed across the map are small different colored metal blocks, indicating the locations of various units.

A soldier walks into the room after them, sits down at the table, and begins typing on the computer. Next to him, the large printer hums to life and spits out the photos they took of the landfill. JJ walks over, grabs the photos, and attaches them to the whiteboard using magnets. They stand in front of the photos for a minute in complete silence, staring at the pictures of the heavily guarded landfill, contemplating what actions to take.

JJ reaches up and compulsively aligns the photos perfectly. "How are we going to handle this without resorting to bombing them all to hell? Now's a good time for one of your crazy ideas, Tim."

"The landfill is a proper fortress. There's no way we can drive close enough without those guns tearing us apart. We can't fly in on helicopters without the air defense blowing us out of the sky. We need to find a way to get the men to come out willingly."

Just then, the door to the war room opens, and a man walks in and stops in front of the table. "Major Johnson, Air National Guard reporting, Sir."

"Welcome, Major," JJ says, turning and placing his hands on the table. "What resources do you have available for us?"

"Sir, currently on the station, we have eight Black Hawk helicopters equipped with Hellfire missiles and M134 miniguns. Arriving on the train right now are two unmanned Shadow Drones, along with their mobile launch platforms. They'll be fully operational within the hour. We also have a squadron of F-22 Raptors and two B-2 bombers ready and waiting for orders at McConnell Air Force Base."

"Have you had a look at the photos of the landfill?"

"Yes, Sir. The place looks heavily defended. We need to strike before they mobilize their heavy equipment. I can send the F-22s in and blast those air defense turrets, allowing for an air assault offensive."

"Do you think your jets can make it past their air defense successfully? If we lose even a single jet, the General will order a massive airstrike and kill them all. We need to get as many out alive as possible."

Tim rubs his chin and looks at the major. "What we need to do is find a way to trap them inside that bowl and cut off their supplies until they're forced to surrender. Do you have any missiles capable of penetrating the ground?"

"I believe we have a few bunker busters in stock," the major says, looking at Tim confused. "However, I didn't see any hardened structures that would require that sort of ordinance."

JJ stares at Tim and can see the wheels turning in his head. "What are you thinking about, Tim?"

"Remember how the men were complaining about the smell from that massive pile of trash in the center? How do you think they would feel if that mess was all over the entire landfill? We don't need to convince them to come out if they already want to leave," Tim says with an evil smile. "We just need to drop one JDAM in the middle of their access road, and that will trap their vehicles inside."

JJ nods his head. "Spreading that nasty shit all over would probably do the trick. You're a horrible person, and a genius. Major, get one of your B-2s ready with a JDAM and bunker-buster payload."

"Yes, Sir. Give me five minutes, and I'll have confirmation."

JJ looks at the picture of the mountain of garbage in the center of the landfill. "This is going to be the worst thing I have ever done to another human being in battle."

"Even worse than the Shit Creek incident in Baghdad in oh seven?"

"Oh yeah…," JJ replies, making a puking sound. "I take that back. This will be the second-worst thing. Don't remind me of that again."

"Not a problem," Tim replies, laughing.

JJ turns and points to his soldier sitting at the desk. "Get the General back on the line."

"Yes, Sir," he replies, and turns on a TV with an attached camera.

Tim sits back off the camera and watches as JJ prepares for his call. The screen lights up, and the same grumpy general appears.

He looks up from his computer and stares at JJ. "What do you have for me, Colonel?"

JJ talks the plan through with the General, and they debate the possible ramifications of the strike, until the General pauses and looks down at his desk.

"This is the craziest and most disgusting plan I have ever heard of, but I like it. Make it happen, Colonel," the General says enthusiastically. "I'm looking forward to your debrief."

The TV turns off, and JJ turns to Tim. "The mission is a go."

Just then, Major Johnson walks back into the war room and stands in front of the table. "The bomber is fueled, and the payload is ready. The drones will be in the air by the time it reaches us."

"Excellent. Get me a live feed from your drones. I want to watch this," JJ replies.

Tim walks over next to JJ with a grin on his face. "Me too."

The Major sits down at the table and types away on a laptop to access the live feeds. When he finishes, three computer screens flash to life, showing both drones and the bomber's targeting screens. They anxiously wait for about thirty minutes as the bomber flies within striking distance.

"Eagle One, this is Broadsword," the bomber calls over the radio. "We're approaching the target."

They stare at the screen displaying live footage from one of the drones as it circles the landfill from high above. Suddenly, the entire sky surrounding the compound erupts with anti-aircraft gunfire. Smoke trails puff from the turrets as they unleash everything they have at the drones and the bomber soaring overhead. The camera on one of the drones goes black after being struck by shrapnel from the explosions, but the camera on the bomber continues to slowly approach the airspace above the landfill. Little black spots fill the air as the shells explode in every direction.

The Major picks up the mic from the table. "Broadsword, you are clear to drop your ordinance."

"Ordinance away," he quickly replies.

They watch the screen as the targeting camera aboard the bomber follows a little white dot falling towards the road north of the landfill. It smashes into the ground with a spectacular flash, blowing a hole right in the middle of the entrance. The screen suddenly switches to the view from the camera inside the nose of the final missile as it darts left and right through the black starbursts in the sky. The oval perimeter surrounding the mountain of garbage takes shape through the clouds as it dives closer. Tim looks over at the next screen from the drone, which shows the mountain of garbage as the missile impacts it directly on top.

A small splash of trash goes flying upward as the missile drives its way to the heart of the mountain. A second passes, and the mountain appears to grow rapidly. Deep inside this fermenting pile of rubbish was a pocket of methane that had just been punctured by a three-thousand pound rod of explosives. The mountain cracks open like a volcano, spewing putrid trash hundreds of feet in every direction. The sides of the mountain crumble and begin to avalanche down, completely burying the artillery guns that were surrounding it. The landslide of waste topples over the big guns and buries everything within a hundred feet of it.

JJ looks up at Tim with wide eyes and half of a smile, realizing that something extraordinary had just happened. "Their long-range guns are out! Prepare the ground forces! We move out immediately!"

The soldier at the desk picks up the radio and calls out to every unit near the FOB to assemble and prepare for the assault. JJ grabs Tim's arm and pushes him out of the war room and down the hall. They stop by the armory to grab body armor and some rifles before rushing out the door and running to the line of armored vehicles that had already lined up outside. JJ takes off running for the command vehicle in the center of the line, while Tim jumps into a truck towards the front. The M.A.T.V. is like a newer version of the Humvee, but taller and stronger. Tim closes the heavily-armored door behind him and puts on his headset. As he buckles himself into his seat, chatter from the troops fill the speakers. Tim pauses and smiles as he hears a familiar voice using a call sign he hasn't heard in a long time.

"Phantom One, this is Iron Horse Six! Are you ready to roll out?"

Tim hits the switch for his mic and calls back. "This is Phantom One. I'm locked, cocked, and ready to rock."

CHAPTER 10

CROSSING THE LINE

"Wanna play Super Nintendo?" Jason asks, as he sits in his uncle's fluffy recliner.

Tim stares at him while lying upside-down on the sofa, with his feet against the wall and his hands dangling on the floor. "Nooo." He replies with a sigh.

"Come on, my mom just bought me Super Mario Kart," Jason pleads.

"I've heard enough whining from you kids about your fancy video games," grumbles Marco from the kitchen. "When I was your age, we went outside and built forts and chased rats with sticks. Listen here now, I know you'll be turning seventeen in a couple of months, but I'm gonna give you your birthday gift a little early. Come outside, boys. I got something I wanna show y'all."

Tim huffs and slides off the couch like a limp noodle onto the floor. He lazily pushes himself up and follows his dad and Jason out through the back door. Marco leads the boys over to his garage where he stores the tools and big machines. He always keeps his shop locked because the boys tipped over one of his toolboxes the last time he left it open.

Marco reaches up and removes the lock from the door, then looks back at the boys. "Wait here for a minute."

He disappears inside while the cousins wait outside, kicking at the rocks in the driveway. They look up as they hear banging and rustling coming from inside the shed.

The big door slides open a little, and Marco sticks his head out. "Now listen to me closely, boys. What I'm about to show you is not a kid's toy. This is something you need to take care of and treat with respect. You hear me?"

"Yes, Sir," they reply simultaneously.

Marco slides the big door to the side, revealing a strange thing hiding in the dark shed. Tim looks closer to see some small wheels attached to a rusty metal frame. Marco grabs ahold of it and slowly rolls it out into the light. Their eyes widen as the sun reflects off the steering wheel and the black plastic seat. Tim's heart pounds as it rolls completely out into the light, and he can see the shiny silver engine mounted on the back with a chrome tailpipe pointing up.

He jumps and waves his hands in the air, yelling, "It's a go-kart!"

"Happy early birthday, Son," Marco says proudly, standing with one foot on the back tire. "A friend of mine was selling it because it wasn't working anymore, so I bought it and fixed it up for you boys to ride around the farm."

"No way! Thank you, Dad!" Tim replies, leaning over and grabbing the steering wheel. "Does it go fast?"

"Get in, and let's find out."

Tim jumps into the plastic seat, pulling the seat belt over his shoulder, and clicks it in. Marco goes back into the garage and returns with an old, sparkly blue motorcycle helmet with no face shield. He squeezes it over Tim's head and buckles the strap under his chin.

"Look here. This switch turns on the power," he says, flipping on the switch, and a red light illuminates next to it. "This button starts the engine. Give it a push."

Tim reaches out and excitedly pushes the little red button. The engine makes a whining noise for a second. Then, with a mighty growl, it comes to life, sending a puff of smoke into the air. It was much louder than Tim had expected, but he was too excited to be scared of the noise.

Marco leans in and points to the floor. "The right pedal is the gas, and the left one is the brake!"

Tim nods at him and gently pushes the gas, hearing the engine rev up. The go-kart lunges forward slightly, and Tim looks up with the biggest grin he can fit on his face, even with it smashed inside the helmet.

"Well! Go!" Marco yells, pointing forward.

Tim hits the gas a little harder this time, and he takes off racing forward. The little go-kart was much more powerful than he had imagined, but it doesn't take him long to gain control of it. Within minutes, he's flying up and down the driveway like a rocket. As he passes the front of the house, Nancy watches in horror with her hands on her face as her son speeds past at mock twelve. He flies past the house and comes to a sliding stop right in front of the shed, where Jason and his dad are standing. A cloud of dust follows him, completely engulfing everything in sight.

When the dust clears, Jason runs towards him, jumping up and down, yelling, "That was awesome! Let me have a try!"

Still shaking from the adrenaline rushing through him, Tim unbuckles his seatbelt and jumps out of the kart. He takes off his helmet and hands it to Jason, who has a big smile across his face. He was a couple of years younger, so the helmet slides on with ease. After he buckles it, the helmet can almost spin completely around while he's wearing it.

He jumps into the go-kart and struggles to buckle himself in, while the helmet keeps slipping down over his eyes. Finally strapped in, he reaches up for the steering wheel, and gives the gas pedal a gentle tap. The go-kart lunges forward, sending him back in his seat. After a few more bouncing and jolting maneuvers, hesitating to hold down the pedal, he finally gives it some gas.

Jason takes off across the backyard towards the horse barn, kicking up a cloud of dust. They watch as Jason should have turned down the driveway, but he doesn't. Instead, he crashes at full throttle through the fence into the horse pasture and keeps going. Jason frantically tries to steer, but he panics and smashes into a large bale of hay, sending the go-kart tumbling to the side and rolling over upside-down. Tim and Marco run over to the crash site and find Jason hanging with his hands dangling above his head.

"Jason! Are you okay?!" Tim yells, as he spins the helmet around to see Jason's teary eyes.

He groans and looks at his cousin. "I think I'll stick to playing Super Mario Kart from now on."

National Guard soldiers gather in record time, lining up their vehicles in front of the Command Center building. About thirty large armored trucks prepare to roll out. Along with five long fuel and water tankers, and five cargo trucks carrying large containers filled with supplies. Bringing up the rear are two massive tracked vehicles. One looks like a tank, but instead of a cannon on top, it has a large bridge folded in half. The other is the Hercules heavy recovery tracked vehicle, in case of breakdowns or if they need to drive through a building.

Tim listens closely to the radio and hears JJ command the convoy to move out, and they were on their way south. Tim's truck is fourth in the convoy, and when he looks through the rearview mirror, all he can see is the never-ending line of tan vehicles snaking back and forth through piles of trash and charred cars. The convoy turns onto a southbound highway, and off in the distance, he recognizes the four towering apartment buildings where Randy's brother lives.

"Iron Horse Six, this is Phantom One," Tim calls out over the radio. "To the right are four tall buildings. We passed through them on our way north. There are about two hundred refugees camped out inside. They were desperately low on supplies and needed some help. Do you think we can spare a pallet of food and water?"

"I think we can spare some supplies," JJ replies. "Cargo One, this is Iron Horse Six. Have a truck peel off and speed drop a pallet of food and water outside the camp, then rejoin the convoy."

"Roger that, Cargo One peeling off."

Tim looks back through the mirror to see one of the trucks with a container on its back turn right off the highway towards the apartment buildings. He smiles and thinks to himself, "I'm sure Nash will appreciate that."

The convoy pushes forward, heading south, weaving in and out of the debris filled roads. Suddenly, the convoy slows to a stop in the downtown area, and a voice comes over the radio.

"Iron Horse Six, this is Iron Horse One," calls out the lead vehicle. "The road up ahead is completely blocked. It looks like a large group of rioters are fighting with the police. There's no other direction we can go. How do you want to proceed? Over."

"This is Iron Horse Six. It's about time we show these crazies who's in control of this city. Take four trucks ahead and assist the police. Load your rubber bullets, though. We want to make a point, not cause a massacre. Show those people how the Kansas National Guard does things."

"Roger that! Moving out!"

Tim's driver hits the gas and follows the first three trucks in the convoy towards the skirmish. A fierce battle is raging ahead across all five lanes of the inner city street. Large brick buildings line either side, with all of their windows and doors boarded up. Positioned with their backs toward the convoy are a mob of about fifty rioters wielding baseball bats and pipes, swinging wildly and yelling. A line of police officers with riot shields closes off the opposite side, as rocks and glass bottles bounce off of their riot shields.

As the lead truck approaches the unruly nest of violence, the driver makes a sharp right turn and positions the truck with its side facing the crowd. The following trucks do the same, boxing in the rioters between them and the police. The crowd shifts their attention to the new threat from behind and starts chucking things at the armored vehicles.

Tim's gunner pushes his head up through the top of the turret with his M4 in his hands. He spots a man lighting a rag on fire that's hanging from a bottle of alcohol. He takes aim and fires before the rioter has a chance to throw it at the convoy. Rubber bullets hit the man in the chest, causing him to fall back in pain and drop his bottle. The Molotov cocktail explodes at his feet, setting him and three others standing around him on fire. The rioters scramble to avoid the flames, stomping and jumping like crazy chickens.

Another man attempts to throw a brick at the trucks, but he's quickly dropped with a rubber bullet bouncing off his leg, sending him spinning to the ground in pain. The angry mass quickly dies down as they realize they were trapped. From the other side, the line of police officers realize what was happening and advances. They pull the rioters through their line one by one and slap zip cuffs on their hands and feet.

As he remembers what the unruly kid did to him and his family in Dallas, Tim's heart begins to race. So he decides to get a closer view of the justice. "Let's step out, and say hello."

Hydraulic doors hiss as they swing open on the trucks, spilling out soldiers into the street with their rifles at the ready. They line up on the inside of the tan armored wall and face the rioters. The now outnumbered and outgunned mob scowls at the soldiers. As the hatred reaches its boiling point, someone from the back yells to charge. Like a battle in ancient times with swords and shields, the mob rushes toward the National Guard soldiers. They scream their battle cries and sprint forward assuming the soldiers would just stand there and take it like the police have been. Unfortunately for them, these are not ancient times, and these soldiers will not stand idly by and take a beating.

Tim aims his rifle at the charging swarm and yells, "Open fire!"

The line of soldiers take aim and fire their rubber bullets at the fast approaching idiots. One by one, they fall in pain as the rubber pellets bounce off their legs and bodies. Their angry screams quickly evolve into moans and cries of pain as they roll on the street. Stopped dead in their tracks, those who remain standing frantically look around for somewhere to avoid the slaughter. But their efforts are useless, as boarded-up windows and concrete buildings entirely box them in.

The police quickly move forward, shoving them to the ground and binding their arms and legs as they go. When the last person is subdued, one of the police officers stands up and removes his helmet revealing blood dripping down the side of his face. He waves and shows appreciation to the National Guardsmen as they stand proudly over the victorious battlefield.

Tim lowers his rifle and turns around. "That'll be all boys. Let's get out of here." He says, as he loads back up into the truck and puts on his headset. "Iron Horse Six, this is Phantom One. The road's all clear. Continue through slowly."

"Good job, Phantom One. Continuing mission."

Vehicle after towering vehicle slowly pass the defeated crowd as they lie face down on the street. Grateful police officers look up, waving their shields and cheering as they pass. Tim can only imagine how much relief it must bring to them, knowing that the National Guard is finally helping to return the city to order. The convoy continues through the war-torn streets, avoiding roadblocks and piles of cars until the road finally clears. Soon, they enter the farmlands, heading south.

"This is Iron Horse Six. All units, there's a town coming up. We'll be stopping to refuel and regroup before we move on."

The convoy slows, and Tim looks out the window to see a familiar sight as they drive through the smoky ruins of Chesterfield. All of the trucks line up outside the town, while the fuel tankers drive down Main Street and set up a temporary fueling station. As Tim steps out of his truck and stretches his legs, he watches as the massive recovery vehicle rumbles past. It drives through town and pushes the destroyed buses out of the end of the road so the trucks could pass once they were done fueling. He walks over to Rose's Diner and takes a seat at one of the outside tables, as JJ walks up with a roll of paper under his arm.

He unrolls a map onto the table and looks down at it. "Ok, Tim. There's one main road leading to the landfill from here, and many smaller back roads. We should be able to surround it easily. Video from the remaining drone shows that the R.R.'s long-range guns are still completely buried, but their heavy armor looks functional. No movement has been seen yet, though. We should be able to get to the main gate quickly and take out any outer defenses with our Javelin missiles. As long as we stay back out of the range of the mortar positions, we can effectively trap them inside that rotting bowl of trash until they're ready to leave voluntarily."

"Sounds like a plan, JJ. We should get there in a couple of hours if we leave immediately after we're done refueling."

Both of them look up as a soldier comes running over from the other side of the street, looking concerned. "Sir, we just intercepted some radio traffic from the R.R. Some men just attacked a farm not far from here. They said something about finding people hidden inside an underground bunker."

Tim looks up at JJ with wide eyes. "My family's in that bunker. JJ, I gotta go now!"

"Take that truck and crew that are fueling up right now," JJ says, pointing at the truck sitting beside the fueler. "We'll meet you at the farm after we're done here."

Tim runs over to the truck, waving with his rifle in his hands. "Jump in! We're rolling out now! Colonel's orders!"

While the others quickly buckle up inside, he jumps into the driver's seat and starts the engine. Tim hits the gas and makes a U-turn in the center of town, narrowly avoiding the massive hole in the street. The heavily armored truck leans hard to one side, and the tires squeal as he punches it and flies out of the small town.

The thirty-five thousand pounds of armored truck barely flinches as it bounces down the bumpy dirt road at top speed. All Tim can think about is his family and if he's too late to help them. His hands shake as he turns the steering wheel and speeds down the driveway towards the farm. He slams on the brakes just before the shed, and the truck skids to a stop, sending up a cloud of dust as he jumps out. Tim runs for the bunker, fearing the worst as he sees the torn-open hatch.

He lands on the edge of the hole and stares down into the darkness. "Hello! Is anyone still here?!"

For a second, he waits for a response, but no one replies. He quickly turns around and climbs down the ladder. The smell of burning plastic and gunpowder still lingers in the air. When he takes a step off the ladder, his feet land on something soft. Startled, he jumps to the side to see the body of a bearded man who was cut down by a shotgun blast to the face. He turns and pulls the pistol out of his holster as he looks at the nightmarish bunker. A deathly silence fills the air as the lights flicker and spark on the ceiling. Another body, dressed in black, lies lifeless in the living room next to a broken TV. He cautiously walks through the destroyed room not knowing what to expect. He notices the door to the bedroom hanging off its hinges, so he walks through to find another dead R.R. soldier hanging half off the bed.

Tim lowers his pistol and looks around in shock, feeling helpless because he was too late to save his family. Now, they were all gone. He returns to the living room with his head hung low, looking at the spent shotgun shells scattered on the floor. Standing in silence for a moment, he hears what sounds like a muffled child's cry and notices that the door to the pantry was still closed.

He moves closer and presses his ear against the heavy steel door. "Hello? Is anybody in here?"

"Tim, is that you?" replies a familiar voice.

He leans back in surprise and holsters his pistol. "Yes, it's me. Are you guys alright? Open the door."

Tim stands impatiently as he hears the metal scraping of a bar sliding free, and watches as the door cracks open, revealing four scared faces staring back at him. Nancy sits at the back of the room, holding Victoria, while Garrett and Marco stand by the door with rifles in their hands.

Marco puts down his gun and reaches for Tim. "Son, thank God it's you. They took Randy and Mary. We did everything we could to keep the baby safe. I'm so sorry."

"They took them to the landfill," Garrett says, looking scared.

Tim turns and looks at the devastation left behind in the living room. "These guys have crossed the line this time. Don't worry. I'll get them back. I have the National Guard with me, and we're heading to the landfill right now to put an end to this."

He stomps through the bunker and up the ladder to find the soldiers standing around the farm. He waves to them and quickly jumps back into the truck. As he gets situated, a large cloud of dust approaches the farm from the road behind him, so he turns the truck around and meets the other National Guard trucks as they pass.

"Iron Horse Six, this is Phantom One. They took Mary and Randy to the landfill. We need to get there now. Are your soldiers ready?"

"Ready and waiting. Let's do this. Drivers, you know where to go. Roll out!"

The convoy splits into three groups of ten trucks, each taking a different road to the east in order to completely surround the landfill. Tim follows behind JJ as they drive down the road leading to the main entrance on the north side. JJ knows that the R.R. has roadblocks along the route to the landfill entrance, but they were ready.

"Gunners, lock and load your weapons," JJ calls out over the radio. "We're not stopping for anything. If you see any R.R. roadblocks, you're free to open fire."

From the turret, the satisfying clank of a fifty-caliber machine gun chambering a round echoes as they continue down the road. As predicted, two trucks manned by soldiers from the R.R. stand at a large intersection up ahead. The militia men open fire, and small caliber bullets harmlessly bounce off the front of JJ's truck. Immediately followed by the sweet sound of half-inch diameter bullets blasting from the machine gun. The high velocity rounds effortlessly punching holes in the civilian vehicles. As they quickly approach, the R.R. men jump out of their trucks and run just as they explode in a satisfying ball of fire.

Without slowing down for a second, the ten massive, tan vehicles speed past the burning trucks, not even bothering to look back.

"This is Iron Horse Six. HQ reports that the drone has picked up two tanks hidden outside the main entrance. They must have been outside before we destroyed the main road. Gunners, prepare your Javelin launchers. When we're in range, take out those bastards before they have a chance to fire."

Tim looks back and watches a soldier handing a long, green missile launcher to the gunner in the turret. He slides it into place on the shield and prepares to fire once they were close enough.

The hill surrounding the landfill appears in the distance and grows larger as they approach. Soon enough, the entrance to the landfill comes into view around the corner, followed by a massive explosion that erupts to the right of the vehicles. Clouds of dust rise from the entrance as the tanks repeatedly fire at the approaching vehicles. Another round impacts the truck behind Tim's, sending it rolling off the side of the road.

"Take your shot!" Tim yells to his gunner.

A loud hiss and a blast of smoke comes from the top of the truck, followed by a flare of fire as the missile takes flight. The trail of smoke climbs high into the sky and comes down directly on top of one of the tanks. A powerful blast of fire and smoke surrounds the tank, causing its main cannon to spin to the side. Another blast comes from JJ's truck, propelling the second missile through the air and impacting the other tank, rendering it charred and lifeless.

As the trucks close in on the main gate, the ground in front of them explodes as mortar shells impact the road, forcing them to stop in their tracks.

"Everyone, halt! We're almost within range of the mortar teams," JJ calls out.

The trucks spread out along the field, about one and a half miles from the entrance, and aim everything they have at the opening. Plumes of smoke rise from the two tanks that were destroyed on either side of the gate. Tim jumps out and moves over to where JJ is standing, and looking through his binoculars.

"What do you think?" Tim asks.

"Well, they're not stupid enough to come out shooting with all of our firepower standing here. They have nowhere left to go. So, now we wait."

Tim pulls JJ away from his binoculars and looks him in the eyes. "We can't just wait! My wife's in there."

"There are far too many soldiers in there to simply burst in shooting like crazy people. If anyone's going to make it out of this alive, we need to be smart and play this right. We've cut off their food supply, so they can't last forever."

"They'll kill Mary before that happens! We need to do something to get those men to come out now!" Tim pleads.

JJ throws his arm up, pointing at the exploding field in front of the convoy. "Then use that big brain of yours and come up with a plan! I'm all ears!"

With his heart racing and mind spinning, Tim looks over at the landfill entrance as another mortar round explodes fifty feet in front of them, serving as a steady reminder of their strength. A strong stench of rot and gunpowder lingers in the breeze coming from the volcano of rubbish.

Having an idea, he looks back at JJ and grabs his shoulder. "Your man said that he intercepted a radio signal earlier, right? Are they still able to hear that signal? More importantly, are they able to send a transmission back to it?"

"You figured out a plan, didn't you?" JJ replies smiling. "I'll go get the commo guy and find out."

JJ walks to the back of the line of trucks and soon returns with one of his soldiers.

"I need to talk to the R.R. Can you get that radio signal again for me?" Tim asks.

The soldier nods his head confidently. "Yes, Sir. Give me five minutes, and I'll have it ready."

The soldier runs to his truck, grabs a black tough box from the back, and runs back. He sets the case on the ground and opens it, revealing a long-range antenna and a battery-powered radio. He sets up the antenna, aiming it towards the landfill, and then plugs everything into the radio receiver. He slowly turns the dial, honing in on the signal coming from the landfill, until the speaker crackles to life with chatter.

"Hey Sarge. I'm starting to think that going to jail was better than being stuck in this shithole, waiting to get bombed. I don't know if I want to fight for these hillbillies anymore."

"You agreed to fight for these men months ago. You can't change your mind now. Now do what you're told, Private. Get off the damn radio and get back to digging out that artillery."

Tim keeps listening to the radio chatter, hoping to hear them say something about his wife, but they never do. Another mortar shell explodes in front of the truck as he picks up the microphone and takes a deep breath.

"Attention prior US Army soldiers! Attention all prior US Army soldiers! This is the Kansas National Guard! We are not here to fight you! If we wanted you dead, that missile we dropped would have been much bigger!"

A filthy soldier stops digging in the trash pile and turns to his radio.

"Our command wants to drop a MOAB on you and move on. We do *not* think you deserve that. We understand that you were tricked and forced into joining these men who think that they're doing something good for the American people. I'm here to tell you that they are not."

A group of soldiers standing in a mortar pit turn up their radio and listen closely.

"They are burning cities to the ground and killing innocent people every day. You were all once proud American soldiers. I'm here to tell you that you still have a choice. You can live to see your families again, or die in this trash-filled grave beside a madman."

Several elderly men sitting at a picnic table, look around at each other with disappointed faces.

"Leave this rotten landfill and your corrupt leadership behind. Simply walk out of the front gate unarmed, and I give you my word that you will not die today. Stay, and the thousands of soldiers surrounding this landfill right now will show you no mercy as we come over the walls."

General Grant grabs his radio off his desk and throws it against the wall next to Wallace. It explodes into tiny plastic pieces upon impact. "What the hell are they trying to do, Wallace?! You had better get your ass out there and stop your men from leaving!"

Wallace turns and walks toward Mary and Randy, who are strapped to chairs. With their mouths covered in tape, they both laugh and taunt Wallace as he passes. He shoves the door open and slams it behind him as he leaves. As he stomps down the hallway, R.R. soldiers watch him with confused faces. He bursts through the main door and steps out into the Texas sun, then looks around. Soldiers that are standing around talking to each other, turn and stare at him in with his arm in a sling.

He angrily steps up onto the picnic table between the elderly men, pulls a pistol out of his harness, and fires a shot into the air.

"What are all of you doing?! You don't seriously believe that man on the radio! Do you?! He's just feeding you with lies to trick you into giving up! What we're doing is saving the American people, not killing them! The US government is who's killing them!"

A soldier stands up from behind a stack of boxes and yells, "So, who is that you have inside the office?! We saw you drag two people in there earlier! Are we taking hostages now?! That sounds like something a terrorist would do!"

A couple more men stand up, nodding their heads and scowling at Wallace.

Filled with rage, he points his gun down at the man. "Those people are a direct threat to our cause!"

"Some lady and a skinny guy are a threat to all of this?! We were told that we would be stopping the government from enslaving the American people! Not taking them from their homes!"

More soldiers stand up and agree with one another as a large group of bearded men come out of the main office and gather around Wallace.

One of them walks up and stands next to the table, yelling out to the crowd of soldiers. "Freedom is not free! Everyone must pay the price for this revolution! *We* are ready to do whatever it takes to reclaim our country! Are *you?!*"

One of the older lieutenants steps forward. "I gave eighteen years of my life to this country. I've paid my dues. I only went along with this because they threatened to send me to prison. I'm starting to think prison would be better than living in hell with that asshole."

The crowd of soldiers behind him cheer and walk forward.

Wallace fires his pistol over his head once more before aiming it down at the group of ex-Army soldiers. "If you're not willing to fight for this revolution, maybe you should just die right here."

Clicks and pops from weapons echo through the yard as the soldiers pick up their rifles and aim them at Wallace and his men.

"The last time I checked, *Colonel,* we had you outnumbered ten to one. If you really want to start a fight you cannot win, go ahead and pull that trigger."

Wallace looks out with wide eyes at the hundreds of men aiming their rifles at him, and realizes what he had just done. Knowing he can't win this fight; he turns his pistol up and slowly holsters it. As he steps down from the table, he looks out at his bearded entourage staring back at him. Fuming with rage from the humiliating situation, he barks orders at his militia men. "Let them go! We don't need them to win this battle! Tell your men to assume the mortar positions and prepare for a fight!"

Another mortar round explodes in front of the National Guard line, but then suddenly, they stop. The only sound they can hear is the static from the radio and the wind blowing through the weeds. Ten impatient minutes pass without a single sound from the landfill.

Then, the radio crackles with a man's voice. "Hey, National Guard. This place stinks like shit. We're coming out now. Please don't shoot us."

JJ looks through the binoculars towards the main gate, as figures begin appearing from behind the destroyed tanks. More and more emerge from the landfill, and soon a parade of people begin walking through the field towards the National Guard. As they move closer, JJ notices that they look like hell, as they're covered in filth and dirt from their little sabotage. The smell of rotting garbage intensifies as they cross the open field. Tim looks out and sees that these men are clean-shaven and fit. Not like the pudgy, bearded men he had seen before.

Tim punches JJ in the arm. "Looks like the soldiers who were forced to follow this regime finally decided to change their minds."

JJ looks through his binoculars. "Yup, I don't see any of those bearded guys in the crowd."

About eight hundred men slowly approach the convoy but stop fifty feet away. One of the older men walks forward to meet Tim and JJ.

He stops in front of them and looks on with sad eyes, wearing a tattered uniform that's covered in dirt and filth. "Which one of you assholes blew up that shit pile?"

Tim smiles and raises his hand. "That was me. Sorry about that."

The soldier stares at Tim with a tired scowl. "That was a real dick move. But pretty damn effective. If you're going to take us prisoner, does that mean we get to take showers?"

"First, we need to get inside and take care of that madman in charge," JJ says, pointing at the landfill. "How many men are still inside?"

"There are about a hundred hillbillies left. We tried to convince them to come out, but apparently, one of you burned down their bar, and they're still pretty pissed off."

Tim raises his hand again. "Ya, that was me too."

"Looks like you have your hands full, then." The soldier replies, laughing. "I saw a couple of civilians being carried in earlier. They're holding them in the main building. Try not to blow *that* up on your way in."

JJ turns and points at the trucks in the line. "You guys can go to the back of the trucks and wait. Downwind, preferably. We'll call for some transport to take you and your men back to town and set you up with some showers."

As Tim holds his nose while they pass. The stinky group of dirty, sad faces walk by and head for the back of the convoy.

JJ walks back to his truck and pulls the radio mic from the door. "Alpha Team, prepare for the assault. Bravo and Charlie Teams, begin your push over the hill on the south."

Thirty National Guard soldiers and four gun trucks gather at the edge of the field, facing the main gate of the landfill. Sixty more men are climbing the hill to the south and will meet them on the inside.

JJ looks at Tim with excited eyes. "Are you going to make it, old man? When's the last time you ran anywhere?"

Tim looks down at his belly and slaps it. "These days, I only run out to buy more beer, but you don't need to worry about me."

JJ looks around at Alpha Team and points his hand towards the front gate. They take off jogging across the mile-and-a-half of open field toward the entrance, while the four trucks follow along for fire support.

About fifty yards in, the thump of mortar round launching starts again, followed by the whistle of the round flying overhead. It explodes far off to the right of the soldiers as they run along. It appears that the ex-Army men disabled the targeting equipment on the mortars before they evacuated the landfill. Another one explodes a little closer as Alpha team starts running faster towards the gate.

As they reach the halfway point, bullets impact the ground around them. Men dressed in all black run out of the gate, but they are quickly halted as the gunners in the trucks open fire, forcing them to take cover behind the destroyed tanks. A soldier running next to Tim falls hard as a bullet hits him in the chest.

He quickly moves behind one of the vehicles and yells, "Take cover behind the trucks!"

As Alpha Team pushes forward, they scramble left and right, trying to avoid the line of fire. Another mortar round lands directly behind the trucks as they continue to lay down suppressive fire. Metallic pings and pops ring out from the trucks as bullets bounce off the thick armor. Tim looks out from behind the truck and spots a man standing atop the hill. He takes aim and hits his target, sending the man tumbling down and scattering his gear in all directions.

Onward, they follow their heavily armored rolling shields until they reach the destroyed tanks just in front of the entrance. Tim runs past the truck and pushes up against one of the tanks for cover and to catch his breath. JJ follows and kneels down beside him. JJ signals for the trucks to move forward and enter the gate, so they drive through. Their gunners continuously firing at the militia men as they pass. They're forced to stop halfway down because of the massive hole created by the bomb, so they honk their horns, signaling the soldiers to proceed.

JJ peeks around to see if it's clear to move forward. "Once we get through the gate, the trucks won't be able to cover us anymore. So keep your eyes open."

Tim pats him on the back. "Good luck then, brother. Let's do this."

JJ stands up and signals for the rest of Alpha Team to advance. He and Tim sprint through the entrance and are soon caught up with the trucks. The entrance is about a hundred yards long, with weigh stations located on either side halfway through. As the assault team advances to the left, Tim and JJ move to the right and take cover behind the weigh station.

They both hit the white building wall at the same time and sit down, out of breath. With their eyes wide open, they creep along the backside of the building until they find a door, and JJ kicks it in. Bullets pierce through the wooden walls as they sneak through the building towards the front. Glass shatters from a window as rounds impact all around Tim, forcing him to take cover behind a desk. Seizing the element of surprise, the two sneak up to the front windows and pop up, firing at the R.R. soldiers as they cross the open road.

As the men run back and forth, Tim and JJ continue to thin out the crowd of black uniforms until a few soldiers jump into the hole in the road and take cover. The two thought they were fairly well covered until a machine gun in one of the towers zeros in on them. Suddenly, the walls of the building splinter and explode as bullets smash through, obliterating everything inside. Narrowly avoiding the barrage, they retreat through the rear door and take cover behind the building once again. JJ looks over at one of his sharpshooters in the hole and signals for him to look up at the tower. The soldier rolls over and comes back up with his rifle, which has a long scope attached. He takes his shot and watches as the machine gunner falls from the tower, landing hard on the ground.

Tim looks around the corner of the building to his right and sees that the path ahead is clear to move. He taps JJ and waves for him to follow. Together, they run forward, firing at anyone who sticks their head out. As they reach the end of the entry gate, they post up behind a pile of sandbags to the right.

Just beyond them sits a field that's about three hundred yards wide, with Humvees and piles of equipment scattered throughout. On the other side of the field stands a large, white metal building that serves as the main office. The rest of Alpha Team rushes towards the entrance upon hearing a loud explosion coming from the other side of the compound. The other teams were making their way through the field of trash and abandoned tanks.

Tim peeks to the right of the sandbags and sees a Humvee parked nearby. He swiftly jumps over the barrier and opens the door, only to find that the steering wheel wasn't chained. So, he jumps in and starts the engine. He honks the horn, and JJ looks over the sandbags with a smile.

Tim waves back and yells, "Hey JJ, our Uber is here! Need a lift?"

He leaps over the sandbags and runs up to the truck. "I like your style."

As he slides into the passenger seat, JJ waves to a couple more soldiers and signals them to jump in the back. Once everyone was onboard, Tim takes off through the field like a bat out of hell.

As he slides around the field, Tim imagines himself playing Mario Kart as a kid. Instead of bananas, this go-kart is equipped with a team of soldiers shooting at anyone wearing black as they go. A couple of men shoot at them from behind a pile of boxes, so Tim accelerates and drives towards them. The two-door Humvee rams into the boxes, sending the men jumping to the sides as pieces of wood and weapons fly in every direction.

When they finally get close to the main building, Tim slides the truck into a small garage on the side, and parks it sideways for some cover. They jump from the truck smiling, and run into the garage, looking back at the trail of destruction left in their wake. Once they were safe, they stop outside the main buildings door and stare at each other.

"You ready for this, JJ?"

"Ready, Tim! Let's go and get your wife back."

Tim reaches for the doorknob and slowly pushes it open. He peeks with one eye through the crack and sees a dark room filled with desks and a couch. The room appears clear, so he waves to JJ before pushing the door open and steps inside. With his rifle at the ready, Tim slowly walks through what looks like the reception area of the office. Couches line the walls, with one large desk in the back with a computer monitor on it. On the wall in front, a large tinted window looks out at the battle raging outside. Dull thumps of gunfire echo through the walls as the two slowly make their way to the door leading to the offices in back.

Tim reaches for the door handle, but he stops abruptly as he hears footsteps approaching. They immediately kneel on either side of the door and patiently wait. The door between them starts to creak open, and a man steps through, with his eyes fixed on the window looking out. Before he has a chance to look down, Tim swings hard with an uppercut directly to the man's groin. The man leans over and drops his gun into Tim's arms, while JJ reaches over his back and puts him in a chokehold. JJ pulls hard and struggles for a second until the man loses consciousness in his arms.

He lays the man down quietly and looks at Tim with disgust. "Did you really have to punch him in the dick?"

"I was hoping it was Wallace," Tim replies with an innocent grin.

"You're a *monster*," JJ says mockingly as he moves through the door. "Let's go."

They quietly move down the hallway, passing empty offices, and listening closely to each door. Just as they hear voices coming from the back office, they freeze in the middle of the hall. Tim slowly approaches the door and peeks an eye through the small glass window in the center of the door. Two men are standing next to Randy and Mary, who are strapped to chairs with duct tape. In the back of the room, Wallace and Grant are standing next to a table, talking to each other.

Tim ducks down and looks over at JJ, pointing to his eyes. He shows the number two on his fingers, then points to either side of the room with both hands. JJ replies with a nod, tightens the grip on his rifle, and pulls it in against his shoulder. Tim stands up and backs away from the door, preparing to kick it. He takes a deep breath and nods to JJ. After giving a thumbs up, JJ counts down on his fingers. Three... Two... One...

Gritting his teeth, Tim kicks the door as hard as he can, sending it bursting open and startling the men who were standing inside. JJ immediately slips around the corner and shoots the man standing on the left before he has a chance to react. Before the first man hits the floor, Tim follows through and takes out the one to the right with two rounds to the chest.

Wallace and Grant jump at the sound of the gunshots and stand up in the back of the room, stunned. With rifles aimed straight ahead, Tim and JJ walk slowly past Randy and Mary. Tim lowers his rifle and kneels down in front of Mary, carefully pulling the tape from her mouth.

He gives her a kiss and smiles. "Hey babe. How's it going?"

With stars in her eyes, she stares back at him. "Not too bad, considering the circumstances. I could still be trapped in that tiny bunker with your parents."

Tim smiles and turns to Randy. He reaches over and not so gently peels the tape from his mouth.

Randy looks up and puckers his lips. "What? No kiss for me too?"

Tim smiles and shakes his head as he turns around. His expression immediately transforms into one of hatred. Focused forward, he raises his rifle and aims it at Wallace, who is cowering in the back of the room.

Grant slowly walks around the left side of the table, staring at Tim. "This must be the famous retired soldier I keep hearing about. It's a shame that Wallace couldn't convince you to join us."

"It is, Sir," replies Wallace as he moves around the table to the right. "This is the asshole who blew up the entire town and broke my damn arm."

Wallace reaches out for his pistol on the table, but Tim takes a step forward and aims his rifle directly at his face. "Go ahead and grab it, Wallace. You crossed the line by kidnapping my wife. Now, I have to kill you. And you're done here, Grant. There'll be no more of this madness, destroying lives for your own gain."

Grant narrows his eyes and stares at Tim. "You can go ahead and kill me too, then. There are thousands more just like me who want to take back this country for the people."

"We're taking you north to hold you accountable for your war crimes, Grant," JJ says, stepping forward.

"Not if I have anything to do about it!" Wallace yells as he grabs for his pistol.

Tim squeezes his trigger without remorse and watches in slow motion, savoring every millisecond as the bullets tear through Wallace's chest. Without blinking, he watches as the stupid expression on Wallace's face turns blank, and his body collapses onto the floor, lifeless.

Grant looks down at his body, then back up at Tim. "Good riddance. He was an idiot that lost tons of money and equipment for the revolution." Grant quickly grabs the pistol from his hip and aims it at JJ. "What? You're not going to shoot me like you did him?"

JJ aims his rifle at Grant and scratches his finger against the trigger. "I already told you that you're coming with us alive."

As his hand begins to shake, Grant stands there, looking down the sights of his pistol. Suddenly, he jerks the pistol back and attempts to put it to his head, but JJ takes a shot. Grant's pistol flies back with a splash of sparks as the round bounces off it. He stares at his empty hand in disbelief at what has just happened.

"Not today, Grant," JJ says as he quickly walks behind him and puts the General's hands in handcuffs.

Grant tries to say something, but Tim quickly grabs a roll of duct tape from the table and wraps it tightly around his head a few times.

He throws the tape onto the floor and looks over at Randy, who's bouncing in the chair he's still taped to. "Give me a gun, Tim! I wanna shoot Wallace a couple of times too!"

Tim pulls out his knife, cuts the tape off of Mary's arms and legs, and helps her to stand on her feet. Relieved that it was all over, he pulls her in tight and gives her another big kiss.

"Me too! Me too!" Randy says, bouncing in his chair. "The cutting part. Not the kissing part. Unless you want that too," he says, puckering his lips again.

"Alright, calm down." Tim laughs as he lets go of Mary. "I'm coming."

He goes over to Randy and cuts his arms free. Before Tim has a chance to reach for his legs, Randy leans forward and gives him a big hug around his waist. "I love you, man. No homo."

Tim pats him on his back and pushes him back into his chair. "Love you too, you crazy animal."

He cuts Randy's legs free, and everyone walks back down the hall to the reception area. Through the front tinted window, they can see a small group of R.R. men on their knees surrounded by National Guard soldiers. They walk out through the side door and over to the Humvee, Tim had parked in the garage.

He opens the passenger door and bows to Mary. "Your chariot awaits, my lady."

"My hero," she replies as she steps in.

Randy jumps into the back while Tim gets into the driver's seat and closes the door. He puts his elbow out of the window and watches as JJ hands Grant over to his men then walks back to the truck.

JJ puts a hand on the roof and looks through the window at Tim. "I guess this is it, then? You sure you don't want to come with us and finish this fight?"

"I'm still retired, and I plan on keeping it that way. I have a family to look after and a farm to rebuild."

JJ reaches out his hand for a handshake. "If I'm ever back in your area, I'll stop by and see how the farm's doing. You still owe me some biscuits and gravy."

"Yes, I do. Take care of yourself, *Sir,*" Tim replies mockingly, while shaking his hand.

JJ squeezes his hand overly firmly. "Take care of your family."

Tim lets go of JJ's hand and starts the truck. As he drives for the exit, he takes one last look through the rearview mirror at JJ waving goodbye.

CHAPTER 11

THE LONG ROAD HOME

"Are you gonna help me pack sometime today?" Mary asks, while walking past Tim with her hands full of stuff.

Tim looks up from his relaxed position on the couch. "Sorry, I'm retired. I can't lift anything heavy for another six months. Doctor's orders."

Mary gives him the stink eye. "Okay then, I guess I'll just throw away all this old Army crap piled up in the garage."

"Okay," Tim casually replies, waving his hand. "Grab me a beer while you're over there."

He throws his arms up in defense as a shoe comes flying across the room and hits him in the chest. Before he has time to recover, Mary follows up with a full-on flying ninja attack, landing on his lap and almost flipping over the couch.

She playfully slaps his head. "I'll show you no heavy lifting.

You've been retired for six weeks now. It's time to get off of this couch, or you'll turn into a super-fat forty-year-old couch potato."

"That's exactly what I was going for. How did you know?" He replies with a smile.

Mary crosses her arms and stares at him while sitting on his lap.

Tim stares back for a second, then breaks. "Ok, *fine.* I'll get up and help you pack."

"Thank you," she replies and stands up, satisfied.

As soon as Mary turns her back, Tim lays back down on the couch. "Just after a quick nap."

"Ahhhhh!" Mary yells as she jumps back on top of Tim and laughs.

"Okay, I'm getting up for real this time," Tim squeezes out, as Mary bounces on top of him.

After Mary finishes her attack, she pulls Tim from his properly formed spot on the couch. He walks over to the kitchen, where brown cardboard boxes and rolls of packing tape cover the countertops. He looks left at the mess, then to the right at the fridge. Reaching for the door, he glances down at his watch that reads two pm.

"It's five o'clock somewhere," he says as he grabs a beer and pops the top.

While taking a drink of his refreshing cold beverage, he walks through the door to the garage where Mary is pulling old gardening stuff from a shelf and packing it into a box on the floor. She reaches for a stack of plastic flower pots, but they slip from the shelf and scatter apart all over the floor at her feet.

She huffs and looks up at Tim, who is standing with his beer. "Why are we moving to Dallas anyway?"

"Three words, Drive Through Margaritas," he replies proudly. "That, and my parents will be nearby in case you ever decide to open the baby factory."

"Ha," she laughs. "I have to teach screaming children every day. Why would I want to come home to one?"

"Because kids can be useful. He could go get me a beer from the fridge, or start a billion-dollar company from our garage. You never know!"

Mary waves her hands at the messy garage floor. "Not in this garage, but I'll think about it."

Tim shuffles through all of his old Army clothes and equipment that "magically appears" in his garage following every deployment. After spending twenty-two years in the Army, one tends to acquire a large number of souvenirs. All sorts of memories flood Tim's mind as he smells the desert sand and dry-rotting rubber.

Mary stands over the pile with her hands on her hips. "For serious though, we would have half as many boxes if you got rid of some of this crap."

"Never!" Tim says proudly. "You never know when I'll need some of this stuff again. Most of this stuff, you can't just buy in any store. It's earned on the battlefield or taken from other people's containers."

Mary shakes her head and returns to packing her stuff. They spend the next week packing up the rest of the house and shoving all of the boxes into the back of a long rental truck. On the final day, they close the front door for the last time and say goodbye to the old house. Tim jumps into the U-Haul, and Mary gets into the car as they set off for Dallas, Texas.

They leave North Carolina and make the long trip across half of the country to the Southwest. As they drive over a hill and catch a glimpse of the city below, Tim sees a sign that reads "Dallas – Ft Worth fifteen miles." The sun is just starting to set, and the buildings are lighting up with all sorts of colors, from green to purple. One building even has a massive ball on top, covered in gold lights. After passing through the busy downtown area, they pull off the highway and enter the suburbs where their new home is nestled in the back of a quiet cul-de-sac.

He slowly drives down the narrow streets, passing children who are playing and riding their bikes back and forth. Through the house's windows, he can see families sitting down at their dinner tables and eating. As they finally stop in front of their new home, it really looks like a peaceful place to live. The house looks small, with only one story and a double garage on the right side. The doors and windows are painted white, while the siding is grey. However, Mary insists that they repaint it a brighter color as soon as possible. They step out of their cars and stand in front of their new house holding hands.

"Welcome to your new home, Babe," Tim says, pulling Mary closer.

She smiles and gives him a big hug. "This does look like a good place to start a family."

As Tim drives toward the main gate, he looks around at the destruction left behind by the assault. In the end, he always wonders how he manages to survive everything. He drives past the soldiers who are guarding the R.R. men as they kneel down in shame. He notices the expressions on their faces and no longer sees them as enemies. What he sees is a group of people who now represent change. This battle changed how they will see each other forever and changed how all of them will live after this.

Just as they reach the exit, the massive tracked vehicle extends a long bridge out over the hole left by the bomb. Once it's finished, he drives over the metal bridge and notices the destroyed white weigh station that he and JJ were just inside. It's hard to believe how one small decision in the opposite direction would have ended up with both of them lying dead inside. They approach the destroyed tanks at the entrance and pass by, while smoke slowly rises from their newly acquired holes.

A sense of relief falls over him as he leaves the landfill and drives down the road to the north. Mary looks out the window to her right and sees the field, now full of craters that resembles the surface of the moon.

"How did you ever make it through all of that?" She asks, looking out the window in amazement.

"Luck," Tim replies, without hesitation.

Luck is not something that can be taught, nor can it be learned by watching. You either have it, or you don't. Luck is still one of the main deciding factors on the battlefield, even to this day. Tim does feel lucky to be alive sometimes, and even luckier to look over at his beautiful wife sitting next to him. He often finds himself on the side of luck, but deep down, he knows that his luck will eventually run out.

They make a left turn and drive towards the massive group of ex-Army soldiers as they climb onto the back of empty cargo trucks to be taken to town. Tim watches and can't even imagine what it's like to be where these poor men are right now. They were forced to change sides or be thrown into a detention center. Now, as they've flipped again, they'll likely be charged with something new and probably thrown into another jail. On top of everything, they got covered in rotting garbage. Talk about bad luck.

"These guys really stink!" Randy comments from the back.

Tim continues down the road and slowly passes the National Guard truck that was hit by a tank round. Several men stand next to the overturned truck looking pretty banged up, but still alive. As they pass, Randy waves to them, and they wave back.

Cruising down the long road home, they pass heaps of smoking shrapnel from a couple of R.R. trucks that were destroyed by the convoy. A few miles later, they pass pastures full of multi-colored cows, with a couple of overturned Humvees lying peacefully in the grass. Next, they drive past a massive, bright green cornfield with a trail of black smoke rising from the center of it.

Finally, they make it to the driveway leading to the O'Connell's farm and turn in, only to see that the farm is a complete disaster. A pair of tractors are dragging shredded Humvees up the driveway that were chewed apart by the minigun. To the right, in the middle of the field, one truck sits smoking and looking like an expensive piece of lawn art. Behind the main house, one of the grain silos is missing, as it lies on the ground with its contents spread out in every direction.

As they approach the house, they see Sammy standing outside. Randy stands up in the back and waves his arms, so Sammy doesn't try to shoot at them. Tim drives around the shattered fountain in the middle of the driveway and parks. The front door of the house had been removed, with a trail of bullet holes punched into the walls around it.

Randy jumps out and runs over to Sammy, excitedly shaking his hand. "You have no idea what we just went through."

Sammy shakes his hand and laughs. "I'm glad y'all made it out alive."

"What do you plan on doing with all of these destroyed trucks and dead bodies?" Tim asks, shaking his hand.

"I guess we'll bury the bodies out back. I'm sure someone'll come looking for them eventually. I'll have the guys line up the trucks alongside the road with the old tractors as a reminder of what happens when people mess with the O'Connell's."

Tim looks over at the front of the house as Garrett and Celia walk out. Garrett's wearing his leather tool belt, with a hammer hanging from the side. Celia, of course, is wearing her oversized fur coat and high heels. She watches the ground closely, trying not to trip over anything as she walks out.

Garrett walks towards Tim with a remorseful look on his face. "I'm sorry I let Mary get taken from your parents' farm. You have to believe me that I did everything I could to help them."

"Don't worry, Garrett,:" Mary says, as she walks over from the truck. "I'm sure he understands that you did everything you could."

"You should have seen it!" Randy says, excitedly. "Garrett was all like, 'take these shotguns,' as the guys came down the hole. Then me and Mary blasted like ten of them, then Mary hit one of them with the TV.”

“There were just too many of them,” Garrett explains. “Your mom grabbed the baby, and your dad and I locked the door before they could get to all of us.”

Tim looks at Randy and Garrett. “You both were very brave and did the right thing. Thank you both for everything.”

“Oh, and don’t worry about those horses you guys lost.” Sammy comments. “They each have a GPS tracker in them, and my men are already out rounding them up.”

“How can we ever repay you for your help, Sammy?” Tim asks.

“No need to repay anything. As far as I’m concerned, we’re even after you saved my son’s life and got him away from those maniacs.” Sammy replies, putting his hand on Garrett’s shoulder.

Tim looks at Garrett and grins. “Your son is the hero here, Sammy. He saved all of us when we were trying to escape the landfill.” He turns to Celia, who is staring at the front of her house. “Sorry about the house, Celia.”

She stands with her hands on her hips, looking up at the large hole. “I never liked that god-awful front door that Samuel picked out anyway. This gives me a chance to choose something more Victorian Era for the house.”

Tim laughs and turns back to Sammy. “We need to be getting back on the road. Thank you again, Sammy, and stay safe.”

“Come back anytime. My door’s always open to you and your family,” he replies, waving goodbye.

“Hey Tim, do you think you can drop me back in town? They probably think I’m still dead,” Randy says, laughing. “I wish I had my zombie costume on.”

Tim waves to Randy and jumps into the truck. “Yeah, we can drop you off. Come on.”

Everyone waves one last time to the O’Connells as they drive away from the house. As the tractors align the charred Humvees alongside the road as war trophies, Mary watches in amazement out the window. Soon after, the smooth driveway turns into a dirt road, and they head towards town.

While driving down the road, Tim looks over at Mary, as she stares out of the window with her long, dark hair waving in the breeze. He recalls something called a victory lap that follows most battles. When you sit back and reflect on the things you just lived through. For him, it was usually in the back of a C-17 flying home with the rest of his battle buddies, while they reenact and share stories from the deployment. Once they landed, they would all go their separate ways and do it all over again the next time. Never before was he sitting next to someone whom he loved and cherished. The events they lived through together will forever be a part of them, and he feels closer to Mary now than he ever had before.

"Watch the road, dumbass!" Mary yells as she grabs the dashboard.

Tim looks forward and quickly turns the truck back onto the road before going into the ditch. "Oops, sorry."

"You need me to drive?" Randy yells as he bangs on the back of the truck.

"NO!" Mary and Tim answer at the same time.

The sky over Chesterfield is clear of smoke as they get closer to town. The National Guard had extinguished all the fires and began clearing the charred debris left behind by the R.R. As Tim drives the Humvee into town, he sees a few locals that had volunteered to help in the cleanup, and were working alongside the soldiers on Main Street. Tan cargo trucks line the street, filled with scrap wood and destroyed machinery. One of the local farmers brought a truck full of dirt and filled the holes caused by the explosions. As they pass the ruins of the bar, Tim hears Randy make a sad noise from the back. They stop in front of the old church, and Randy jumps from the back of the truck.

He walks towards the crowd with his hands in the air, yelling, "I have returned," as if he was some kind of apostle.

An old man walks up to Randy in disbelief and shakes his hand.

"How are you alive? We thought you were in the bar when it burned down."

A loud squeal echoes through the town as the twins jump up and run toward them. With their matching denim overalls and dirty, white sleeveless shirts, the Swanson sisters frantically run towards Randy. He throws his hands in the air and runs towards them in a simulated slow-motion jog, until the three collide in mid-air and fall to the ground, laughing and screaming. Mary looks over at Tim with the weirdest expression on her face.

"You don't want to know," Tim says, laughing. "Bye, Randy!" He yells out of the window.

A thumbs-up pokes out of the top of the pile of twisted bodies, and Tim turns the truck around and leaves town, heading back to the farm.

As the sun begins to set, the long, bumpy road seems to go on forever. When they finally pull into the farm, Marco and Nancy run towards the truck. Victoria hangs onto Nancy's shoulders while her little head bounces back and forth. Tim stops the truck next to the house, and Mary jumps out, grabbing the baby from Nancy. She lifts her up in the air and spins around in a circle, then pulls her close and plants a big kiss on her cheek. Tim goes to his mom and dad, hugs them, and reaches over to touch the baby's head as Mary squishes her.

"We were so worried about you two!" Nancy says, crying. "We didn't know what to do. I'm so glad you're both home safe now, and all of this is over."

"This mess is far from over, Mom. But we're safe for now."

"Come on inside, Son. Dinner's on the stove," Marco says, turning towards the house.

Tim puts his arm around Mary and walks towards the house behind his parents. As everyone else goes through the door, he stops and looks at the sunset. He turns around and stands facing the white rails of the porch, gazing out at the bright green cornfield swaying gently in the breeze. The sky is slowly turning orange and yellow as the sun sets on the horizon. Small trails of black smoke rise from different places across the horizon, creating a black shadow trailing off into the clouds. Tim leans sideways against the wooden post and rests his hand on the pistol attached to his hip.

He stands in silence for a moment, taking in the view and thinking to himself. "What a beautiful country."

Acknowledgments

Special thanks go out to my family for helping me put this together, and allowing me to use their names. Thank you to my Mom and Dad, RIP. My brother Randy, his wife Kari, and their son Nash. My brother Garrett, and his wife Melinda. Most of all, my beautiful wife Mary, and baby V.

About the Author

I was born in Midland, Texas, Nov 5, 1983. I have 2 younger brothers who are twins. We lived in Texas for 10 years, then my dad got a job in Northern Michigan, so we hopped in a car and drove all the way there. We then froze to death in the frigid tundra of Michigan for another 10 years, until I joined the Army at the age of 20 in 2004. I turned 21 in basic training at Ft. Jackson, NC.

After completing Basic Training and AIT as a tracked vehicle mechanic, I was chosen to attend the first ever STRYKER Maintenance course offered to Army soldiers, followed by an Advanced Electrical course. After all of the malingering in training was done, I was stationed in Ft. Lewis, Washington where I married my first wife, then deployed to Iraq in late 2005.

A few months later I was moved to Baumholder, Germany where every road is uphill both ways. The birth of my first baby girl named Katelyn happened not long after. Good food and better beer were the highlight of the "Armpit of Germany", until I deployed to Iraq again in 2007 for an experimental 15-month deployment. I safely returned and froze for a German winter, then deployed to Afghanistan in 2009.

After returning I was moved to Ft. Irwin, California where I had the pleasure of being stationed in the biggest NTC in the states. I then spent 3 years dressing up in a man dress and throwing smoke grenades at training troops as they practice reacting to contact drills.

At this point in my carrier, I was 10 years in and getting tired of the Regular Army BS. I wanted to experience the other side of the Army for a change. So, I applied for Psychological Operations. After preparing for a year, passing the Special Operations Selection Course, then a brutal year of PSYOP Q-course and Language training, I finally passed and was a part of coveted Psychological Operations.

After that I moved to Ft. Bragg, North Carolina where my second baby girl was born named Madison. I had a short Airborne refresher course, and was deployed to the GCC, where I was a part of a PSYOP team operating out of Kuwait, Qatar, Oman, Bahrain, UAE, and KSA. I loved every minute of it. 5-star hotels, rental cars, and a hefty Per Diem pay. Daily I would drive back and forth to the local Military installation where the "Regular Army Schmucks" stayed.

While working in Abu Dhabi, I met my current wife, Mary, playing pool in the hotel I was staying in. Long story short, this Eastern European and I hit it off and the rest is history.

After the defeat of divorce, I was then faced with the hardest decision of my life. Stay in the Army for another 5 years and lose someone that I had been looking for my whole life, or take an early retirement and join my beautiful lady in a foreign land. I chose the latter and moved to Abu Dhabi to be with her. Since then, we have lived 3 years in Abu Dhabi, 1 year in Eastern Europe, 3 years in Oman, and now living in Dubai for the last 3 years.

During my time in Oman there has been Covid lockdowns, the birth of a beautiful baby girl named Veronika, and plenty of time to write some outstanding books. More to come.

About the Publisher
TACTICAL 16

Tactical 16 Publishing is an unconventional publisher that understands the therapeutic value inherent in writing. We help veterans, first responders, and their families and friends to tell their stories using their words.

We are on a mission to capture the history of America's heroes: stories about sacrifices during chaos, humor amid tragedy, and victories learned from experiences not readily recreated — real stories from real people.

Tactical 16 has published books in leadership, business, fiction, and children's genres. We produce all types of works, from self-help to memoirs that preserve unique stories not yet told.

You don't have to be a polished author to join our ranks. If you can write with passion and be unapologetic, we want to talk. Go to Tactical16.com to contact us and to learn more.

All of Tactical 16's books are available on our online bookstore, T16Books.com. Visit it today to see more books from our selection of authors and to find a new adventure to read!

* 9 7 8 1 9 4 3 2 2 6 9 7 9 *